INTO THE DARK

ROBERT J WALKER

❀ Created with Vellum

*S*ipping contentedly on an ice-cold beer, Frank watched the sun setting over the distant valley, which was mostly dry scrub dotted with large boulders and the odd tree. The sweltering heat of the dying day was rising up into the darkening sky, in which the first stars were already sparkling, and the cool air of the hills had a pleasantly crisp feel to it. Frank was the only person around for miles, and he liked it that way. He had been hiking and camping in these hills and mountains for over six decades now, and being alone in the great outdoors still revitalized him as much as it had in those distant years when he'd been a young boy out here under the stars with his father.

While Frank was the only human being around for miles, he wasn't alone. He reached down and gave Boris a scratch behind his ears. Boris, a four-year-old German Shepherd, was one of Frank's best friends in the world, and, as the sixty-three-year-old former Green Beret liked to say, was one of the two things in life he knew would never under any circumstances let him down. The other was his trusty .357 8-shot revolver.

At this moment, though, Boris did not respond to Frank's gentle fingers in his usual affectionate manner. Instead, he growled, his hackles raised.

Frank spun around, suddenly feeling the eerie sensation of eyes locked on his back … unfriendly eyes. His right hand, moving with the mechanical speed of perfect muscle memory from years of training, shot instinctively down to the holster on his left hip … but his fingers curled around nothing but air, and with a sudden, sinking feeling of dread, Frank realized that his trusty revolver was sitting on his camping stool across the campsite, where he'd just finished cleaning it.

And staring down at him with baleful eyes from the top of the low cliff against which he'd made his camp was a massive male mountain lion. It was the biggest one Frank had ever seen; easily over two hundred pounds, perhaps closer to two-twenty. His .357 was thirty feet away – a distance the huge cat could cover in a single leap. And now, standing where he was, unarmed, there were a mere twenty feet separating him from the mountain lion.

Next to Frank, Boris started barking frantically, and above him the mountain lion let out a low, rumbling growl, its ears pressed flat against its skull, its fangs bared and its powerful muscles tensed, ready to pounce.

Most people would have frozen with sheer panic at this point and would have been completely paralyzed with terror. Frank, however, was not like most people. The cogs in his well-oiled mind were already spinning rapidly, and he knew that at this crucial juncture, his best defense was a strong offense. The beer can in his hand was half-full, and while it wasn't much, it had a little weight to it, enough to provide a distraction and give him a window to get to a more substantial weapon. Without a second thought, he flung the beer can as hard as he could at the big cat's face, and it snarled and flinched as the projectile came flying through the air toward it.

Frank didn't wait to see what effect his impromptu attack had had on the beast. Instead, the instant the beer can left his hand, he darted across to the campfire and whipped out a stout four-foot-long burning log. With this improvised weapon in his hand, he spun around just in time to see the mountain lion leap down the twenty-foot-high cliff in a single bound, landing a mere six feet from him.

Boris half-charged at the huge cat, but Frank yelled a curt, sharp command to the dog, and Boris, supremely well-trained, immediately stopped in his tracks, growling and barking aggressively at the mountain lion but staying still. As tough a dog as Boris was, Frank knew he didn't stand a chance against a big male mountain lion.

He held the burning log in front of him as if it were a spear and waved the end of it with an aggressive slash at the mountain lion's face. The predator growled and flinched, afraid of the fire. Despite the intensity of the situation, a reflection crossed Frank's mind: this was how it must have been for men tens of thousands of years ago, facing down ferocious predators with nothing but wood and fire in their hands. And, like those distant ancestors of his, he would not back down from this challenge, and he would use these crude but effective tools to defeat his adversary.

"Back Boris, back," he said calmly to his dog, who knew this command and began retreating, still growling and snapping at the mountain lion, who snarled and tensed his muscles, getting ready to attack.

As Boris backed away from the big cat, so too did Frank, waving the burning log aggressively at it and keeping his eyes locked on the creature's as he inched closer and closer to his revolver, which was still a frustratingly large distance away.

With a spitting hiss and a vicious snarl, the mountain lion half-charged forward, but Frank counterlunged with a purposeful swipe of the burning log. The arc of fire through the chilly dusk air got the big cat to stop in his tracks, skidding across the dusty rock floor of the campsite before the challenge posed by the flames. As he waved the burning log, Frank yelled and shouted at the top of his lungs, giving his voice a deep, aggressive rasp, doing his best to intimidate the big cat into backing down.

The mountain lion darted off to the left, trying to circle around Frank and come at him from his flank, but he spun around, keeping the end of the burning log between himself and the cat. The flames on the end of the log were beginning to shrink and falter, though, and he knew that if the fire went out he would be in deep trouble; those weakening flames were the only things keeping the deadly predator at bay.

Even so, Frank managed to keep calm. He kept moving slowly toward his revolver, shouting and yelling at the snarling mountain lion while lunging and taking swipes at it with the burning log every time it half-moved in his direction. Boris, meanwhile, growled and barked and gave a few half-charges, but remained obedient to Frank's commands and did not attack the mountain lion.

The flames on the end of the log were now almost dead, and the mountain lion was growing bolder. Frank was still a few paces from his revolver, and it didn't look like the flames would last for more than a few more seconds. He had a decision to make, and he knew that his life depended on how quickly he made it and how well he executed the move he was about to make.

With one final roar of aggression, he flung the log as hard as he could at the mountain lion, and then dived across the gap of the last few yards between him and his revolver. He snatched it off the camping stool in midair, and then, as he hit the ground, he rolled and came up firing, blasting shots in the direction of the mountain lion without even bothering to take aim.

He had expected it to have pounced on him by now, but no claws raked his skin and no fangs sank into his neck. Surveying the entire campsite through the sights of his .357, Frank, with adrenaline racing through his system, searched the shadows for any sign of the beast. The smoldering log lay close to where the mountain lion had been moments earlier, but now the creature was gone. Boris was still growling, but he was staring in the direction of the trees at the edge of the campsite, where the shadows were dark and thick.

Frank breathed out a sigh of relief; the mountain lion had run off, having been finally scared off by the burning log flung at it and the loud booms of the shots fired immediately thereafter.

"Thank God," Frank murmured. He only noticed now how rapidly his heart was racing. Just to be sure the big cat had been scared off, he fired a few more rounds into the darkness of the forest. After the echoes of the bangs had faded away, he lay back on the dusty ground, staring up at the starry sky and breathing in a slow, even rhythm to calm himself.

Boris came up close and curled up next to him, and when Frank ruffled his dog's coat, he noticed his companion was trembling. "You've never seen a mountain lion before, huh?" Frank said. "That was one big bastard, I'll tell you that, and we came awfully close to becoming his dinner. We'd better get inside the tent and stay there for the rest of the night in case he decides to come back and try to turn us into cat food again."

In his pocket, his cellphone buzzed. He pulled it out and smiled when he saw a text message from Diana on the screen. Diana, an attractive fifty-two-year-old widow, owned a trading store in the small town closest to Frank's homestead in the hills.

After his wife had passed away from cancer ten years ago, Frank – a lifelong loner – had sworn to never get married again, or even get into another romantic relationship, but in the last few years he and Diana, with whom he shared a surprisingly intense attraction, had grown very close.

He opened the message, but immediately frowned when he read its contents.

"Frank, there's trouble in town," the message said, cutting straight to the chase. "Armed, masked men packing a lot of firepower are rolling into town in Humvees. I don't know who they are or what they want, but I don't like the look of it. I don't know if they're government or Army troops, or what's going on. I'll keep you updated. XXX."

Before Frank could type out a reply, he saw a curious and worrying sight: flashes of light just beyond the distant horizon. They were bright and numerous, and as a military man, he had seen them before and knew exactly what they were.

"Oh shit," he muttered, scrambling to his feet. "This is not good, this is not good at all…"

What Frank was witnessing in the night sky was a

missile attack on the city fifty miles away. This, along with the message he had just received from Diana, got his mind racing and got his old combat instincts kicking in.

He started typing out a reply to Diana, telling her to get out of town to his homestead right away, but before he could hit send, his phone went dead. The LED light hanging in his tent also died at the same time, and when he pulled the small flashlight he kept in his pocket out, he found that it was dead too. In the distance, the sparkling lights of a faraway town all simultaneously went black.

At this point, a stunning realization hit him with the force of a speeding truck. He could scarcely believe what he was seeing, what was happening, but he knew without a doubt what had just happened.

"Oh my God," he murmured to himself, with the small campfire now providing the only light for miles around. "It's an EMP attack. The world as we know it … is gone."

2

*D*iana had her eye on the strange man at the back of the store. She didn't think he was going to try and rob the store or cause any trouble, but he did seem like a relatively suspicious character. There was something about the way he carried himself, as well as the hard look in his dark, deep-set eyes, that suggested he was hiding something.

He looked like he was in his late thirties, or was perhaps a hair over forty. A few streaks of gray lightened his long, jet-black hair, which was tied up in a ponytail. His features marked him as a full-blooded Native American, but his ethnicity had nothing to do with the fact that Diana found the man to be a little menacing and unsettling; rather, it was because of the long scar at the left end of his mouth, which marred his strong-featured face and twisted his lips into a permanent scowl.

He had pulled up outside on a big Harley, whose

thumping twin mufflers had rattled the display windows of the store, and immediately made Diana suspicious of his intentions. On the rare occasions there had been trouble in this part of the world, it had come from bikers – as well as from Mexican drug runners from across the border.

The suspicious man had been browsing through the fishing gear at the back of Diana's trading store – which she had inherited from her late husband when he had passed away a couple years ago – for some time now. Diana had asked him if he needed help with anything, but he had simply given her a shake of his head and a grunt under his breath.

At the age of fifty-two, Diana could easily have passed for someone at least ten years younger. She was graying, and there was at least one white hair for every three chestnut brown strands on her head, but she wore her gray hair and the fine wrinkles that lined the corners of her eyes with pride. She was pretty in a dignified manner, and her penchant for hiking, archery, swimming, mountain biking, and other vigorous outdoor activities meant that she was just as healthy in body as she was in her sharp, analytical mind.

She also knew how to use a gun and kept a 9mm pistol under the checkout counter where the cash register was. She didn't expect anyone to try to rob her store, not in this small desert town, but she lived by the motto that it was always better to have something and never need it than to not have it when you needed it – especially when the item in question was a firearm.

Diana's attention was drawn away from the strange man at the back of the store, though, by the sound of a number of large vehicles coming along the winding road that led past her trading store into the center of the town. Giving the man at the back one last glance, to make sure he wasn't surreptitiously slipping anything into his pockets while her back was turned, she walked out to the front door to get a better look at who or what this incoming cavalcade might be.

She was surprised to see that there were a large number of Humvees coming up the road. She wasn't surprised to see military-style vehicles around here, because there was a large US Army base out in the desert twenty or thirty miles away, but rather, she was surprised at the look of the vehicles. They weren't painted in the usual US Army colors; instead, they were a deep shade of blue, and in them were people who looked like soldiers, but who did not seem to be members of the US Army. For one thing, they were dressed in dark blue uniforms, and for another, they were all wearing navy blue balaclavas that covered their faces.

Diana didn't like the look of this at all, and alarm bells immediately began ringing in her head as her sixth sense kicked in. She grabbed her phone and typed out a hasty message to her boyfriend, Frank, who she figured might know something about who these mysterious armed strangers were and what they might be doing here. Were they part of some secret government branch she had never heard of, or perhaps a new special ops unit? If anyone would know, it would be Frank.

She sent him a message and then watched as the Humvees rolled past the store. One of the armed men leaned out of the passenger side windows of one of the Humvees and pointed his M-16 at her. "Get inside and lock your store up!" he yelled as the vehicle went past. "That's an order!"

His tone was aggressive, and the look in his eyes was one of cold, intense hardness. It frightened Diana and made her quite worried about exactly what it was these people were up to. Frank hadn't replied to her message yet, but she was quite sure he would tell her to lock the store up and head straight home.

She turned to speak to the Native American man. "I'm sorry sir, but if you're not going to buy anything, I'm going to have to ask you to leave. I need to close the store up now, and—"

Before she could finish speaking, there were a series of bright flashes on the horizon, and a few seconds after that, all the lights in the store went out, plunging the space into gloom in the thickening dusk. "Dammit," Diana muttered under her breath and got her phone out to use its flashlight app. However, when she got her phone out, she found that it was dead.

She kept a number of emergency flashlights around the store, and she headed over to the nearest one. When she tried to turn it on, though, she found that it was as dead as her phone was. At this point, the alarm bells in her mind began pealing even louder. Something far more serious than just a power outage had just happened.

"Sir!" she said, peering through the gloom in the direction of the Native American man, who appeared as a mere silhouette in the shadows now. "I'm sorry sir, but you really do need to leave now."

Before he could respond, though, the front door, which Diana had not yet locked, opened behind her. She turned around and saw that three of the strange soldiers in blue had just stepped into her store. Her gut instinct told her that they weren't here to make a social call, and her heart suddenly began pounding with fear.

"We're closed," she said to the three men. "I'm sorry, I don't mean to be rude, but you need to leave, please."

"Get over there, now," the closest soldier growled at Diana, gesturing with his M-16 rifle behind the counter. "You're closed when *we* say you are."

"I don't—" Diana began, but the soldier swung his rifle up, aiming it at her chest from point-blank range.

"Are you deaf, stupid, or just plain fucking suicidal, you dried-up old cow?" he snarled. "Get behind the counter and stay there with your hands behind your head. We need a few supplies from this shithole, and we're going to take them whether you like it or not. Move!"

With her heart thumping with fear, Diana raised her hands in a gesture of surrender and walked slowly over to the counter, where she stood with her hands behind her head. While she walked, she glanced over to where the Native American man had been standing. Strangely enough, he seemed to have vanished into thin air, like a phantom dematerializing.

Diana stared down at the grip of her 9mm pistol, which lay easily within reach, poking out from its drawer under the counter. She was half-tempted to grab the gun but knew that it would be a terribly stupid thing to do. There were three soldiers with automatic rifles close by, and she knew she didn't stand a chance against them. As much as she hated to see her store looted by these thugs, she knew that the best thing to do now was just to comply and keep her hands behind her head while they took whatever they wanted.

Two of the soldiers began taking food from the shelves, scooping items into a bunch of large duffel bags they had brought with them. The third soldier – the man who had initially threatened Diana – walked over to the counter where he could keep an eye on her.

"Who are you people?" she asked softly, avoiding eye contact with him so as not to provoke him.

"Shut the fuck up, bitch," he snapped. "Keep your damn mouth shut unless you want your fucking teeth shattered."

Diana swallowed slowly and kept silent, praying that the men would just take what they wanted and leave her unharmed.

"It's getting dark in here, I can hardly see what I'm doing," one of the looters complained.

"Light the gas lamps then, you moron," the man at the counter grumbled.

One of the looters got two gas lamps out of his backpack and lit them up. Whatever this strange power outage was, they seemed to have been prepared for it, Diana noted. Once they had lit up their lamps, the man at the counter called one of his buddies over to keep a gun trained on Diana while he got out his own gas lamp and lit it up. Once it was burning, he stuck it on the counter, and it illuminated Diana clearly in its warm white glow.

"Hey, she don't look so old in this light," the second soldier remarked, leering unabashedly at Diana. "Damn, she's got a nice pair of tits on her."

The first man chuckled darkly. "Yeah, she does, doesn't she, Ray? She's a good-looking one, a bit of a cougar, huh? Yeah, look at those lips, I bet she could suck—"

"Please just take what you want and leave me alone," Diana pleaded. She didn't like the way these men were looking at her, and especially didn't like the things they were saying.

The first man lunged across the counter and grabbed her by her collar, and dragged her forward so that he could get his balaclava-clad face right up in hers. "Don't fucking interrupt me, you dirty old whore," he snarled, his rancid breath hot and humid in her nostrils. "I'll kick your fucking teeth in if you interrupt me again, you understand?"

"Y-, yes, I'm sorry, I'm sorry," she gasped, so racked

with raw terror that she felt as if her legs would buckle beneath her.

"What do you say we have a little fun with her, Jim?" the second man said. "Phillips won't care if we come back a little late, and I bet this old cougar hasn't had the kind of lay we can give her for years. She wants it, Jim, look at those pretty eyes and those blowjob lips, she wants it all right…"

The first man grinned evilly. "You know what, Ray? I think you're right. I think she wants us. Tom, lock that door there so nobody can interrupt the fun we're about to have," he said to the third man, who was still looting the shelves of canned food and other items.

"No, no, please, please," Diana begged, paralyzed with fear. The 9mm was within reach, but she just couldn't bring herself to grab it. Terror seemed to have caused every muscle in her body to freeze up.

"Shut up!" the first man roared, delivering a backhand slap that landed with such force across Diana's cheeks that it sent her flying.

She hit the ground hard, and all the wind was knocked out of her. She lay there, stunned and groaning, expecting the disgusting men to pounce on her and start their terrible act within seconds. Instead, though, she heard two dull, wet thuds and a grunt of pain, followed by two heavy thumps which sounded suspiciously like two bodies hitting the floor. Then there was a brief scream of fright, which was cut abruptly short and followed by another ominously loud, dull thump … and then there was only silence.

Diana groaned and gasped and tried to struggle to her feet. She screamed as two hands gripped her under her armpits – but then a new voice spoke from behind her, and the hands gripping her were helping her to her feet, not molesting her.

"They're dead, and they won't be hurting you or any other women now," the Native American man said. His voice was deep and sonorous, and oddly soothing, in a way.

Diana, now on her feet thanks to him, turned and looked at him with a mixture of fear and relief on her face. She saw that a tomahawk, the blade of which was dripping with fresh blood, was tucked into his belt. The three soldiers were lying on the floor, with blood spreading from their split-open skulls.

"Oh my God, oh my God…" Diana murmured. She wanted to throw up.

"I'm sorry, but I did what I had to do," the man said. "I'm Clay, by the way. Clay Blackelk, bounty hunter. These scumbags aren't the first men I've killed, and I suspect they won't be the last either."

"Th-, thank you for saving me, but we, we have to, we have to call the police," Diana stammered.

"No, we have to get out of here, right now," Clay said. "There's no more police, not anymore. Someone just hit the reset button on the world a couple minutes ago, and nothing at all is ever going to be the same. Trust me on that."

"Reset button? N-, nothing ever the same? What on earth are you talking about?" Diana gasped. She pulled out her phone and tried to turn it on again, but found that it was still dead.

Before either of them could say anything else, though, a pair of headlights stabbed through the thickening dark outside, blazing bright light through the storefront window as another blue Humvee pulled up.

More soldiers had arrived … and once they came in and found their comrades dead on the floor, there would be hell to pay.

3

"Hey Chuck," Adrian said excitedly, pointing at a pile of rocks behind a large cactus, the shadows of which were long and dark from the low, late afternoon sun in the desert, which was still viciously hot despite the approaching dusk. "I think there's something under there! I saw something moving, I know I did!"

Chuck shook his head and rolled his eyes with a world-weariness that belied his fourteen years. He and Adrian had been close friends for the past five or six years, ever since Adrian's family had moved into the house next door. Adrian was a fun kid to hang out with, but being hyperactive and suffering from a mild form of ADHD meant that he was often a bit of a handful, especially for a boy like Chuck, who was level-headed, even-tempered, practical, and wise beyond his years.

Chuck had his mother's good looks and curly red

hair. He was tall, athletic and strong for his age, like his father had been as a boy, but he had his grandfather's mind, down to a tee. Like his paternal grandfather, Frank – his only living relative on his father's side, since both of his parents had been killed in a car accident three years ago, and he and his younger sister now lived with his aunt on his mother's side – he enjoyed his own company and greatly valued solitude. And like Frank, he was stoic, proud, and tough as nails.

He had been hoping for some solitude on this camping trip deep into the southwestern desert, organized by his school's hiking club, but Adrian, who had never been on a hiking trip before – unlike Chuck, who, like his grandfather Frank, took every opportunity he could to spend time in the woods, mountains, and desert – was a city slicker through and through. Although Adrian had far more interest in video games and phones than he did the great outdoors, he had nonetheless joined the school hiking club so that he could accompany Chuck on this trip. And part of Adrian's reasoning behind doing this, Chuck thought somewhat sourly, had been just to annoy him.

"Whatever's behind those rocks, dude, just leave it alone," Chuck said with a sigh. "Come on, let's get back to the campsite. You haven't finished setting up your tent, and Mr. Redman is gonna be pissed if you don't move your ass. You said you were just coming out here to take a leak, Adrian, and you've done that, so let's go."

"What are you guys doing out here?" a new voice

called out. It was a girl's voice – that of Melissa Tilley, Chuck's younger sister.

A precocious child, like Chuck, she had had to grow up a lot faster than most girls her age when both of her parents had unexpectedly passed away. While she shared her brother's red hair, pale skin, and bright emerald eyes, her long hair was wavy rather than curly, and although the siblings' attractive facial features marked them as related by blood, their personalities couldn't have been more different.

Melissa, thirteen years old, had her deceased mother's bubbly, extroverted personality, and like her she was an artist to the core, dreamy and creative with her head in clouds, unlike Chuck's which was firmly rooted in practicality and the real world. Melissa was an extremely talented guitarist and could sketch amazing portraits with pencil and ink, but she was not the most practically-minded person.

"Have you finished setting up your tent?" Chuck asked his sister as she wandered over to him. There was a blatant tone of annoyance in his voice, but Melissa took no notice of it.

"I haven't even taken it out of its bag," she said with a cheeky grin.

"You know how Mr. Redman is!" Chuck complained. "Jeez, now I've gotta get you *and* Adrian back to the camp and help the two of you do something you should both have done yourselves! Man, I feel like a freakin' kindergarten teacher here."

"Chuck, check it out!" Adrian blurted out excitedly.

21

He had picked up a stick and was poking around in the pile of rocks. He was a chubby boy with a shock of jet-black hair, and the baggy hip-hop jeans and garishly colored ice hockey jersey he was wearing out here in the desert made him stand out like a sore thumb among the other kids, who were all dressed far more appropriately for a desert camping outing.

"Adrian, come on dude, stop it, I told you not to do that!" Chuck grumbled. "It could be a rattlesnake or a Gila monster, and trust me dude, you do *not* want to mess with either of those. Come on, just—"

A piercing scream of pain and terror shattered the dry-heat silence of the late afternoon. Fear ripped through Chuck's veins, for it was Adrian who had just howled in agony and horror.

"Oh my God!" Melissa shrieked. From the spot where she was standing, she had seen the whole thing. Adrian had been poking the pile of rocks, despite Chuck's repeated warnings, and Melissa had watched in horror as a snake lashed out and sank its fangs through Adrian's jeans into his lower left leg. "Chuck, Adrian just got bit by a snake!"

"Dammit, Adrian!" Chuck yelled, running over to help his friend, who staggered back, yelling both with fright and in pain, and tripped over a rock. "I told you not to do that!"

"Oh my God, oh my God, what do we do, what do we do?!" Melissa cried.

"Go get Mr. Redman!" Chuck yelled. "Hurry!"

Melissa nodded and ran off to fetch the teacher.

The first thing Chuck did was check that, aside from the bite wound, his friend was okay. Despite how annoyed he was with Adrian for repeatedly ignoring his advice, he felt really bad that Adrian had been hurt like this and was in pain.

"Ow, it hurts, Chuck, it really hurts!" Adrian whined, lying on his back and gripping his leg.

"Hold on buddy, I'll help you in a sec, I just need to ID the snake that bit you," Chuck said. "In the meantime, just try to stay calm, focus on breathing slowly and evenly, okay?"

He picked up a long stick – one that was twice the length of the twig Adrian had been foolishly poking around in the rocks with – and cautiously approached the pile of rocks. Once he got close to it, he carefully shifted a few rocks out of the way, and in a hollow beneath them, he soon saw a very angry-looking snake coiled up in the shadows. He could identify most snakes and reptiles by sight, as he had an avid interest and did a lot of reading up on them, so he determined right away that the creature that had just sunk its fangs into his friend was a rattlesnake. A threatening rattle from the snake's tail confirmed this.

Keeping his eyes on the snake, Chuck backed slowly away, being careful to avoid falling victim to the same fate that had befallen his friend. When he was a safe distance away and felt sure that the snake wasn't going to come out and attack, he knelt down next to Adrian, who was panicking, his eyes wild and white and his nostrils flared.

"Dude, just do your best to stay calm," Chuck said.

"Quickly man, you gotta suck the poison out before it freaking kills me!" Adrian whimpered, on the verge of tears. "I don't wanna die, Chuck, I'm scared, I'm really scared, I don't wanna die, I don't wanna die…"

"That doesn't work, the whole sucking the poison thing out," Chuck said calmly. "The best thing to do is get up. We need to keep the bite wound below the level of your heart. Since you got bit down near your ankle, that should be easy enough."

"I don't wanna die, I don't wanna—"

"You're not going to die, dude," Chuck said, doing his best to keep his friend calm. "Most rattlesnake bites aren't fatal. You'll feel real sick for a day or two, but you'll be fine, trust me. You need to be calm, that'll slow down the spread of the venom in your body."

Just then, Mr. Redman came running over with Melissa. Mr. Redman was a young teacher in his mid-twenties and was pretty new on the job. He was a thin man with brown hair, prematurely balding, and the sweat that glistened on his forehead and scalp was not just from the heat of the desert – he was panicking.

"Oh no, oh no, I can't believe this is happening, this isn't happening!" Mr. Redman said.

Chuck rolled his eyes and shook his head, realizing that he would have to be the one who took control of this situation, despite being a good ten years younger than his teacher. "Mr. Redman, it's a rattlesnake bite, I ID'd the snake," he said. "We need to—"

"We need to get Adrian to a hospital right away!"

Mr. Redman said, pulling out his phone. "We need to get an ambulance chopper flown in! Oh God, if this kid dies on my watch, I'll be the most hated man in America once the media gets hold of this story! Oh God, my career is over, my life is over!"

"Mr. Redman, it's gonna be okay," Chuck said calmly. "As long as we can all stay calm, Adrian will be okay."

"There's no reception out here! I can't get any signal!" Mr. Redman said. "Melissa, get your phone out, call 911!"

Melissa took her phone out of her pocket, but shook her head. "I don't have any signal either," she said.

"Dammit, dammit, dammit," Mr. Redman said, pacing back and forth. "Okay, okay, be cool, be cool … I'm gonna have to drive him out, it's the only way, it's the only way." He looked up at Chuck. "Chuck, you're the most experienced hiker here. Do you uh, do you think you could be in charge of the camp and the other kids for a couple hours? If I drive fast, I can get this kid to the nearest hospital in two and half, maybe three hours. Then I can be back here by around midnight, I guess?"

"I don't think that'll be necessary, Mr. Redman," Chuck began, "because the bite is—"

"I'm not having a child die on my watch!" Mr. Redman snapped. "No way! We're going to the hospital right now, and you're in charge until I get back, Chuck. Now come on, help me carry him to the 4x4!"

25

Chuck shook his head; he could see that Mr. Redman had made up his mind. He, Melissa, and the teacher helped Adrian to the 4x4, which was the only vehicle here, seeing as they were many hours' walk from the nearest signs of civilization. The teacher jumped in, fired up the engine, and then took off without another word, driving off at speed into the sunset and leaving Chuck, Melissa, and the three other kids alone in the desert.

"I hope Adrian's gonna be okay," Melissa said, looking concerned.

"Trust me, he'll be fine," Chuck said. "Now come on, let's get your tent set up, sunset is in an hour."

Chuck and Melissa explained to the other kids what had happened, and that Chuck was in charge until Mr. Redman got back. Chuck, a natural leader, ran the small campsite like a well-oiled machine, and made sure everyone had their tents set up before dusk. He made sure to get a good fire going. He delegated dinner preparation tasks to various kids, and soon everyone was busy and working productively.

Around sunset, though, everyone was distracted by a series of bright flashes on the distant horizon.

"What on earth is that?" Melissa asked, spellbound. "It looks almost like a meteor shower, but at ground level."

Just then, all the LED lights around the campsite simultaneously went dead. A few murmurs of panic flitted around, and the kids all got their phones out to use their flashlight apps … but they quickly found that all of these were dead too.

An ominous realization dawned on Chuck, and Melissa too, for thanks to the time they had spent with their grandfather and the lessons he had taught them, they both knew exactly what had just happened.

Chuck looked at his sister in the falling dark, and the same word emerged from both of their lips, almost at the same time: "EMP."

This was it, this was the thing Frank had warned them about … and it had just hit at the worst possible time. They were stuck out in the desert, dozens of miles from anywhere, without any adults around and with only enough food and water for the night and the next morning … and with the following day predicted to be one of the hottest of the year.

As calm and collected as Chuck usually was, panic started to crash against him now like an incoming tide.

"We're in trouble," he whispered to himself, with cold fear racing through his veins. "We're in deep, deep trouble…"

4

***

rank didn't waste any time worrying or debating with himself over what to do. He had never been one to sit and agonize over problems and issues; if something came up, he dealt with it immediately, in the most efficient and direct manner, no matter how difficult or dangerous that path might be to take. He didn't intend to deal with this new catastrophe any differently.

Unlike the vast majority of the rest of his countrymen, Frank was prepared for this scenario. He hadn't, of course, been prepared for an EMP to hit while he was solo camping deep in the mountains, but in the cellar of his homestead, he had a Faraday cage in which he kept a number of important electronic items. These would all be perfectly functional after an EMP strike due to the protection offered by the Faraday cage. His first mission was to head straight back to his cabin on the homestead to retrieve a few of these, after which he would proceed to town to find Diana. Finally, when she was safe, Frank knew he would have a long trek ahead of him, for he would have to journey south and head deep into the desert to find his grandchildren.

He knew that Chuck and Melissa could handle themselves and survive for a time on their own – especially Chuck, of whom Frank was immensely proud – but that didn't change the fact that there would be dangerous predators skulking about in the wake of the attack ... predators of the two-legged variety, the worst kind.

He had friends in law enforcement, and he had been hearing worrying things about Mexican drug cartels becoming ever bolder with their illegal border crossings in recent times. This was happening in the vicinity of where his grandchildren were camping. What was more, he had heard that crystal meth and dope weren't the only things these gangsters were smuggling – they were trafficking human beings, too. He suspected that in this new post-civilization era, in which all semblance of law enforcement would invariably break down, the cartel would only step up these nefarious activities.

Speaking of Chuck, Frank had received a text message from him just a few hours earlier. His grandson had been happy to be out in the middle of the desert, far from civilization, but had been complaining about his teacher, Mr. Redman, who sounded like quite a rookie. Frank doubted that the young, inexperienced teacher would be able to take care of himself out in the middle of the desert, let alone a bunch of frightened kids. He hoped he could find them before they got into any serious trouble.

A more immediate concern, though, was the worrying message he had received from Diana about the strange, unidentified military-style cavalcade of Humvees that had rolled into town just before the EMP had hit. Frank had no idea who these people could be, but strongly suspected that they had something to do with what had just happened.

He hastily took down his tent and packed up his camp, working by firelight. In the back of his mind, he was worried that the mountain lion might return and try to ambush him again, but even with such a danger lurking in the shadows, he couldn't afford to wait around. He would just have to take his chances with the big cat, for with Diana and his grandchildren in increasing danger, he would not be sleeping or resting tonight. Not until he got to Diana at the very least.

When he had packed everything up into his backpack, he lit a gas lantern, brewed a quick, strong coffee over the fire to give him a caffeine boost, and then, after downing it, he put out the fire.

"Come on Boris," he said to his faithful canine companion. "We gotta go. You keep those eyes and ears and that sharp nose of yours open for any signs of that big, nasty pussycat, you hear? This time I'm ready for him."

Boris gave an eager bark in response. He was an energetic creature and excited for the upcoming night hike.

Frank was indeed ready to take on the mountain lion should it return. In his left hand he carried his gas lantern, but in his right was the comforting weight of his .357 revolver, full loaded and ready to shoot at the first hint of danger. With Boris at his side and his firearm in his hand, he set off into the darkness, the lantern blazing a trail of light ahead of him through the close-packed trees.

Frank and Boris journeyed quickly through the dark woods, making brisk progress along the trail. It was one Frank had hiked many times before, and he knew it well enough that he could have followed it even without the aid of his lantern. As for the mountain lion, if the creature was still nearby, it didn't come close to Frank and Boris, or at least not close enough for Boris's sharp canine senses to detect its presence.

Despite being in his sixth decade of life, Frank was far fitter than most men half his age. It was an eight-mile hike back to his cabin, which took a few hours, but he was by no means exhausted by the time he got back home.

Home for Frank was a large wooden cabin on a few acres of hilly land, with a small creek running through it. He kept chickens and turkeys, but no other livestock, and grew a large variety of crops here. Usually the lights of the nearby town would have lit up the valley a few miles away, but aside from a few fires and what

looked like lights from gas lamps, the valley looked
ominously dark.

"All right buddy, we made it back here without that
big ol' cat hassling us," Frank said, bending down to
give Boris a good rubbing behind his ears. "We'll have
ourselves a quick meal to replenish the old energy
stores, and then we'll head on down to town to find
Diana."

He opened a can of dog food for Boris and cooked
up a quick meal of pork and beans on a small gas stove
in his kitchen for himself. After he had wolfed this
down, he packed as much perishable food as he could
fit into his backpack – it would all have to be eaten
soon or it would rot, now that his refrigerator was
dead – and then he headed down into his cellar to pick
up the supplies he would need for the difficult path
that lay ahead.

The first thing he did was open his bugout Faraday
cage. This small Faraday cage protected a few little but
essential items that would be needed in the event of
making a hasty retreat from his homestead in the wake
of an enemy attack. Inside were two LED headlamps, a
set of simple two-way walkie talkies, some extra
batteries for the aforementioned items, and a personal
GPS navigation unit that he knew may or may not
work, depending on how powerful the EMP attack had
been and whether it had knocked out any major
satellites.

Frank had some other electronic items in a larger

Faraday cage, but these were not portable enough to be carried on a mission like this, so he left them locked up. Next, he unlocked his rifle safe. He loved his .357, but he knew that it had to be a sidearm, and that if he was faced with multiple armed opponents, he needed something more suitable for combat purposes. For this, he had an AK-47 rifle, purchased as a semi-automatic, but which he had converted to a fully automatic.

After clipping a shoulder strap onto the AK and sticking some spare ammo clips into his tactical belt, he got two bulletproof vests off a shelf and put one on. It was a standard military-issue item, but the other was a much rarer and more expensive piece of kit, one that he had gladly splashed out on.

"Come here, Boris," he said.

Boris came obediently over and waited patiently while his master fitted the special K9 bulletproof vest onto his body. Frank had already trained Boris extensively with the K9 vest, so he was quite used to wearing it and running around in it. What was more, the K9 bulletproof vest had a number of large pouches on it, so Boris could be used as a pack mule of sorts to carry some extra equipment. Most of the pouches, though, Frank filled with high-quality dog food sachets.

"You're carrying your own food on this trip, buddy!" he said with a grin, ruffling Boris's shaggy fur.

In addition to the stuff Frank had just packed, he already had the ultra-lightweight camping gear he'd taken on his ill-fated hike, so he was ready to camp out anywhere and live off the land. The immensely efficient NASA-spec water purifying bottle he carried with him everywhere meant that he and Boris would always have fresh water to drink, even if the only source of water was a dirty brown puddle on the side of the road. Short of radioactive water or water contaminated with seriously potent chemicals, this bottle could purify pretty much anything. Frank also had a number of spare filters for the bottle in his backpack.

He also had an ample supply of bug spray and sunscreen. The latter item was especially important; the next few days were predicted to be some of the hottest of the year, and venturing out into the scorching heat of the desert could prove deadly to those who were unprepared.

In the barn on his homestead, Frank had an early '80s Toyota Hilux 4x4 that was not only completely EMP-proof, but also bulletproof. He also had a pair of '70s-era two-stroke dirt bikes that were also ready to go and unaffected by the EMP.

He decided to leave them here for the time being, though, at least until he had extracted Diana from the occupied town. While they would be useful for covering large distances across the desert, he didn't want to draw attention to himself by driving anything with a motor now. No, he needed to sneak into town silently and stealthily on foot.

At this point, he was ready to go. He gave Boris a determined look and a nod.

"All right boy," he said. "We have a lot to do before sunrise … so let's go do it."

Armed to the teeth and ready for anything, he and Boris jogged off in the direction of the ominously dark town in the valley.

5

"Oh no, oh no, what are we gonna do?" Diana asked fearfully. "When they come in here and find out what you've done, they'll kill us both!"

"Not if we act fast," Clay said. "You got a sink back there?"

"Uh, yeah, but—"

"Go wash the blood out of this," he said, cutting Diana off before she could finish protesting. He yanked the balaclava off the head of the nearest corpse and tossed it over to her.

She instinctively caught the item, but the instant she felt the warm stickiness of the dead man's blood on her hands, she shrieked with fright and dropped it. "Oh my God, it's, its…"

"It's just a bit of blood," Clay said as he hastily stripped the clothes off the dead soldier. "Not much different to cooking a nice, rare steak. Look, lady, if you don't move your ass and wash that balaclava, we're both dead. Not now, because I'll gun these bastards down before they shoot us – but the gunfire will draw the rest of them, and against that many I can't prevail. Go, move it!"

Realizing that she had no option but to do what Clay said, Diana nodded, doing her best to steel her nerves, and she picked up the blood-soaked item and ran into the back room of the store, where there was a small sink. There was a simple gravity-fed water tank on the roof, so the flow of water through the faucets was uninterrupted by the EMP. She hurriedly washed the balaclava in the sink, and when she'd gotten the blood out of it, she hurried back to Clay, flinching with fright as she heard the Humvee doors slamming shut right outside the store. The soldiers would be coming in any moment, and she had no idea how Clay was going to explain the sight of the dead bodies on the floor to them.

When she got back to the main section of the store, she saw that Clay had put on one of the dead men's uniforms and was holding one of their M-16 rifles. He had slung the bag of looted supplies over his shoulder.

"Hurry, toss me that balaclava!" he said.

The soldiers outside were already walking up to the front door of the store. Diana felt as if her legs were about to buckle beneath her and her heart was about to explode with fear, but she managed to throw the balaclava to Clay, who hastily pulled it over his head.

"Come over here and play along with the act! Do exactly what I say! Hurry!" he snapped.

Diana hurried over to him, and he grabbed a fistful of her hair, making her yelp with surprise and pain.

"It's just an act," he whispered. "Play along, or we both die."

Then, pulling her by her hair, he strode out of the front door just as the first of the soldiers opened it. His body and Diana's blocked their view of the corpses on the floor, but if either of them moved from their position, the soldiers would certainly catch a glimpse of their dead comrades.

"Move aside," the soldier grunted to Clay, who now looked exactly like one of the blue-uniformed soldiers.

"We're finished in here," Clay growled back, imitating the voice of one of the men he'd killed. He had heard two of the men calling each other Jim and Ray, so he used these names before the man at the door could respond. "Jim and Ray have already moved on, this bitch here told 'em about a house down the street where there's a guy who's got a lot of guns and ammo in a safe. I got this bag of supplies, but there ain't nothing more in this little dump worth taking."

He thrust the duffel bag at the soldier, who took it and opened it to briefly search through the contents. He nodded, satisfied. "Nice work," he said. "I thought there'd be more in here, though."

"There isn't," Clay said. "Nothing else worth taking."

"What are you gonna do with this cougar?" the soldier asked, an edge of evil mirth to his voice.

"She told me she's got some diamonds and shit in her safe back at her house. I'm gonna take her there and relieve her of those items, then have a little fun with her in private. She ain't bad-looking for an old whore, is she?"

The soldier chuckled darkly. "I wouldn't mind having some fun with her myself. But I've got some stuff to take care of for Phillips first. Which house did you say Jim and Ray went to?"

"Tell him where you told my friends to go, bitch," Clay growled at Diana, tightening his grip on her hair and giving her head a rough shaking.

"Ow, ow, I, I told them to go to Mr. Eaton's place, he's got a lot of ammo and guns there, it's four blocks away, on Fifth Street, uh, you'll see a brand new silver Mercedes sedan parked outside his house. I, I told them to go there. Please, please don't hurt me, don't hurt me…" She didn't have to put on much of an act, for she was genuinely terrified at this moment.

"All right, and this Mr. Eaton asshole," the soldier said to Diana, "he isn't going to welcome Jim and Ray with a spray of hot lead, is he?"

"No, no, he's away on a f-, fishing trip," Diana stammered, "that's why I sent them there, it's, it's totally safe." This part was true, even though everything else she'd said was a lie. Mr. Eaton was away on a fishing trip and his house was empty. There were no guns or ammo in it, though.

"I'll meet you boys there when I've relieved this whore of her jewelry and given her what I've got," Clay said. "We can meet up there shortly."

The soldier nodded. "All right. I'll tell Phillips, and we'll meet up with you, Jim, and Ray soon."

The soldiers turned around and got back into the Humvee and then drove off. Clay softened his grip on Diana's hair, and they both released a sigh of relief when the men left, even though the tension and threat level remained high.

"Okay, they bought it, thank God," Clay said. "But they'll find out the truth soon enough. Let's drag these bodies away, where they can't be seen from outside, and then you need to lock up the store."

"And after that?" Diana asked. Her mind was still reeling with fear and confusion, and she could hardly believe that all of this was really happening.

"One thing at a time," Clay said calmly. "Let's move the bodies."

They went into the store and dragged the dead bodies into an aisle where they couldn't be seen from outside. After that, Diana locked the front door.

"What do we do now?" she asked. "Can we get away on your Harley?"

Clay shook his head. "I love my bike, but it's as useful as a damn boat anchor right now, and that beautiful V-twin motor is never going to roar again. No, the EMP has killed most vehicles. We have to move on foot for the moment. We might be able to steal one of their Humvees if the opportunity arises, but for now, let's just get out of here before they discover the dead guys. You're going to have to pretend to be my hostage again. I won't hurt you, but we're going to have to put on a convincing act if we come across more of the soldiers."

"Okay, okay, I understand," Diana said. "Let's go to my house. My boyfriend Frank, he's an ex-Green Beret and a prepper, he'll be coming for me there. He told me that if any sort of disaster scenario happened, I should go wait at my house for him. He'll know what to do."

Clay nodded. "All right, I'll help you get there. If you've got some food we could share, I'd be mighty grateful for that. After that, I'll head out on my own."

"Thank you again for saving my life," Diana said. "I don't know how to repay you."

"We're not out of the woods," Clay cautioned. "So don't go thanking me just yet. A hot meal – if you've got a camping stove or something at home – will be payment enough. Come on, we'd better go."

They left out of the back entrance to the store, and Clay marched Diana through the streets at gunpoint, keeping the muzzle of the M-16 pressed into her back. A Humvee drove past them at one point and slowed down to shine gas lanterns on them, but when Clay gave them a salute, they drove on without stopping and hassling them. As they walked through the eerily dark town, where almost no lights shone aside from one or two camping lanterns and some candles, they saw that the soldiers had looted more stores. Alarmingly, a number of gunshots and screams that came from the other side of the small town shattered the silence with disturbing frequency, but both of them realized there was nothing they could do to help whoever the soldiers were attacking and harming. They could only take care of themselves.

They finally got to Diana's house, but when they arrived, relief was not a feeling either of them experienced. Instead, both were hit with a sinking feeling of dread … for a Humvee was parked outside her house, and soldiers were waiting on her porch.

6

"*A*re you sure this is an EMP?" Melissa asked her brother nervously.

"It's gotta be," Chuck said, his head spinning with the implications of what this meant. "What else could have taken out every single piece of electronic equipment at once?"

"So … we're totally screwed then, aren't we?" Melissa murmured. "Grandpa isn't here to help us, and neither is Aunt Olive. And Mr. Redman is gone, and if Grandpa is right about what an EMP does to cars and stuff, he won't be coming back…"

"Grandpa is right about everything he's told us about EMPs," Chuck said. "Trust me, I looked it all up on Google. And yeah, Mr. Redman and Adrian are gonna be stuck somewhere in the middle of the desert, unless they made it to a town before the EMP hit. I don't know what's worse, though, being out here all alone in a situation like this, or being in a place where people are gonna be going crazy and doing all sorts of crazy stuff because they don't understand what's going on."

"In a town or city there'll be food and stuff, at least for a while," Melissa said. "We've got barely enough food and water for a day. Mr. Redman was supposed to drive us out of here tomorrow morning."

"Nobody's gonna be driving us anywhere, not ever again," Chuck said glumly.

"So … what are we gonna do? How are we gonna get out of the desert? Where are we gonna go? What are we gonna eat and drink? What are we gonna tell the others? Who's—"

"Quit asking so many questions!" Chuck snapped. "You're driving me nuts! Just, just gimme a moment to think, okay."

"Sorry," Melissa murmured, tracing a pattern in the sand with her toes. "I'm just … I'm scared, Chuck."

"I'm scared too," Chuck admitted. "But we can't panic. That's Grandpa's number one rule in a sticky situation: don't panic. Use your head. It's never as bad as you think it is, and if it is, you're gonna die anyway so just accept it. That's what he always said. So, uh, it's bad, yeah, but let's not panic."

"But seriously, what are we gonna tell the others?" Melisa looked over at the other children, who were getting agitated about the fact that nobody's phone would turn on, and that every piece of electronic equipment in the camp was now dead. "They don't know anything about this EMP stuff, and if we tell them, will they even believe us?"

"They have to believe to us," Chuck said. "They don't have a choice. How else can they explain what's just happened?"

"All right, so they believe us about the EMP," Melissa said. "What then? What are we gonna do?"

"We have to get out of the desert," Chuck said. "That's our mission. Tomorrow is gonna be one of the hottest days of the year, and we're going to be in serious trouble if we run out of water. So the first thing I'm going to do is ration our food and water. We're gonna have to have a very light dinner, and then pack up camp."

"Pack up camp?"

"Yeah," Chuck said. "We have a long hike ahead of us tonight. We can't afford to sit around and wait for help that's never going to come. And we sure as hell can't hike under the heat of tomorrow's sun, which will roast us alive and dehydrate us real fast if we're out hiking. No, we have to use the night to hike. No sleep tonight; we need to get as far as we can before the sun comes up."

"That sounds crazy, Chuck," Melissa said. "How will you even know where to go?"

"I've got my compass, and Grandpa taught me how to navigate using the stars. It's a clear evening, and I'll be able to tell exactly where I'm going."

"And where exactly *are* we going?" Melissa asked.

"We'll head to Aunt Diana's place. It's not the closest

town, but at least we'll be able to get some help there. And Aunt Di won't mind helping the other kids out and giving them a place to stay for a while until we can figure out how to get them back to their parents in the city."

"That's really far away, Chuck."

"Well, do you have a better idea? I figure we can get there in maybe … three days, if we hike through every night and rest during the day."

"Three days?! But … we've barely got enough food and water for one day!"

"I know, I know," Chuck said. "But like I said, do you have a better idea? Nobody's going to come out here and rescue us, and if we stay put we'll … well, I don't think our chances are very good."

"But the water!" Melissa gasped. "We won't have water for at least two days!"

"We might be able to find some," Chuck said. "We can live without food for three days, but water … yeah, it'll be a problem. If it comes down to it, we can drink small amounts from a fishhook barrel cactus. Grandpa showed me how to identify 'em, and how to drink from 'em. Only in a real emergency, though, coz you can only drink a little cactus water before it makes you sick. Anyway, enough questions, let's go tell the others what's up."

Chuck and Melissa returned to the group and explained to the other children exactly what had just happened, and what an EMP was, and what it meant for them. As they had expected, the other kids were somewhat reluctant to accept the idea at first, but when Chuck explained things in more detail and pointed out that every single electronic item in the camp had died simultaneously, shortly after they had seen the strange flashes of light on the horizon, the others were convinced. Nobody was happy about the idea of hiking through the night, but they realized that due to the danger the heat of the following day posed to their survival, and the fact that they would have to severely ration their supplies, they accepted the idea and began packing up the camp.

Once everything was packed up, Chuck rationed out some food and they cooked a small meal over the fire and ate it in glum, worried silence before putting the fire out. Then they each had a sip of water, slipped their backpacks on, and set off into the night, with Chuck leading them, navigating through the dark desert by the bright starry sky above, and with each silently worrying about what new dangers and difficulties the coming day would bring.

$\mathcal{T}$he journey to the town in the valley was one Frank usually did by truck or motorcycle, but he had nonetheless done it on foot before. What was around a half-hour drive was now a four-hour hike – and that was hiking at a rapid pace that would have left a younger man breathless. Coming out of the hills, the trees thinned in density and then disappeared as he and Boris started to get into the sandy, scrub-covered terrain that surrounded the town.

Cover was limited around here, and Frank knew that he had to keep a low profile and move with stealth in case any of the mysterious militiamen were patrolling the outskirts of town. The strange soldiers – terrorists, rather, for that was who Frank was sure these men were – were not the only dangers he was worried about, though. While he knew he had left the hungry mountain lion far behind, he certainly didn't want to step on a rattlesnake or any other sort of poisonous viper, and snakes were active in the dark. He hoped that Boris's sharp canine senses would detect any snakes before he stepped on them.

Diana's house was on the outskirts of town, which was a good thing for what Frank wanted to do: get in quick, and get her out just as fast, hopefully without having to fire a single shot or slip his hunting knife into anyone's windpipe.

From what he could see from the point he reached at around five in the morning, shortly before sunrise, the town was mostly shrouded in darkness, with only a few lights burning here and there. He got out his binoculars to get a better look at things. Diana had told him that the terrorists had arrived in Humvees, but he couldn't see any of those from his vantage point, which was at the top of a small hill that overlooked the western section of the town, where Diana's house was. He was sure that they were there, though.

One of the buildings in the center of town was on fire, and Frank suspected that the blaze was no accident. He doubted that the terrorists wanted to completely annihilate the town, but he guessed that they would engage in some acts of destruction to throw their weight around and intimidate the townsfolk.

He was about to head down from the top of the hill and make his way to Diana's backyard, which bordered the open desert, when he saw them: two headlamps cutting through the dark streets of Diana's neighborhood. He raised his binoculars to his eyes to get a better look at the vehicle and saw that it was a Humvee painted a dark shade of blue. Two terrorists in blue uniforms, armed with M-16 rifles, with balaclavas hiding their faces, were leaning out of the passenger windows of the vehicle, peering all around and obviously searching for someone. They rolled along slowly, with the Humvee sweeping the glow of its headlamps across dark houses and empty yards at a crawling pace, before they finally disappeared down one of the streets, where they continued their search.

"So the bastards have taken the town, have they," Frank growled to himself. It infuriated him to see that terrorists had simply walked in and taken over the town like this. He knew that the sheriff was notoriously lazy and inept, but surely the man and his deputies could have at least put up some sort of token resistance?

Boris growled and then let out a few sharp barks, interrupting Frank's thoughts.

"What's up, boy?" he asked after getting Boris to quiet down.

He didn't want to use any of his LED headlamps, for they would make him stick out like a sore thumb in the dark, but as it turned out, he didn't need any light to identify the threat that was nearby. An ominous rattle cut through the silence of the desert night, and in the gloom, Frank managed to make out the gleaming scales of a rattlesnake a mere few feet away.

"Well spotted boy, well spotted," Frank said to Boris in a soft, calm tone before backing slowly away from the rattlesnake, taking care not to startle it. As long as he and Boris left the snake alone and didn't antagonize it, he knew that it would leave them alone too.

When they were a safe distance away from the rattlesnake, Frank decided that it was time to head straight for Diana's house. Sunrise was only forty-five minutes away, and if he didn't get her out before it was light, his mission would become more difficult and dangerous by an exponential degree.

He and Boris headed straight for her backyard, which was a few hundred yards from this spot. They moved swiftly across the desert, with Frank staying low and moving from bush to bush for cover; even though it was still dark out here, he didn't want to take any risk of being spotted. He also kept his eyes open for any more rattlesnakes, but knew that he was likely safe from them since Boris was undoubtedly on high alert for snakes after having just seen one.

They got to Diana's backyard, and Frank let himself and Boris in through the gate that opened out onto the desert. The house was shrouded in darkness, and Frank wasn't sure whether this was a good sign or a bad one. Either way, he had to hurry; sunrise was getting ever closer, and the dark sky was becoming lighter with every passing moment.

He and Boris hurried across the yard and got up to the back door, which he slipped his spare key into, quietly unlocking it. He put his AK-47 over his shoulder and took out his .357; the revolver would be better for close-quarters combat, if it came to that. He also loosened his hunting knife in its sheath, just in case.

"Wait here, boy, stay, there's a good boy," he said to Boris. Boris knew this command well, and no matter what happened, he would stay right here until Frank called him again. He sat down by the door in obedient silence.

Frank then drew in a deep, calming breath, which he held in his lungs for a while, and he opened the door and stepped into the dark house, moving on light feet as subtly and quietly as any phantom. He crept through the kitchen and stepped cautiously into the hallway … where he came face to face with one of the terrorists, who was armed with an M-16 rifle.

8

"Oh no, oh no, what do we do now?" Diana asked anxiously as she and Clay ducked into the dense black shadows beneath a tree on the sidewalk.

Clay peered at the four soldiers who were standing on Diana's porch. They seemed to be waiting for someone else who was likely inside the house, for the front door was open. They were looking out at the street, but not watching it very intently.

"Besides working in that store, do you do anything else in this town?" Clay asked, whispering. "By that, I mean do you have any sort of authority here? Do you have any connections to powerful or influential people, or the Army or government?"

"No, nothing at all like that," Diana whispered back. "I just own my little trading store and live a modest life here, that's all."

"What about your husband?"

"He passed away a few years ago, and no, he wasn't connected to anything like that either. The store belonged to him, and that was all he did when he was alive. He wasn't involved in the military or government or anything like that," she answered.

"Then these goons aren't likely looking for you. They're probably just looting your house because nobody's home. Let's just wait here until they're done and they move on to someone else's place."

"Are you sure?" Diana asked nervously. "You don't think they might have, you know, found the bodies in the store?"

"Even if they had, how would they know you live here? Is there anything in the store that would lead them to your house?" Clay asked.

"Um, no, I don't think so," Diana answered.

"Then they're probably just looting. Let's wait here for them to finish, and when they're gone, we'll sneak in."

They waited with bated breath in the shadows beneath the tree, carefully watching the men on Diana's porch. After a few minutes, another soldier came out of the house carrying a duffel bag bulging with items. Diana winced at the sight of it, knowing that the bag was likely filled with her most valuable possessions that these thugs were shamelessly stealing, but she held her tongue and stayed still; her life was a far more valuable possession than anything in that duffel bag, and she wasn't about to throw it away.

"Looks like I was right," Clay whispered. "Sorry about your stuff, but it's only stuff, right?"

"Right," Diana muttered sadly.

The soldiers loaded the duffel bag into the back of the Humvee and then drove slowly on down the street, looking for houses that seemed unoccupied – those that didn't have the lights of candles or gas lamps burning gently in the windows. When they found another seemingly unoccupied house down the street, they pulled the Humvee up in the driveway. Clay and Diana watched as the heavily armed soldiers went up to the door and pounded on it, demanding that whoever was inside open up. The men did this a few times, and then, when there was no response and it was obvious that nobody was home, one of them kicked the door in while holding an empty duffel bag, ready to loot the place of whatever valuables he found, as he'd done in Diana's place.

"The good news," Clay said, "is that now that they've looted your place, they won't come back to it, at least not for a while, now that they think it's unoccupied. You should be safe for a little bit."

"I guess you're right," she said. "Should we move now?"

"Not yet," he said. "I don't want to risk being spotted. Wait for them to finish looting that house; when they're done, they'll probably go around the corner and continue their thieving on the next street. It'll be safe to move then."

They waited in silence in the shadows for what felt

like hours. Finally, the man emerged from the house with his duffel bag bulging with looted valuables, and he and his companions got into their Humvee and drove around the corner. Once they were gone, Clay checked quickly up and down the street, making sure that there were no more of the soldiers hanging around, and then he and Diana jogged briskly but quietly across her front lawn and slipped into her house through the open front door.

"Oh no, they've ruined my door!" she complained; the men had kicked in the front door and completely destroyed the lock and door handle mechanisms.

"A broken door handle is going to be the least of your concerns on a night like this," Clay said dryly. Since he was finally safe, he was able to take off his balaclava, which he tucked into one of the back pockets of his combat pants, in case he quickly had to put it back on. "Wait here, I'm going to make sure there ain't nobody waiting in the shadows to give us a nasty surprise."

He crept through the house with catlike stealth, his senses on high alert. After spending a while checking things out, he found that the house was, thankfully, empty.

"It's all clear," he said upon returning to the front hallway, where Diana was waiting. "We're safe … for now."

"Thank God," she murmured, feeling as if a hefty weight had just been lifted from her shoulders, although a good measure of fear, worry, and anxiety remained and continued to percolate in her guts. "But what do we do now?"

"If you've got anything nutritious to eat, that'd be great," Clay said. "I've got a long journey ahead of me tonight, and I need some fuel for it."

"All right, I've got some stuff in the fridge I can cook up on my camping stoves," she said. "I'm not too hungry after everything I've seen and been through tonight, I have to say, but I know it'd be a wise move to get some food in me and keep my energy levels up. I expect when Frank gets here, he's going to want to take me back to his cabin in the hills, which will be a long hike."

"Sounds like he's got his head screwed on right," Clay said. "With everything that's just happened and this strange new world we've transitioned into, the remains of civilization are gonna be the last place anyone will want to be. The more remote and isolated you are, the better chance you have of surviving what's coming."

"The living room is over that way," Diana said. It was dark and gloomy inside the house, but with the gentle moonlight coming in through the front door, Clay could make out where she was pointing.

"Great. It'll be a welcome break to sit down and rest on a sofa for a while," Clay said. "I'll head over that way. Oh, and uh, you got a chair to prop up against the door here, just to keep it closed? It ain't a great solution, but it'll at least temporarily stop one of those goons from just wandering in here without warning if they do come back."

"Sure, there's a wooden chair just down the hall to your left. I'll be in the kitchen if you need anything else."

"All right. Just be careful with using your gas lamps," Clay said.

"I go camping a lot," Diana said. "I know all about using gas safely."

"No, I meant the light itself; we don't want people outside to see that there's anyone here. Block up your kitchen windows, or cook in a room where the light won't be seen from the street."

"Ah, yes, of course," she said. "Good thinking. I'll take the stoves to the spare bedroom and cook in there."

Around half an hour later, Diana had cooked up a quick but nutritious meal, which she shared with Clay by candlelight in the spare bedroom, with both of them sitting on the floor.

"You said you've got a long journey ahead of you," Diana said as she ate. "Where are you going?"

"I'm heading south, into the desert," Clay said. "Chasing a bounty."

Diana was quite surprised to hear this. "But … what's the point of doing that, now that society and civilization have been turned upside down? Who's going to care about bounties now, or money, even?"

A hard glint shone in Clay's eyes, and his scarred mouth curled into a dark scowl. "It ain't about money anymore. It's about justice. The guys I'm after, this Mexican cartel leader and his top lieutenants, they murdered my partner and his wife. I was headed down there to capture 'em and get the satisfaction of not only locking their evil asses up for the rest of their natural lives, but also the big reward offered for them. Now, though, I'll be content just to blow their ugly heads off and know that Nathan and Betsy's deaths have been avenged."

"Are you sure that that's … wise?" Diana asked. "I understand that you want to avenge your friends' deaths … but at a time like *this?* Isn't it far more dangerous to do something like that now than it was before?"

Clay shrugged. "What the hell else have I got left to live for? I don't have no wife, no kids, nothing like that. Nathan and Betsy were pretty much the only family I had, and those scumbags took them away from me. Sure, I could run off deep into the wilderness and save my ass, and live off the land pretty much indefinitely … but knowing that those scumbags who murdered my best friend and his woman were still out there, walking around free after what they did, it'd eat me alive. No, screw that. This is what I'm gonna do, regardless of what happened. It's what I *have to* do."

"I understand," Diana said. She remembered vividly just how devastated she had been when her husband had died many years ago, and although his death had been from natural causes, she knew that if he had been murdered, she too would have felt a burning desire for vengeance against those who had done the deed.

They ate mostly in silence after this. Diana was a fantastic cook, and even with the limitations imposed by the complete lack of electricity and equipment, and only being able to use small camping stoves, she had been able to whip up a tasty and nutritious meal. Both of them felt a lot better after their bellies were full.

"When are you going to leave?" Diana asked. "I'm sorry," she added hastily, "I'm not trying to drop a hint that I want you to go. I'm just asking, because I don't know how long it'll be before my Frank gets here, and … well, I'm a little scared to be here on my own with those horrible men on the prowl, and everything that's happened."

"You don't have a gun here?" Clay asked.

"I did have a pistol, but those awful people stole it, along with all the ammunition that was in the drawer," Diana answered.

"Hmm, you don't have any other weapons here to protect yourself with?"

"I've got my compound bow and a few arrows," she said. "Archery is one of my hobbies, in case you were wondering why I have that. Not that they'll do much good against a man with a gun…"

"Better than nothing," Clay said. "And if you're a good shot with that bow, you could take a man down with it easily enough, as long as you shoot him before he spots you. But all right, I'll hang around until your man shows up, if that'll make you feel safer. I guess I could use a few hours of sleep before my trek into the desert anyway. But if your boyfriend hasn't showed up by dawn, I'm afraid I'm going to have to leave you on your own then. I have to leave town while it's still dark; I can't risk traveling in the open in daylight."

"I understand, and I really appreciate that," Diana said. "I'll get you a blanket and a pillow; the sofa is very comfy."

"Thank you," Clay said. He took the dishes to the kitchen while Diana got the sofa ready for him.

"It's all done and ready for you to take a nap," she said. "I'm going to get a few of my things together – just a few little things of sentimental value that I'm going to take with me when Frank comes. I'll pack a bunch of food and stuff, and I'll pack you a backpack of supplies and stuff for your trip too."

"Thank you kindly, I appreciate that," Clay said.

"Don't mention it," Diana said with a shrug. "The food would all be going to waste anyway. I might as well give it to a good person."

"Wake me if there's any sign of trouble, or whenever your man shows up," Clay said. Then he took off his boots, curled up on the sofa, and was asleep in seconds. As a bounty hunter, he was accustomed to sleeping in all sorts of places in stressful situations, so he had no trouble falling asleep.

Diana, meanwhile, busied herself with sorting out a few things by candlelight. Now that Clay wasn't awake to witness it, she broke down, weeping softly on her own in her bedroom. She was still reeling from everything that had happened, and the implications of what the EMP meant for her in this terrifying new world into which she been so viciously and suddenly thrust. She had been mentally preparing herself to move out of this place and into Frank's place, but she hadn't counted on it happening so soon. She had lived in this house for the last thirty years, ever since she and her former husband had gotten married. There were so many memories in these walls, and it was hard to simply leave them all behind like this without looking back, even though she knew that that was the only thing she could do.

After spending an hour or so quietly mourning for the loss of her former life, she steeled her will and got busy with the task at hand. She sorted out all of the perishable and semi-perishable food in the pantry and started packing various items into three spare back-packs she had. She also had a few water purification bottles, which she added to the packs. Once she had done this, she packed a few essential items of clothing and got her bow and arrows. She was a brilliant shot with her bow, and had taken first prize in a number of archery contests. She wasn't sure how useful the bow would be when she was up against men armed with assault rifles, but like Clay had said, it was better than nothing.

By the time it was past midnight. Diana was weary, but she didn't think she would be able to get any sleep, not with her stress and anxiety levels being at their current levels. So, instead of sleeping, she just went quietly around to each room in her house and spent some time in it, recalling all the memories associated with each room, knowing that it would be the last time she got to experience that memory in the room in which it had been created.

The town was mostly quiet, strangely enough, aside from the odd burst of gunfire and shouting in the distance, and the sound of Humvees occasionally driving along the street outside. If it weren't for those scattered bouts of frightening noise, it could have been just like any other night she had spent under this roof in the last three decades.

Finally, in the early hours of the morning, she felt tired enough to catch an hour or two of sleep. She wondered if she should wake Clay up so that he could stand guard, but decided against it; he was about to set off on a long journey and needed his sleep, and despite the worrying situation she was in, it didn't seem as if there was any clear and present danger. She figured it would be safe to just get some sleep for an hour or two.

She lay down on her bed and closed her eyes. She wasn't worried about oversleeping; her body's natural alarm clock had always been very accurate, and if she set out to sleep for exactly two hours, she would naturally wake in almost exactly that amount of time. She made a mental note to wake up in two hours, and then closed her eyes and finally fell asleep.

It barely felt as if she'd closed her eyes when she felt as if she was jolted awake. She got out a cigarette lighter and in the dim orange light of its flame, she glanced at her watch – a vintage mechanical wind-up wristwatch from the early 20th century which was working just fine, and completely unaffected by the EMP – and saw that she had indeed slept for two hours.

She yawned, not feeling very refreshed, and struggled up onto her feet. She got dressed, parted the drapes to look outside, and saw the sky was growing light with the approaching dawn. She sighed, feeling a tide of fear, worry, and disappointment crashing in, for Frank had still not arrived, and sunrise was just around the corner.

She walked over to the door, intending to wake Clay up so that he could be on his way before first light … but before she could open it, a sledgehammer of pure terror slammed into her as a deafening, thunderous barrage of gunfire erupted in the hallway mere feet away.

9

"What if one of us steps on a freaking rattlesnake or something?" asked Kenneth, a skinny, long-limbed fourteen-year-old boy with close-cropped blond hair. "I uh, I think we should have just stayed at the campsite and waited for the grownups to come find us."

Kenneth was perpetually worrying about things, and while Chuck was usually able to keep a level head and remain calm in situations of stress, Kenneth's constant whining was starting to get to him. They had only been hiking for an hour, but Kenneth had been complaining for most of that time.

"Kenneth, we're not going to step on any rattlesnakes as long as everyone keeps tapping the ground with their sticks while we walk," Chuck said. "Snakes aren't dumb; they don't want to be stepped on, and as long as we make some noise while we move, they'll make sure they aren't in our path."

"But if someone gets bit, what are we gonna do?" Kenneth whined. "There's no car and no grownup to drive us out of here, and—"

"Just shut up, Kenneth!" Chuck snapped, temporarily losing control of his temper.

"Kenneth, we've already explained many times why this is the only thing we can do in this situation," Melissa said, stepping in before her brother's temper got too heated. He was a slow burner, and it took forever to get his temper up, but in situations when someone did prod him enough to get him to lose it, he would usually explode in a spectacular fashion. This was the last thing any of them needed. "Jeez, do you even know how obsessed Chuck is with snakes and reptiles and stuff?" she continued. "He spends all his time reading up on them and watching YouTube videos about snakes and lizards and other gross critters like that. My point is, he totally knows what he's talking about, so if he says that snakes will stay out of our way if we keep hitting the ground while we walk, I totally trust him – and you should too."

"Okay, okay," Kenneth muttered. "But if I get bit, it's Chuck's fault!"

"Are you sure you know where you're going?" asked Priscilla, a pretty, quiet, and introverted thirteen-year-old girl of Japanese ancestry. "Navigating by the stars, I mean. I um, I don't see how anyone can see any patterns in all those thousands of specks of light."

"Trust me, I know where I'm going," Chuck said, calming down even though he was still highly annoyed with Kenneth. He had a bit of a crush on Priscilla, so it was easy to cool his temper off when she was asking him questions rather than Kenneth. "My grandpa taught me how to do this. He's super cool, he was a Green Beret, he knows pretty much everything there is to know about survival and stuff like that."

"You can really tell the difference between all those stars up there just by looking at 'em?" Priscilla asked.

Chuck grinned, any semblance of annoyance gone now that his attention was focused on Priscilla. "Sure!" he replied enthusiastically. "I can show you some of the constellations. Once you can pick out the patterns in the sky, they're easy to spot. See those three stars over there? Those three are Orion's belt. And the rest of Orion, the hunter, is easy enough to make out once you've located his belt."

As they walked through the dark desert, tapping their sticks on the ground, Chuck showed Priscilla the rest of Orion, as well as some other easy-to-spot constellations. Melissa and Kenneth followed behind them, and bringing up the rear was Joe, a chubby, shy African-American boy who rarely spoke, but who was honest, smart, and dependable.

"I don't know what I'm gonna do without my phone," Kenneth complained. "Are you guys serious, no phones at all will work anymore because of this EMP thing? Man, that's crazy. No phones, no TVs, no game consoles, no tablets, no computers … I can't even begin to imagine how crap my life is gonna be now."

"Why are you in the hiking club if you like all of

that stuff so much?" Melissa asked. There was nothing sarcastic or sardonic in her tone, though; she was genuinely curious why someone who seemed to love technology so much would be voluntarily going on a camping trip in the middle of the desert. "You sound like you'd rather spend your time staring at screens than being out in nature."

"My stupid dad made me join this club and go on these stupid hikes," Kenneth muttered. "He says I spend too much time staring at screens..."

"Gee, I wonder why," Melissa said, rolling her eyes.

They walked along, quietly talking among themselves, for another hour before Chuck called a halt and allowed each of them to have a carefully rationed sip of water and a small morsel of food. Kenneth tried to sneakily take more than his fair share, but Chuck spotted him and was quick to snatch the bottle away from him before he could glug down half the precious contents.

"Come on, Kenneth!" Chuck said harshly. "I know that you're thirsty, we *all* are, but this water is all we've got and it might be the only thing we get to drink for three days. Please dude, you need to take this seriously and be considerate and forward thinking, okay?"

"Okay, okay," Kenneth muttered, his cheeks hot with both embarrassment and anger at having been caught trying to take more than his fair share. Despite the darkness that surrounded them, he was sure that he could feel the other kids' eyes staring angrily at him and burning holes in his back. Instead of feeling guilty and remorseful about what he had done, he felt angry that Chuck had seen him doing it, and he quietly resolved to get revenge on him for supposedly humiliating him in front of the others.

"All right everyone, we've had our rations, let's get moving again," Chuck said, oblivious to the silent rage radiating from Kenneth in the darkness. "I know you're all tired from the long hike, but we have to get going. Tomorrow's heat is going to be crazy, and we won't be able to move at all while the sun is up, so we have to cover as much distance as we can now while it's cool enough to do that. Let's go."

The children set off into the night. They hiked for another two hours, and by the time they stopped for their next rations of food and water, they were all quite exhausted. This time it was not only Kenneth who was complaining; Joe was weary and unhappy, as was Priscilla. And even though she knew that they had to cover as much ground as they could while the night was cool and the sky was dark, Melissa was exhausted too. Her legs and feet ached, her throat burned, and her stomach was starting to hurt from hunger.

Chuck, of course, wasn't immune from the same discomfort and pains suffered by his peers, but he bore his suffering with his grandfather's stoic defiance, and urged them all to press on through their pain and tiredness. Soon, though, their pace slowed to a crawl, and it didn't take long for the other kids, spurred on by Kenneth's ceaseless whining and complaining, to start to rebel against Chuck.

"All right, all right," Chuck eventually said, breaking under the unending pressure. "We'll stop and sleep here. There's only an hour or two until dawn anyway, I guess we can't have gone much further."

"Let us have some more water!" Kenneth demanded. "I'm so thirsty it feels like I haven't drunk for days!"

"No," Chuck said firmly. "I already gave you your rations for tonight. We have to make this water last."

"Come on, man," Joe, who was usually so reticent, pleaded. "My throat's so dry my mouth tastes like sand. Can't we all just have a small sip, just to wet our mouths?"

"Please, Chuck?" Priscilla asked.

Chuck looked over at his sister, hoping for some support from her corner. She shrugged, unsure of what to say. The truth was, she was just as thirsty as the others, and was finding it harder and harder to justify not asking for an extra sip, even though her brain told her it was necessary to ration the water in this manner.

"Okay, okay," Chuck said, unable to stave off the mounting pressure any longer. "One tiny sip. We can each have one very small sip. But that's all."

Everyone took a small sip, including Kenneth, who, this time, made a show of taking a smaller sip than anyone else.

"Why should Chuck be the one who gets to keep the water and ration it out?" Kenneth said to the others after he had taken his sip. "How do we know that he isn't gonna wait until we're all asleep, and then drink a whole bunch himself?"

"Come on man, you know I'm not gonna do that," Chuck said, doing his best to stay calm despite a sudden flare of anger within him at this blatant attack from Kenneth.

Thankfully, Melissa jumped to his defense immediately. "Don't be ridiculous, Kenneth," she said. "My brother is the most trustworthy person I know. There's no way he's gonna do anything like that."

"Yeah dude," Joe added. "I've known Chuck since first grade. I trust him."

"I also think he's the best person to keep the food and water," Priscilla added. Over the last few hours of walking and talking with Chuck, she had found that she had started to develop a crush on him.

Chuck grinned triumphantly, happy both that his peers trusted him so much, and that Kenneth's attempt at stoking a rebellion had backfired. Kenneth, meanwhile, scowled darkly and quietly clenched his fists. His determination to get revenge on Chuck had now grown even fiercer. He pretended, however, to be nonchalant. "Okay, well if you're all cool with Chuck keeping the supplies, I am too," he said calmly. "I was just checking."

They got out their sleeping bags and tents and set up camp by the light of one of the gas lamps. They got set up quickly enough, and it didn't take long for them to fall asleep … everyone but Kenneth, that was. He waited in the dark until he was sure that everyone else was asleep, and then he quietly slipped out of his sleeping bag and crept over to the bag of supplies, smiling evilly.

"*Nobody* makes Kenneth Johnson look like an idiot, *nobody*," he whispered, staring maliciously at the sleeping form of Chuck. "And *you're* about to find out what happens when you do that, Chuck, you asshole…"

He quietly unzipped the bag and began his nefarious work.

$\mathcal{F}$rank may have been retired from the military for many years, but his soldier's instincts, drilled so forcefully into his body and mind that they had become muscle memory, were as sharp now as they were twenty years ago.

The instant he saw the terrorist in the hallway of Diana's house, he opened fire, pumping three shots from his .357 directly into the man's torso. The terrorist went down, but he was far from dead, and he opened up on Frank from the ground, spraying the walls with a ferocious burst of automatic fire from his M-16 rifle.

Frank dived to the ground as the bullets tore through the walls and rained down masonry dust and chunks of plaster on him, rolling to get behind the cover of a large wooden bookshelf in the hallway. He immediately returned fire from his position of cover, blasting three more shots at the man, who had crawled into the cover of a doorway and was groaning with pain.

"Clay!" a familiar voice screamed from Diana's bedroom. "Are you okay?! What's going on?!"

"Di!" Frank yelled back. "It's me! Who the hell is Clay?! I just shot some sonofabitch terrorist who was skulking around your house!"

"I ain't no damn terrorist!" Clay groaned from the doorway. "Don't shoot, dammit, don't fuckin' shoot me again!"

"He's a friend!" Diana screamed. "Both of you, stop shooting! Don't fire another shot!"

Diana ran out of the bedroom, carrying a gas lantern to illuminate the hallway. Her ears were ringing with a shrill whine from the brief but furious barrage of gunfire, and the hallway smelled like gunpowder smoke. The walls had been ripped apart from the gunfight, and it looked like a grenade had exploded in here.

"Frank!" Diana gasped, running over to him and throwing her arms around him. Then, however, she shoved the lantern into his hands and ran over to Clay, who was groaning in pain on the floor.

"Oh my God, Frank, what have you done?!" she murmured, staring at Clay in horror. "This man saved my life earlier! And now you've … you've…"

"I'm sorry, I thought he was a terrorist," Frank muttered, getting up and dusting himself off. "He sure is dressed like one."

Diana dropped down onto her knees next to Clay.

Waves of panic were crashing against her, for she thought he was dying.

"I'm … okay," he managed to groan, grimacing with pain. "Probably cracked a few ribs … and my chest is gonna be black and blue from bruising for the next few days … but I'm … okay. Bulletproof vest … level two."

Frank walked over to Clay and sheepishly knelt down next to him. "I'm sorry, friend, I honestly thought you were one of them, coming here to do my Diana harm," he said.

"It's okay," Clay groaned. "Wrong place … wrong time, bad timing. Thank God I decided to put this damn armor on, though."

"Let me help you up," Frank said. He gave Clay a hand and helped pull him up to his feet. In the light from the gas lamp, they could see the three holes ripped in his bulletproof vest where the .357 rounds had slammed into him. They had put three big dents in the plate at the base of the armor, but hadn't gone through it.

"I'd be dead right now if it wasn't for this armor," Clay said. "You're a deadly shot, sir."

"Call me Frank," Frank said. "And again, I'm real sorry about almost killing you."

"Water under the bridge, Frank, water under the bridge," Clay said, still grimacing from the pain. "I'd have done the same in your shoes. I'm Clay, by the way."

From outside came a loud bark. "I'd better let Boris in," Frank said.

ROBERT J WALKER

"Boris?" Clay asked.

"My dog," Frank answered. "He's more than just a pet, before you ask. Best trained German Shepherd this side of—"

"We've got a problem," Diana said, interrupting their conversation. "Listen!"

The men fell silent and listened intently, and soon heard the sound that was causing Diana alarm. From outside came the sound of two Humvees racing up the street and screeching to a halt in Diana's drive.

"Shit," Clay muttered. "I guess someone heard the gunfire. We're in trouble now."

"You got a working vehicle, Clay?" Frank asked, the gears in his mind whirring with efficient speed and cool focus despite the unfolding crisis.

"Nope," Clay answered, popping out his M-16 clip to check how many rounds he had left.

"You will soon enough," Frank said, grinning. "There are two of those Humvees outside – one for you, one for me. We just have to take care of the current owners."

Clay nodded grimly. "I'm with you there, buddy. But I suspect that *doing* that is gonna be a lot harder than *saying* it."

"Maybe not as hard as you might think," Frank said. "Despite the fact that we're considerably outnumbered. Di, do you still have that antique wind-up phonograph in the living room?"

"Yeah I do," she answered, "but I don't see how that will help right—"

"It'll help, trust me," Frank said. "Grab it and that old record of Truman's speeches, wind it up, and get it playing in the bedroom closet. Go, hurry!"

Diana knew not to argue or question Frank's plan; there was no time to do anything but what he said anyway.

"Clay," Frank continued. "I need you to get behind this coat rack at the end of the hall and stand real still. You strike when they line up outside the bedroom; you'll be able to cut a few of 'em down in mere seconds."

"Roger that," Clay said, nodding. "I see what you're trying to do here, and I think it'll work."

Frank hastily helped Clay hide himself among the jumble of coats and hats on the hat rack, and piled some boots around his feet to hide his lower body.

"What are you gonna do?" Clay asked.

"Draw 'em in, then get outside and around to the front, and mop up whatever sons of bitches come running out the door. That reminds me – do *not* come running out the front door, whatever happens. Stay in the house."

"Got it. Good luck, Frank," Clay said, gripping his M-16 and waiting at the ready behind the coats.

Diana returned with the old antique wind-up phonograph, which, due to its entirely mechanical clockwork mechanism, worked just fine despite the EMP attack.

"Hurry, put that in the closet in the bedroom, playing Truman speaking," Frank said, "just loud

77

enough that you can hear it from outside the closet, but not loud enough that you can make out what he's saying. Then get into the bath and lie down, and blast whoever steps through the door full of lead," he said, thrusting his .357 into her hands. "Me and Clay will announce ourselves before stepping anywhere near the bathroom, so if you don't hear our voices, you know whoever's coming in there is an enemy." He gave her a quick, tight hug and then a kiss. "Go, quickly!" he said, "they'll be coming in here any second now!"

Now armed with his AK-47, Frank jogged down the hallway to wait for the terrorists to burst in. He hoped that Boris wouldn't get shot; some of the men would undoubtedly be checking out the yard, where Boris was waiting. There was no time to do anything for his beloved dog now, though. He could only pray that Boris would be okay.

He got to the living room, the door of which opened out into the entrance hall, and heard voices whispering in urgent tones on the porch. From the sound of it, there were six or seven men, possibly more. He couldn't make out what they were saying, but guessed they were adding the final touches to whatever plan they had for their attack on the house.

He got down behind the sofa, which gave him some cover as well as a clear shot at the door; whoever came in first would get peppered with AK rounds.

"Yo MacDuff, are you in there?" a man called out from the porch. "Is everything clear in there? We heard some gunfire."

The men waited for a few tense moments, and then called out once more. "MacDuff, if you're in there and you don't say something, you're gonna get shot – just like whoever else is in there is about to get their asses killed! Last chance, buddy! If I don't hear nothing in the next two seconds, whoever is in there, whoever killed MacDuff, you're fucking dead, you hear me?! Dead, anyone who's in this shithole!"

Frank prepared himself for the coming onslaught. His mind was clear and his breathing was controlled, and his every action and reaction was one that came from decades of intense training and supreme discipline. "Amateurs," he whispered to himself as he lined up the front door in the sights of his AK. "These punks are nothing but a bunch of amateurs."

One of the men kicked open the front door, but nobody charged in … not yet. Instead, Frank heard a hiss from outside, and then saw a canister, belching out thick plumes of smoke, come rolling through the doorway into the entrance hall.

It was either a smoke grenade or a teargas canister. Frank couldn't tell which in the dim half-light of the imminent dawn, but he hoped it wasn't the latter. He had two gas masks, but they were in his backpack, which he had left in the kitchen. All he could do at this stage was improvise, so he yanked the small decorative tablecloth off the nearby coffee table and tied it around the lower half of his face like a bandanna, tucking the bottom into his collar to make a rough seal. It was a poor substitute for a mask, but it would at least filter out some of the smoke and make it a little easier to breathe.

The men outside waited for the canister to billow out its contents, and then, after two or three minutes, when the front section of the house was thick with smoke, they came charging in. Because of the gloomy light of the dawn combined with the choking thickness of the smoke, Frank could barely make out their forms. Even though there was no chance of making an accurate shot, which now put Frank's entire plan in jeopardy, he knew that he had to do what he could.

The men would be wearing armor, the same as Clay's. To take them down, he needed to hit them in their heads – which was a difficult thing to do when it was dark and when smoke was obscuring his vision. He unleashed a burst of rapid fire at the height of the men's heads, his thundering AK shattering the tense silence with sudden violence, and then, before even waiting to see if any of his shots had hit home, he sprayed another burst of fire at leg level; anyone who hadn't been hit by his first spray of fire would have instinctively ducked, and the lower shots would surely hit a few of them.

Then, as the entrance hallway started rocking with the hammering thunder of M-16s blasting return fire in Frank's direction, he took off through the house. Instead of running through to the kitchen, where he could get out via the back door, he bolted down the stairs into the basement.

He prayed that Diana hadn't moved anything

around, because it was pitch dark in here and the only source of light was the narrow window at the far end. Frank knew the layout of the basement well, as he'd helped Diana install some new shelving in it a few months earlier. He knew it well enough to navigate it with his eyes closed – which was what he essentially had to do in this situation.

He hurried through the darkness toward the window, praying that Diana hadn't left a box or a crate out for him to trip over and break his neck. Thankfully she hadn't, and he reached the shelves below the basement window without tripping over anything.

He climbed up the shelves and peeked out of the window into the yard, which was now light with the grayish illumination of dawn. This section of the yard was clear, so he quietly opened the window and crawled out of the house. Stealth would play an important role in his strategy here, so he crept along the side of the house, keeping his body pressed against the walls, and headed around to the backyard.

Despite the barrage of gunfire that had erupted earlier, and the shouting, Boris was still waiting obediently for Frank outside the back door. "Come here, boy," Frank whispered. Boris ran over to his master, wagging his tail with joy, and jumped up to greet him.

"Shh, shh, quiet boy, quiet," Frank whispered before Boris got too excited and started yapping. Boris knew this command and obeyed, whimpering softly as he suppressed his desire to bark with excitement at seeing Frank.

"We've got some work to do, boy, and you're going to help me," Frank said. "Come on, this way!"

Meanwhile, inside, the terrorists were sweeping through the house, which was slowly filling up completely with choking smoke from the grenade. They were wearing gas masks and were thus immune to its effects, but Clay, hiding behind the coats, was starting to feel the effects of it as it grew thicker in the hallway. He knew that if he coughed, he would give his position away and possibly lose his life in the process, so he held his breath. An experienced swimmer, he could hold his breath for over two minutes. He hoped that would be long enough.

Diana was safe from the suffocating smoke in the bathroom, seeing as the door was closed – but only temporarily, for tendrils of smoke were creeping under the door and slowly filling the small bathroom too. She waited on her back in the bathtub in the dark, the cold weight of the big revolver in her shaking hands. She had the weapon aimed at the door, but didn't know if she had it in her to actually pull the trigger if someone came barging in. She would find out soon enough...

A minute had passed from the time Clay had started holding his breath, and the smoke in the hallway was growing thicker. He could hear the terrorists coming closer, but would they fall for Frank's trap before he ran out of breath and then gave himself away by inevitably coughing when he was forced to suck in a lungful of smoke? His hands were growing clammy on the M-16, and a bilious fear was starting to bubble in his guts. If the men didn't come this way soon, the entire plan would fall apart, and the three of them might end up dead.

A minute and a half passed, and Clay's lungs were starting to feel as if they were on fire. It felt as if an elephant had just sat down on his chest, and he was growing light-headed. Every cell in his body was screaming out for him to suck in a breath of air ... but the instant he did that, he would start choking on the acrid smoke and give his position away.

Still, there was nothing else he could do at this point. It was either breathe or pass out – in which case his fainting body would come crashing out of his hiding place and give his position away anyway.

And still the men did not come. The weight on his chest now felt like that of an entire skyscraper, and the burning in his lungs was as if someone was pouring red-hot molten steel down his throat. He couldn't hold his breath any longer. He started counting down ... a countdown that would likely end in his own death. He only hoped he could take down two or three of the terrorists before they inevitably cut him down.

In his mind he counted down, on the verge of passing out: *five, four, three, two...*

*P*ablo Cortez was about to take a hit of crystal meth when all the lights went out. "Shit," he muttered. "Esteban, go see if the generator is out of gas again."

Esteban stood almost a head taller than the short, stocky Pablo, and he was a tough, seasoned brawler and killer with plenty of scars and prison tattoos to show for his exploits, but in Pablo's presence he always felt small and weak. Pablo didn't look particularly menacing – not to an outsider, anyway, who would likely have been far more scared of the hulking, tattooed Esteban – but everyone who actually knew who Pablo Cortez was feared him, and rightly so. He may have looked more like a respectable businessman than a Mexican drug cartel boss, but beneath the expensive, tailored Italian suits and perfectly slicked-back hair, cut and styled by a celebrity stylist, was a

sadistic, violent brute who was among the most ruthless of the cartel leaders.

"I uh, I put some gas in the generator half an hour
ago, boss," Esteban said nervously. "I filled it up, it
should have lasted for another twelve hours at least."

"Well then why the fuck are the lights out?!" Pablo
roared. "Go check that fucking generator or I'll have
your skin mounted on my wall before tomorrow's sun
rises!"

"Okay boss, I'm going, I'm going," Esteban said.

In the thick darkness into which the warehouse had
been plunged, Esteban got up from the table where he,
Pablo, and some other members of Pablo's gang had
been packing and weighing crystal meth to smuggle
across the American border, and walked outside, where
the sun had just set. Just before he turned to go around
the back of the warehouse where the generator was
located, he saw a strange, dazzling series of flashes just
beyond the distant horizon.

"What the fuck is that?" he murmured to himself.
He took out his phone to try to record some footage of
the strange lights but found that it was dead. "Son of a
bitch, just my luck," he muttered, shaking his head
before shoving his phone back into his pocket.

He got to the generator and popped the gas tank
cap off. Even though dusk was falling, it was still light
enough to see inside the tank, and he could see that it
was almost full. He muttered a curse under his breath
and then tried to start the generator, but after a

number of attempts with no sign of it sparking to life, he quickly realized that something was wrong with it.

"Generator's bust, boss," he said when he went back into the dark warehouse. "I tried starting it, but it's totally dead." He cringed, waiting for the inevitable torrent of curses and abuse that Pablo would surely hurl at him.

Instead, however, Pablo spoke with uncertainty in his tone. "Are you sure it's dead, hombre? You checked the spark plug and all that shit?"

"Uh, yeah boss, I checked everything," Esteban replied. "It's totally dead."

"All our phones our dead too," Pablo said. "Something weird is going on."

"I don't know if it's got anything to do with this," Esteban said, "but when I went outside to check the generator, I saw all these strange flashing lights on the horizon…"

"That is strange … very strange," Pablo mused. He didn't know exactly what had happened, but he did suspect that this was something far more significant than a mere power outage. "Esteban, get in the Jeep and drive to town, see what's going on there, if the same shit is happening there."

"All right boss," Esteban said. He walked outside to where a couple of brand-new Jeeps were parked and hopped into the closest one. When he turned the key in the ignition, though, nothing happened. Nothing on the dash lit up, there was no sound, not even an impotent clicking. "What the hell…" he murmured.

He got out and tried another Jeep and found that it was just as dead. He tried all of them, and none of the new vehicles showed even the slightest sign of life. Shaking his head with confusion, he went back inside and explained what had happened to Pablo. Even stranger was the fact that Pablo didn't explode with vicious rage at the news that his entire fleet of brand-new Jeeps were completely dead.

"Interesting," was all Pablo murmured. "All right, there's one more thing to try," he said to Esteban. "Go give the old Yamaha a kick, see if it starts."

"Sure thing, boss." Esteban went back outside to the shed where a few old Yamaha dirt bikes – 70s and 80s-era machines – were parked. Pablo's lower-tier drug mules used these cheap, disposable, and unregistered bikes to smuggle smaller quantities of dope and meth across the border into the United States.

Esteban straddled one of the Yamahas, flipped out the kickstart lever, and gave it a kick. To his surprise, the old bike roared immediately to life, and its single headlamp burned a horizontal pillar of bright light through the thickening darkness of the Mexican desert beyond the warehouse.

He flipped up the kickstand, clicked the bike into gear, and rode it into the entrance of the warehouse, where he put the kickstand back out, hopped off the bike, and left it idling so that its headlamp could serve as a makeshift light to illuminate the inside of the warehouse.

"Ah, good to see that at least something is working!"

Pablo said, rubbing his hands – the fingers of which were thick with gold rings, many of which were encrusted with jewels – together with glee.

Esteban still could not believe that Pablo's incredibly short temper had not yet exploded. He found the fact that his boss hadn't had an outburst even stranger than what was going on with the dead Jeeps and the loss of all electrical power.

"Do you see what's happened, my friends?" Pablo, smiling, asked Esteban and the other cartel members who were sitting around the table.

"Uh, I don't know, boss," Esteban said. "There's some kinda weird power outage, and—"

"No, Esteban, no," Pablo said, his gold-toothed smile gleaming in the light of the dirt bike's headlamp. "It's not just a power outage … it's an *opportunity*. One gigantic fucking opportunity! If this thing is as widespread as I think it is, the *federales* will be totally crippled. We can move a mountain of our shit across the border completely unopposed! We could get more shit across the border tonight than we could in a whole fucking year!"

Murmurs of agreement and excitement rippled around the table.

"We can also get people across the border, boss," Esteban suggested. "Both ways."

Pablo's grin took on a particularly evil nature. "Oh yes, my friend, oh yes," he said. "Some of my friends have been wanting some pretty young American playthings … and now, with this situation, it'll be easier than ever to capture and deliver them. My friends, we need to get every old bike we have! And a couple old trucks from the village. I'm guessing that if our simple old dirt bikes still work, simple old trucks like those pieces of shit from the 60s that the peasants are driving, they'll still work too. Esteban, get on that bike and go spread the word to all my men! Tonight is our night! Tonight … we invade America!"

The children woke soon after dawn broke. There was no cover or shade around them, and even at this early hour, the heat of the rising sun was formidable. While the desert night had been cool and they had been warm and comfortable in their sleeping bags, when the rays of the sun hit them their sleeping bags soon started to heat up to the point of discomfort.

Kenneth was the first to wake up – something he had planned for, and set a mental alarm clock for. He got out of his sleeping bag and deliberately started making noise to wake the others up. He wanted to grin with triumph at having pulled off his dastardly plan for revenge, but he knew that for it to fully succeed, he had to play things cool and act as if nothing was out of the ordinary.

The others groaned and yawned as they awoke, and

everyone felt drained and weary after having had so little sleep.

"All right everyone, let's get our things packed up," Chuck said once he'd crawled out of his sleeping bag and stretched. "We'll have our rations, then get moving. We need to find some shelter where we can hide from the sun and sleep for the rest of the day before it gets too hot."

Everyone lined up to get their rations of water. Again, Kenneth made a show of taking a small sip. Chuck watched this petty display and shook his head but said nothing.

"Okay," Chuck said, "now for some food. We can have those oat bars for breakfast. There's one each, and that's all we can eat until lunchtime." He opened his bag, but found that there were only four oat bars. "Hey, where's the other oat bar?" he asked. "There were five, but one's missing."

Everyone shook their heads and mumbled out confused denials of having taken the missing bar. Chuck immediately suspected Kenneth of having something to do with this, but when he looked up at the boy, Kenneth's face was blank and innocent.

"Come on guys, just own up," Chuck said, feeling a deep anger growing within him. "Who took it?"

"I didn't take it, I promise," Melissa said.

"It wasn't me," Priscilla said.

"I didn't take anything," Kenneth said with a completely straight face.

Everyone turned and looked at Joe. He, being the chubby kid who liked his food, was already subconsciously the prime suspect in everyone's mind – everyone except Chuck.

"What?" Joe said, scowling. "Why are y'all looking at me? I didn't do it. I'm just as hungry as everyone else, but I'm not stupid, I know that food has to last."

Nobody said anything, but the looks in their eyes were cold and accusatory. Kenneth, for all his whining and complaining, was a talented strategist – something he'd learned from the countless hours he had spent playing video games – and he knew exactly how to play this situation to his advantage.

"You're always eating something, Joe," he said. "I've never seen anyone eat as much as you. You just couldn't stop yourself, I bet."

"I didn't do it!" Joe snapped. "Shut up, Kenneth!"

Chuck was sure that Kenneth was somehow behind this, but he couldn't figure out how he could prove this. He also didn't want this situation to blow up any worse than it already was; the last thing they needed now was to argue and fight among themselves. Everyone needed to cooperate in order to survive the difficult times ahead.

"That's enough, Kenneth," he said. "Don't accuse people when there's no evidence."

"Exactly," Joe said, folding his arms defiantly across his chest. "Go ahead, search my bag and my stuff, you won't find any wrappers or crumbs or anything there."

"Yeah, coz you probably buried them already," Kenneth muttered. "You may be greedy, but you're not dumb."

"Shut up!" Joe snapped, balling his hands into tight fists. "I didn't do it, Kenneth, and you know I didn't! I bet *you* did it, and you're just trying to put the blame on someone else to cover your tracks. Yeah, blame the fat kid, right?! Everyone will think it's the fat kid who stole the food! Just shut up already, okay!"

"I didn't do anything!" Kenneth yelled back. "Go on, search my stuff! You won't find anything!"

"Yeah, coz *you* buried the evidence, like you're accusing me of doing!" Joe yelled.

"Guys, stop!" Chuck shouted. "Just stop it! Stop fighting! It's getting hotter every minute, and we need to get moving and find shelter. Just, just forget about the damn oat bar. It's not worth it. What's done is done. I guess I'll just have to protect what's left of the food and water better in the future."

"Oh, so that's it, it's all over now, is it?" Kenneth asked, spinning on his heels to face Chuck. He could barely resist breaking into a triumphant grin, but for the sake of his plan, he kept the smile off his face. "How *convenient,* Chuck…"

"What's that supposed to mean, huh?" Chuck demanded, his temper now rising as quickly as the scorching heat of the day.

"You know what it's supposed to mean," Kenneth muttered, still defying the almost irresistible urge to grin madly with the imminence of his victorious revenge. "You're the one in charge of the food … so maybe *you* took it, huh?"

"What?!" Chuck snapped. "Are you crazy?! I'm the one who put this whole rationing plan into place, and I'm the one who's been emphasizing just how important rationing is! Why would you think I'd be so stupid and selfish as to do something like that?!"

"Uh, Chuck," Joe said, with uncertainty and suspicion coloring his voice, "what's that?"

Everyone looked at where Joe's finger was pointing. Near Chuck's sleeping bag, the rays of the early morning sun were glinting and flashing off a tiny piece of something silver sticking out of the sand.

"Yeah Chuck, what *is* that?" Kenneth asked, the accusation in every syllable blatant. He walked over to the tiny fleck of gleaming silver and dropped down onto his knees while Chuck watched in helpless confusion.

"What is it?" Priscilla asked, turning to glance at Chuck with a look of deep disappointment on her face.

"I don't know!" Chuck spluttered. "It's the first time I've seen anything there. It's just, it's just some litter or something!"

Kenneth started digging in the dirt, and soon unearthed the object … which was an oat bar wrapper – the same brand as the missing one. "A-ha!" Kenneth said, triumphantly holding up the wrapper, which he'd carefully and stealthily buried there a few hours earlier, while Chuck had been asleep. "Look at this, everyone! And what are *these?* What are *these*, huh?" He dropped down onto his knees and picked up some crumbs from the ground next to Chuck's sleeping bag.

For a moment, Chuck was flabbergasted – but then he understood exactly how the wrapper and crumbs had gotten there, and a fast, hot rage boiled up inside him.

"You *asshole*, Kenneth!" he snarled, balling his hands into rocky fists. "You planted those there! *You* ate the damn oat bar, and you tried to frame *me!*"

"Oh please, why would I do that?" Kenneth asked, his smug face exuding fake innocence. "Seriously, dude, you're losing your shit. Just admit that you abused your power as leader and took the food for yourself. The evidence is right here for everyone to see."

"I'm gonna kick your lying, scheming ass, Kenneth!" Chuck yelled hotly, charging at Kenneth, whose face suddenly paled with fear as the stronger, bigger boy bore down on him like an angry rhino.

Melissa, however, hurriedly stepped between her brother and Kenneth. "Stop it, Chuck!" she yelled. "Are you crazy?! We can't fight now, not at a time like this! It's getting hotter every second, and we've barely got any food or water, and I can't see any shelter anywhere! Just stop it – you too, Kenneth," she added, turning to shoot the gangly boy a withering look of condemnation. "Both of you, stop it! Stop fighting!"

"He's crazy!" Kenneth yelled, making sure to position himself with Melissa as a shield. "Look at him, he wants to kill me!"

Chuck was trying to get around Melissa to get to Kenneth, and his wrath was still bubbling and hissing with a terrible fury within him. He forced himself to listen to his sister, though, and calm down. She was right; this wasn't the time to fight, despite the terrible thing that Kenneth had done. Fighting was a complete waste of precious energy. He lowered his fists and let his arms hang limp by his sides.

"You're not fit to lead us!" Kenneth yelled at Chuck, still using Melissa as a shield. "You're crazy, Chuck, and you're a liar!" At this point, Kenneth could no longer hold back his grin of victory, and it spread across his face in a broad, smug smear. He had beaten Chuck, and he had turned the others against him.

Anger flared up within Chuck again, but this time he forced himself to shove it back down before he lost control again. He turned around to face the others and hung his head in embarrassment. "Everyone, I'm sorry I lost my cool," he said. "It was the wrong thing to do, especially at a time like this, in the situation we're in. All I can say is that I promise I didn't eat that oat bar. Cross my heart and hope to die. But this is what I'm going to do, seeing as some of you don't believe me. I'll give up my breakfast ration. So that way everyone else still gets to eat a full oat bar for breakfast."

The smug grin fell from Kenneth's face; this was a development he hadn't planned for. Frustration tore through him like floodwaters from a breaking dam, but those raging waters were thick with helplessness. There was no move he could make now to counter this unexpected checkmate from Chuck.

"Are you sure, dude?" Joe asked. "You're gonna go hungry while the rest of us eat?"

"You don't have to do that, Chuck," Priscilla said.

"Uh, um, yeah he does!" Kenneth spluttered, desperate to try to turn the others against Chuck again. "He's a liar and a thief!"

"Shut up, Kenneth!" Joe yelled. "It was probably you that took the oat bar, I bet."

"Liar! Liar! I never took—"

"Just shut up, Kenneth," Melissa said harshly. "Forget about the oat bar. We're wasting time here."

Everyone murmured their agreement with her, and Kenneth scowled with frustration, observing that the others were turning against him now instead of Chuck. He snarled and spit on the ground, but said nothing else. He wanted to explode with naked anger but realized that he could not; any further stoking of the argument would result in everything backfiring in his face completely.

Chuck, meanwhile, handed everyone an oat bar. He walked over to Kenneth with the last oat bar, but didn't place it in the boy's hands. Instead, he dropped it on the ground in front of Kenneth. "Oops," he muttered sarcastically before turning and walking away, where he sat on a small boulder away from the others, looking glum and feeling the pangs of hunger gnawing painfully in his belly.

While the others ate, Melissa walked up to Chuck and broke her oat bar in half, handing half to him. "Take it, Chuck," she said. "I know you didn't steal the oat bar."

Chuck shook his head and refused to take it. "You need to eat, sis," he said. "I'll go hungry, it's fine. I'm the strongest here, and I've got the biggest energy reserves."

"Don't be silly," she said. "Just take it. You need energy as much as anyone else does."

Chuck reluctantly took half of the oat bar and ate it in silence. After this fiasco, even though he had partly salvaged the situation, his confidence in his ability to lead the others had been diminished. He wondered how much longer they would continue to follow him.

"What do you think Grandpa would do in a situation like this?" he asked Melissa.

"Probably kill Kenneth and hide his body behind a cactus," she answered with a grin. They both laughed, and Chuck was grateful for this moment of levity.

"No, seriously," he said when they'd stopped laughing. "How would Grandpa handle this situation?"

"He'd stick with the plan," Melissa said. "It's the most sensible plan, and it's the plan that's most likely to get us all out of here alive."

"But what if the others don't listen to me?"

"I'll help you," she said. "I'll back you up. And the others don't have a plan anyway. Joe will do whatever anyone else tells him, and Priscilla is too meek to try and suggest her own plan. Kenneth's dumb idea is to just sit around and wait for grownups to come and find us, and I don't think the others are going to agree with that idea, not when we've hardly got any food and water. There isn't really any other choice – your plan is about the only way we're going to get out of the desert."

"Thanks sis," Chuck said. "I'm glad that someone still believes in me."

"No problem, Chuck," Melissa said with a warm smile. "Now, speaking of the plan, we'd better get going. It's getting freakin' hot. It's gotta be over a hundred degrees already, and the sun is barely up."

"Yeah, no kidding, right? I'm boiling here." Chuck stood up and walked over to the others, who were all polishing off the remnants of their oat bars. "All right guys," he said, "we need to get moving. I'm sure you can all feel how hot it is, and we need to find some shelter and shade where we can rest until nightfall. I'm gonna look at my compass and—"

"We don't need to go anywhere!" Kenneth yelled, jumping up excitedly.

"Yes we do," Melissa said firmly. "We'll be roasted alive out here in the open."

"No, uh, I don't think we do," Joe said. He too had scrambled to his feet, and his eyes were wide with surprise. "I don't think we need to go anywhere!"

"Look!" Priscilla yelled excitedly, pointing behind Melissa and Chuck.

The two of them turned around, and when they did, they were both slugged with heavy blows of surprise. On the horizon, racing toward them, was a man on a motorcycle.

"We're rescued!" Kenneth yelled, jumping up and down with glee. "We're saved, we're saved!"

13

Clay was about to exhale when he saw three figures moving through the gloom and smoke. Even though he was on the verge of passing out, he forced himself to keep holding his breath for a short few moments longer – for this could mean the difference between life and death for him.

As Frank had predicted, the sound of the old record player playing Truman's voice in the closet distracted the terrorists.

"He's in there!" one of them muttered. "I can hear the motherfucker whispering!"

"Light up the whole room, just rip a volley through the door and drywall," another one whispered. "Spray that fucking room with so much lead that not even the cockroaches and bedbugs will survive. That fucker killed Billy and Jimmy back there, and now he's gonna pay. On my mark ... three, two..."

The three terrorists aimed their rifles at the door

and walls of the room, completely oblivious to Clay's presence behind the coats. He had to attack at once, for he could barely hold his breath for even a second longer at this point. He couldn't see too clearly, but he could make out the shapes of the men, and that was enough.

He whipped the M-16 up to his shoulder, and in the same motion he kicked the coats out of his way. The men heard the commotion to their side and swung around in surprise, but by the time the coat rack hit the ground, it was too late for them. Clay put a bullet through the first man's skull, and before his body had even hit the floor, he blasted a hole through the second man's head.

The third terrorist had time to drop to the ground and blast a wild, poorly aimed burst of fire in Clay's direction, but before he had even loosed a handful of rounds, Clay was spraying him with furious fully automatic fire. He was dead in seconds, and his bullets smashed harmlessly into the walls a good yard or two from Clay, who finally inhaled … and then, as the acrid, smoky air burned his nose and throat and filled his lungs, he dropped to his knees in a fit of violent coughing.

A fourth terrorist was in the hallway behind his three companions, and the sudden attack startled him. Instead of joining the fight against Clay – as briefly as it had lasted – he staggered back, stricken with terror, and stumbled through the bathroom door.

Inside the bathtub, Diana reacted faster than she

could ever have thought possible. She neither thought about what she was doing nor hesitated; she simply pulled the trigger the moment the man burst through the door. The .357 round hit him through the neck, and he dropped his M-16 and staggered back out into the hallway, clutching his neck and reeling like an inebriated drunk. Diana, whose mind had finally processed what had happened and what she had just done, screamed at the horrific sight as the man stumbled around with blood gushing from his neck. She knew that she had to shoot him again, but now that she had seen the gruesome effect of the first shot, she couldn't bring herself to squeeze the trigger again.

The man dropped to his knees, making a terrible gurgling, rasping sound as he started to drown in his own blood, his lungs filling up with it. Diana kept screaming, unable to deliver the killing blow that would instantly put the man out of his misery.

Then, however, a single shot rang through the hallway and blood sprayed in a burst from the man's skull, and he flopped onto the ground, dead. Clay, coughing and choking on the smoke, which was now billowing into the bathroom too, called out to Diana.

"Diana, it's me, Clay!" he yelled between coughs and splutters. "Don't shoot!"

He came lurching into the bathroom.

"Clay!" Diana gasped. "Where's Frank?!"

Before Clay could answer, a burst of furious firing erupted from outside in the yard, accompanied by the sound of Boris barking frantically. This was followed by a period of ominous silence. Frank was outside somewhere, but whether he was now alive or dead was something that neither Clay nor Diana could know until they saw him with their own eyes.

"Come on," Clay said, coughing, "we have to get out of here!" He offered Diana his hand and helped her out of the bathtub.

They stepped over the body of the dead terrorist in the hall, and then, with Clay sweeping the passage forward with his M-16, they ran through the house to the kitchen, where their bags and equipment were. They hastily gathered these and then prepared to leave the house. "Stay low, and stay behind me," Clay said. "We have to make a break for it out the back door. We'll go around the side and head straight for the Humvees out front. If any of those bastards are still alive, I'll change that real fast."

"Okay, okay," Diana said. Adrenaline was surging through her veins, and everything felt extremely surreal and dreamlike at this moment. She could barely process what was happening, and it felt as if her body was acting independently of her mind, and that she was a mere observer of this whole thing rather than a participant.

Clay yanked open the door and charged out, but instead of opening fire when he got out of the house and into the backyard, he lowered his weapon and exhaled a sigh of relief, for Frank and Boris were standing there.

A wave of intense, almost euphoric relief tore

through Diana when she saw that Frank was okay. With tears streaming down her cheeks, she pushed past Clay and ran over to Frank and threw herself into his waiting arms. She hugged him tightly, weeping into his strong chest.

"They're all dead," Frank said, "they're all taken care of. You're safe now, my beautiful Di, you're safe now."

"Are you sure they're all dead?" Clay asked, scanning the yard, which was now illuminated with the light of the early morning.

"They are, unless there are more of them in the house," Frank answered. "I've taken care of all of the bastards who were outside."

Just then, Diana noticed that there was warm blood all over Frank's left hand. "Frank, you're bleeding!" she gasped. "Oh my God, have you been shot?!"

"It's just a flesh wound, a bullet grazed my arm," he said. "It's nothing. Come on, we have to move. More of these goons are gonna be coming along soon enough."

"But your arm—" Diana began.

"He's right," Clay said, interrupting her. "We can dress wounds later. The sound of the battle we've just fought is gonna draw in every one of these assholes this side of town. We managed to beat this small group, but when five or six more Humvees arrive in a couple minutes, we won't stand a chance. Let's move!"

"Come on, go, go!" Frank said, before Diana could voice any sort of protest.

They ran around the side of the house to the front yard, where the two Humvees were parked. They could already hear a number of Humvees racing through the town from all directions, and it was apparent that the vehicles would all be converging on this spot shortly.

"Shit," Clay muttered. "There are a lot of 'em, and they'll be here in under a minute. You take that one, Frank," he said, pointing at the closest Humvee, "and I'll take this one."

He jumped into the Humvee and muttered a silent prayer of thanks when he saw that the key was in the ignition. He fired up the motor and was about to accelerate away when he saw Frank, Boris, and Diana come running toward him. They yanked open the passenger doors and piled inside.

"The other one doesn't have any damn keys!" Frank growled. "They must be in the pockets of one of the dead guys inside, and we sure as hell don't have time to go looking for 'em."

"One Humvee it is, then," Clay said. "Which way's the fastest way out of this town?"

"Turn left at the intersection over there, then blast straight all the way," Frank said, pointing down the street.

"Hold on to your asses," Clay said, and then he stomped on the gas and tore out of the yard at top speed, praying that his madcap driving would get them out of there before the rest of their enemies caught up to them.

14

*C*huck watched as the tiny speck on the horizon grew larger and clearer. It definitely was a rider on a motorcycle, and a voluminous caterpillar of dust was being kicked up in his wake as he tore across the scrub-dotted desert.

"You lied!" Kenneth sneered. "You said that no cars or planes or anything with a motor would ever work again, but what's that, huh? It's a freakin' motorcycle, with a freakin' motor!"

The others, except for Melissa, turned and stared at Chuck with looks of suspicion on their faces. Even though he knew he was right about the EMP, he couldn't help but feel embarrassed, and a hot blush glowed uncomfortably on his cheeks.

"He's right," Priscilla said. "You said that no vehicles would ever work again, Chuck, but that's clearly a motorcycle coming toward us."

Coming from his crush, this doubt and criticism hit

particularly hard. Chuck racked his mind, his mouth hanging open but no words coming out. How could this be possible, he wondered. Everything else had pointed to the event being an EMP, yet here was a motorcycle speeding across the desert, defying everything Grandpa Frank had said about the effects of an EMP attack. "I ... don't know," was all Chuck could utter, shaking his head and staring at the ground to avoid the damning eye contact.

"This whole 'EMP' thing was just bullshit," Kenneth said. "You just wanted to be our leader, you wanted to control us and make us listen to you like little slaves," he continued, pointing an accusatory finger at Chuck. "It was just a power outage! And the rest of you, when I said we should wait where we were for some grownups to come find us, you voted against me and listened to him instead! Mr. Redman probably came back with the 4x4 last night and couldn't find us! You idiots should have listened to me! I—"

"Shut up, Kenneth!" Melissa snapped. "Just because there's a motorcycle out here doesn't mean that there wasn't an EMP attack, okay? My grandpa told me that it wouldn't affect every single vehicle, actually. Some older ones, like those from the 70s and stuff, they'd be okay because they don't have complicated electrics and stuff. So that might just be a real old motorcycle from the 70s or something."

"Yeah right," Kenneth scoffed. "Even if that bullshit was true, who would be riding around on like a forty or fifty-year-old bike in the middle of the desert?

You're as crazy as your brother is, and, and you're also a liar!"

A lightbulb of sorts had gone off in Chuck's mind when his sister had mentioned the detail about older vehicles being unaffected by an EMP. Come to think of it, he did remember his grandfather saying something about this. Then, when he thought about it a little more, it totally made sense; *that* was why Grandpa Frank still drove an ancient truck from the early 80s and refused to get a new vehicle, he realized. It wasn't because his grandfather was stingy, or opposed to new technology – no, it was because his old truck was essentially EMP-proof. When these thoughts rolled through his mind, his faith in both his judgment and decisions were restored.

"I'm still convinced that what happened was an EMP," he said defiantly, now looking up proudly and staring everyone in the eye with a look of unbreakable confidence. "One motorcycle doesn't disprove my theory."

While they had been talking, the motorcycle rider had been coming rapidly closer, and now he was clearly visible. He was riding helmetless, and from what the kids could see as he approached, he was a young working class Mexican man. The bike he was riding was indeed an older model, a Yamaha from the early 80s.

Chuck wasn't sure what it was about the approaching rider, but for some reason, his sixth sense began to tingle when the man drew closer. Warning bells started to sound inside his head. He glanced at his sister and saw a subtle frown on her face as she stared at the approaching rider, and he realized that she too thought that there was something suspicious about him. Neither of them said anything, though, for outwardly, the man didn't look suspicious or dangerous.

He slowed down and pulled up to a stop a couple of yards from the kids. He was wearing a bulging back-pack, which looked as if it was quite heavy, stuffed as it was with its hidden contents, and his clothes were brown with dust. He had goggles on, and a bandanna was wrapped around his nose and mouth to filter out the dust. He looked quite haggard, and it seemed as if he had been riding for quite a few hours.

He left the bike running, kicked out its kickstand, and hopped off. He lifted his goggles up onto his fore-head and took off the bandanna. He was a good-looking young man in his early twenties, and his face seemed like a kindly one, but Chuck's sixth sense refused to be placated, and he couldn't help feeling suspicious about the man.

"Hello little hombres," the man said, his English colored with a heavy Mexican accent. "What are you doing out here in the middle of the desert?"

"We were on a camping trip, but then *this* butthead made us hike off on our own through the night, and now we're lost," Kenneth said before anyone else could answer. He was pointing accusingly at Chuck.

"You hiked all night, huh?" the man asked. "You

must be tired. You need some food and water, right? Are you lost?"

"Yeah, we're totally lost, and—" Kenneth began. This time, though, Chuck cut him off.

"No, we're not lost," Chuck said calmly. "I know exactly where we are and where we're going. What are you doing out here?"

The man chuckled and smiled, but Chuck noticed him subtly gripping the straps of his backpack tighter. There was something suspicious in the backpack, he was sure of it. While there was a smile on the young man's lips, his eyes looked hard and dangerous. Chuck wondered if any of the others had spotted this. "I'm just delivering something for my boss," the man said. "We live out here, near the border. Listen, you kids must want food and water, yeah? I know some people nearby who can help you."

"You do?!" Kenneth spluttered, bubbling over with eagerness. "Where?! We need food, lots of food, and water too! And soda and juice, oh my God, I'd kill for a cold soda right now…"

"I bet," the man chuckled. "It's gonna be real hot today. Well listen, my friends, they got a fridge with plenty cold sodas in it. And ice cream too, you kids like ice cream?"

"Y-, yeah, I love ice cream!" Joe exclaimed, his eyes lighting up with delight. "Is there really ice cream nearby?"

"Sure, sure, plenty of it," the man said, smiling.

Chuck was still feeling very suspicious of the man's

111

intentions. What was in the bag? And why was the man riding alone across the desert like this? Why was he so quick to evade questions about himself? Something wasn't right here at all.

"Is your phone working, mister?" Melissa asked.

"My phone? No, it ain't," the young man said.

"See," Melissa said to Kenneth. "My brother was right, this is an EMP."

"I don't care," Kenneth said. "I just want some soda and ice cream. Mister, how do we get to your friends?"

The young man smiled – and in his grin was something undeniably predatory. Chuck couldn't believe he was the only one who could see it. All the others – except for Melissa – seemed completely oblivious to the threat, though, and were virtually drooling and slobbering at the prospect of soda and ice cream. He could hardly blame them for this; he was starving and thirsty too, and the heat of the day was rapidly becoming unbearable.

"Oh, it's easy to find them," the young man said. "It's actually where I'm headed now. See those two big outcrops there?" he said, pointing at two huge sandstone rock outcrops jutting into the sky in the distance.

"Yeah," Kenneth said, "we see 'em."

"Walk between them, and keep going in a straight line. It'll take you maybe forty-five minutes or an hour to walk there, it ain't too far. You'll see a ghost town over the ridge. It ain't no ghost town though, there are people there, even though it might look empty at first. Just walk in; you'll see my bike parked up outside one of the buildings. And if you see my friends before you find me, tell them Alejandro sent you. They'll take good care of you. You'll get all the soda and ice cream you can handle."

"Wow, I can't wait!" Kenneth exclaimed eagerly.

"I can't wait either," Joe said, grinning broadly. "Thank you, mister, thank you so much for helping us!"

"It ain't no problem, lil' hombre, it ain't no problem at all," the young man said, smiling strangely. "I'll see y'all soon. I gotta get going now. Remember, go between the big rocky outcrops, and just keep walking straight. See you soon."

He put his bandanna and goggles back on, hopped back onto the bike, and then sped off toward the huge rocky outcrops in the distance, leaving a cloud of reddish dust in his wake.

"Come on, let's go!" Kenneth said eagerly.

"Ice cream and cold soda, I can't wait!" Priscilla exclaimed.

"Let's go, let's go!" Joe said, rubbing his hands together.

Chuck shot Melissa a worried glance, but she just shrugged. Even if they opposed the decision to go there, the other three would outvote them; it was apparent that they had clearly made up their minds.

The five of them set off toward the rocky outcrops, and Chuck prayed that they weren't about to walk unsuspectingly into something truly terrifying … which was the exact thing his sixth sense was warning him about.

*C*lay cut across someone's lawn, demolishing their white picket fence and tearing up the flowerbed as he pushed the big Humvee to its limits. He skidded across the street on the other side, the tires howling in protest, and then he floored the gas pedal, hurtling down the long straight road out of town at speed.

"Any sign of the bastards?!" he yelled to Frank, who was keeping watch through the rear window with his rifle in his hands. Diana, meanwhile, was strapped into the front passenger seat, her hands holding the dashboard with a white-knuckled grip.

"None so far, but I'm sure we'll see 'em any minute! Punch the gas!" Frank yelled.

He glanced down and saw that there was a box of smoke grenades in the footwell, and he quickly realized that these weapons could prove very useful in the event that the terrorists caught sight of them and pursued them.

"Oh my God," Diana gasped. "How fast are you going, a hundred miles an hour?"

"One hundred and five, still accelerating," Clay muttered, his focus razor sharp and his eyes on the road.

Frank knew it wasn't wise to get his hopes up, but he couldn't help but feel triumph rising up within him. A premature celebration was almost always an invitation for disaster, though, so he forced himself not to smile or clench his fist with victory; they hadn't successfully escaped the town just yet.

And then, sure enough, he saw three Humvees careening around the bend a mile or so behind them in hot pursuit. "We've got company!" he said to Clay, who had the gas pedal floored.

Clay didn't bother to check the rearview mirror; at this speed, taking his eyes off the road for even a second could cause a fatal error. "How many?" he asked as they entered a long, sweeping bend in the road, which cut through the vast and empty desert landscape like a long gray serpent.

"Three so far, but I'll bet there'll be more," Frank said.

"If I hold her steady, can you take the drivers out?" Clay asked.

Frank shook his head, the expression on his weathered face grim. "Unlikely," he said. "These windscreens are bulletproof, and trying to get a shot on a target hanging out the window with the wind battering me around, while trying not to get blown out of the vehicle … no, it ain't gonna happen. I do have some smoke grenades back here, though, they could give us a useful screen. We just need to find the right place to use 'em; they're useless out here where the road's mostly straight, or just has a gentle curve like this."

"Is there anywhere up ahead where they might be more useful?" Clay asked, his focus locked on the road ahead.

"Yes! Yes there is!" It wasn't Frank who answered this question with excited enthusiasm, though. It was Diana. She had gotten over her initial burst of fear and was now driven by a fierce desire to get her own back at the men who had destroyed her house and terrorized her town.

"Tell me where to go," Clay said. His eyes didn't leave the road even for a second.

"There's a dirt track that's coming up on your right, around five and half, six miles down the road. It branches off this road, and you'll have to slow down a lot, because it's a real sharp turn. Head down there."

"Where does it lead to?" Clay asked.

"It goes deep into the desert, out to an Air Force base that's been shut down for decades now. But on the way, it passes a small canyon, and there's a section where the road bends right on the edge of the canyon."

Frank's eyes lit up when Diana mentioned this, for now he understood her plan. "Hell yeah Di," he muttered, grinning fiendishly. "That's the perfect spot.

I'll drop the smoke grenades before we get to the bend; it's a tight one, Clay, and it's at the end of a long straight. You'll have to slow down and brake hard for it. These clowns behind us won't know that, though, not with the wall of smoke … and if they're as dumb as I think they are, they'll blast into that smoke at full speed."

"And then, I'm guessing," Clay said, "they'll catch some air."

"Yes sirree," Frank said. "It's a hundred-foot drop into the canyon, and they'll take a real fast ride to the bottom. These Humvees might be bulletproof, but I'm pretty sure a drop like that will destroy 'em and take out anyone inside 'em."

"It sure would," Clay agreed.

Behind them, the pursuing Humvees were gaining on them. Some of the terrorists leaned out of the passenger windows and unleashed bursts of M-16 fire, but while the bullets peppered the back of the vehicle with an alarmingly loud drumming, they couldn't penetrate its bulletproof exterior. However, any triumph or sense of security the three of them might have felt because of this was soon erased when Frank saw one of the men pop out of the leading Humvee's sunroof with an RPG in his hands.

"Oh shit," Frank muttered. "*Now* we've got trouble."

"What's wrong?" Diana asked, her tone urgent.

"They've got an RPG," Frank said, strangely calm despite the deadliness of the threat.

"If they hit us with that, it's tickets for all of us,"

Clay said. "Either I have to dodge rocket-propelled grenades, or you have to take the bastard holding that RPG out before he can fire it at us. Of those two options, number two is the only one that's gonna work in the real world."

"I'll do what I can," Frank said. "Di, I'm gonna need your help here, get in the back with me please."

Diana climbed over the seat into the back with Frank. He, meanwhile, opened up the window next to him. At that moment, the man with the RPG took a shot at them. Clay caught sight of the flash in his rearview mirror and swerved hard, almost causing the Humvee to launch itself off the road into a death roll. The hissing rocket streaked past the Humvee, missing it by mere inches, and hit the desert sand a few hundred yards down the road, exploding in an enormous fireball.

"Shit!" Clay yelled as he fought to get the fishtailing vehicle back under control. "I don't know how that one missed us, but the next one won't! Take the bastard out before he takes us out!"

The terrorist had slipped back inside the lead Humvee to reload his RPG, and since the vehicle was gaining on them, Frank knew that the man wouldn't miss his second shot. If he didn't take him out before he fired another rocket-propelled grenade at them, they would all be dead.

"What do you need me to do?" Diana asked urgently.

"Hold my legs so I don't get blown outta the

window," Frank said. He wished that this Humvee had a sunroof, like the lead vehicle that was pursuing them, for that would have made his task a lot easier. As it was, though, he had to make do with his current circumstances, and that would mean leaning out of the passenger window to try to take a shot on a moving target, while getting buffeted by fierce winds and possibly getting shot at. It wouldn't be easy, but he had to try it.

"All right, all right, I'll hold you tight Frank, I won't let you go," Diana said.

"You'd better not, sweetcheeks, because at this speed I'll get turned into mincemeat in about five seconds after I hit the blacktop. You ready?"

Diana nodded.

"Okay, I'm gonna start leaning my body outta the window," Frank said. "As soon as my torso is out, you grip my legs and hold 'em as tight as if your arms were a sprung bear trap, you got it? Then once you've got me gripped tight, pass me the rifle."

"Got it," she said.

Frank started leaning out the window and immediately felt the buffeting of the wind battering his head, neck, and shoulders like a hundred simultaneous fists. He didn't know how he'd be able to get a bullet within feet of his target while being buffeted like this, let alone shoot with the kind of pinpoint accuracy needed to take out a man wearing a bulletproof vest.

"Damn it," he muttered as he pushed his torso farther out the window. He felt like if he pushed any more of his body out, he would get sucked right out of the vehicle and smashed onto the road, flung there as if by the force of a titan's mighty arm, and dashed to pieces. There was nothing he could do, though, but keep pushing, for he was not yet in a position to be able to set himself up to take a shot.

At this point Diana, who saw that Frank was struggling to remain stable and balanced in the buffeting wind, gripped his thighs tightly, pressing her body weight against them and using it to stabilize his position.

"Is that okay?" she asked.

Frank could see Diana's lips moving, but with the howling roar of the wind in his ears, he couldn't hear anything she was saying.

"I can't hear you!" he yelled. He glanced up and saw that the terrorist was now reemerging from the sunroof with a freshly reloaded RPG in his hands. The vehicle was closer now, and the man wouldn't miss them again, not from this distance.

"I said are you okay?" she yelled back.

"The rifle, hurry, gimme the rifle!" he yelled. There was no time to answer her question.

Diana could hear the desperate urgency in Frank's voice. She hastily passed him his AK-47, and he hauled it up and pressed the butt into his shoulder, doing his best to stabilize his torso against the relentless, hammering force of the wind.

Behind them, the terrorist had his RPG over his shoulder and was taking aim. Frank was finding it extremely difficult to get his sights on the man, owing to the ceaseless beating he was taking from the wind, but he knew that time was running out and he had to make this shot. He figured a few bursts of automatic fire, even if they missed by a mile, might scare his adversary and wreck his aim, so without bothering to get his sights on his target, he squeezed off three bursts of auto fire.

The bullets sprayed the windscreen of the pursuing Humvee – which had little effect, as it was bulletproof – and shot up a few sparks from the vehicle's roof where they hit home, but none of the rapid-fire bullets actually struck the man.

The effect was what Frank had desired, though. The bullets whizzing around him and slamming into the Humvee caused the man to duck and flinch, temporarily ruining the process of his aiming of the RPG. It bought Frank a precious few seconds. Having expended most of the bullets in his magazine, though, he knew that he now only had two, maybe three rounds left. "Hold me tight, Di!" he yelled. "Hold me tight!"

He felt her press the weight of her body more force-fully into his thighs, and despite the hammering wind, he felt more stable than he had a few seconds earlier. He lined up the man – who had recovered from the fright of being shot at, and was now re-aiming his RPG – in his sights.

There was no time to try to get a perfect shot. He fired once but missed. The man got them lined up in the sights of his RPG. Frank fired again, and this time the bullet hit the windscreen. "Shit," he muttered.

The terrorist, meanwhile, prepared to squeeze the trigger of his RPG. Frank's Humvee was lined up perfectly in his sights, and this time he wouldn't miss.

Frank didn't know if his magazine was empty, or if he had one shot left, but he had to try. He growled wordlessly with fierce determination and locked all of the muscles of his upper body tight to try and stabilize himself as effectively as possible. Then he locked his sights on the terrorist's head for half a second of pure stability, and he squeezed the trigger.

The man's head snapped back in a spray of blood, but at that moment his finger squeezed the trigger mechanism of his RPG. The rocket tore through the air and sped by Frank so close that it singed his hair and his face – but the minor loss of aim caused by Frank's shot was enough to cause the projectile to miss. It streaked past the Humvee and exploded in a massive cloud of dirt and debris a few hundred yards up the road.

The dead terrorist's body slithered back into the Humvee, and the empty RPG dropped off the top of the vehicle and bounced and cartwheeled across the road and then disappeared into the desert scrub. They had bought themselves a little more time, but with the enemy vehicles still hot on their heels, Frank wasn't sure if they would survive the chase long enough to get to the point in the road at which they could use the smoke bombs.

All he knew now, though, was that they had to try.

CHAPTER 15

The temperature soared during the hour the five children spent hiking across the desert. Since they knew they would be getting more food and water when they reached the biker's friends, they ate and drank the remainder of their rations – which had been intended to last for the next few days – over the course of the hike.

Chuck and Melissa were still feeling wary and suspicious about where they were headed, but the others were all so excited about getting ice cream and soda that there really wasn't anything the two of them could do or say to dissuade their companions from continuing on this path.

After they passed between the two massive outcrops of sandstone, which towered over them like twin reddish-brown skyscrapers, the desert sloped downward, and they saw a small ghost town shimmering in the heat, almost like a mirage.

"That place gives me the creeps," Melissa murmured. A cold shiver of dread ran down her spine.

"Our friend is down there, and so is a ton of ice cream and cold sodas!" Kenneth said with a grin. "Look, I can see his bike!"

The young man's motorcycle wasn't the only one in the ghost town. There were a number of old dirt bikes parked outside the crumbling, ruined buildings in the dusty streets. Once again, alarm bells pealed loudly in Chuck's head, this time with an even greater urgency than before. A voice in his head was screaming at him not to go any closer to the place, but what alternative was there at this point? They had used up all their rations, and only slow, agonizing death awaited them in the desert. This strange, scary oasis was their only hope now.

"Come on guys, let's go," Joe said, grinning. He was just as excited as Kenneth about the prospect of something cold to drink and sweet to eat.

"I can't wait to get a nice, ice-cold drink," Priscilla said. She, like Kenneth and Joe, seemed to have no misgivings about venturing into the eerie-looking ghost town.

Chuck looked at Melissa and shrugged with helpless surrender, and then set off across the pebble-strewn track down the gentle slope, leading the others to the ghost town. It took them around twenty minutes under the blazing sun to get to the town, which consisted of little more than a dozen old buildings along a single stretch of dirt road. The town looked as if it hadn't been inhabited for many decades, possibly even a century or more. The only signs of life were the 70s and 80s-era dirt bikes parked outside some of the buildings, but the children couldn't see any people.

Now, despite their enthusiasm for the sodas and ice cream, even Kenneth, Joe, and Priscilla were starting to get suspicious about this place.

"Uh, guys, is anyone else feeling a little creeped out

right now?" Priscilla asked. "I uh, I feel like this place is kinda … sketchy."

"Yeah, it's pretty weird and creepy," Joe murmured, his eyes darting nervously from side to side.

Most of the buildings' doors and windows were all boarded shut. Chuck and Melissa were now completely convinced that the young man was some sort of criminal, for surely no legitimate business could be taking place in these sort of surroundings. Everyone now started to stare at Kenneth, for he had been the one who had been most vocal about trusting the young biker and walking blindly into this place.

"I'm, uh, I'm not so sure it was such a good idea to come here," Priscilla said nervously. "I'm actually starting to get really freaked out."

"Pfft, what are you, a first grader?" Kenneth scoffed, but the flimsiness of his false bravado was embarrassingly clear for everyone to see. "There's nothing to be scared of! It's just a bunch of dusty old buildings!"

"Stop pretending you're not nervous, Kenneth," Chuck muttered, scowling. "You're as freaked out as the rest of us. I say we just try to find some water in this place and then get the hell out before anyone sees us. I'll be able to figure out where we are with my compass, and the position of the sun, and—"

"Don't fucking move, little gringos, don't even fucking blink," a harsh, raspy voice growled from behind the kids. "Get your fucking hands up in the air where I can see 'em, then turn around real slow."

They heard the telltale click of a shotgun being

cocked, and they all did what the voice had told them to, raising their hands above their heads and turning around slowly. They saw that a man – who must have been hiding behind a rusted old water tank they had just passed – had stepped out into the street behind them. He was a big, beefy Mexican man in his thirties with hard eyes, a scarred face, and tattooed arms. And he was holding a pump-action shotgun, which was aimed straight at them.

"We're uh, we're Alejandro's friends," Kenneth spluttered. His hands were trembling, and his voice had shot up an octave to become embarrassingly high with fear. "He told us to come here, he, uh, he said you'd help us."

"Oh, so *you* say you're Alejandro's buddies, eh?" the man growled, keeping his shogun leveled at them. "Well, what if *I* think you're a bunch of little narcos sent by the federales, eh?" His voice grew louder and more aggressive with every sentence he snarled at them. "What the fuck do you think you're doing out here, huh?! Why the fuck are you here?! Tell me! You lying lil' fucks, tell me why the fuck you came to this place!"

"Sir, there's been some sort of misunderstanding," Chuck said, doing his best to remain calm despite the fear that was pulsing through his veins. "We met Alejandro in the desert, he was on his bike. You see, we were on a camping trip, but my friend Adrian got bit by a rattlesnake, and—"

"Shut up!" the man roared, aiming the shotgun at

Chuck's face. Priscilla and Melissa screamed with fright. "Did the federales think if they sent a bunch of kids here, we wouldn't kill 'em like we'd kill any other federale who set foot in this place? Is that why they sent you here?! Tell me, you lil' fuck, or I'll blow your fucking head right off your shoulders! I don't give a fuck, I'll kill a fuckin' kid, I'll kill all you lil' fucks!"

"Hey, Carlos, chill out my man, chill out," a familiar voice said. "I know them, they ain't no federales."

Alejandro stepped out of the side door of one of the derelict buildings. The children, who were trembling with fear, had never been more relieved to see someone in their lives. Their relief, however, was to be short-lived.

"You know these fucks?" Carlos snarled.

Alejandro gave him a wink and said something in Spanish. Chuck didn't like the way Alejandro was smiling; it was the smile of a reptile; an alligator waiting to drag its unsuspecting prey into the depths of a swamp. Whatever Alejandro said, it changed Carlos's attitude right away. The big man lowered his shotgun and smiled at the children – but his false smile was also that of a dangerous predator preparing to strike.

"I am sorry, lil' amigos," Carlos said, grinning wolfishly. "I thought you were someone else. Come, come in, we'll give you some of that ice cream and soda Alejandro promised you, eh?"

Kenneth had almost soiled himself at this point, and the relief on his face glowed as brightly as the fierce summer sun overhead. "Yes, yes please!" he said eagerly. "We'd love to have some ice cream and soda, wouldn't we, guys?"

Nobody else was fooled by the men's fake smiles and put-on friendliness. Everyone now knew that these men were criminals of some sort, and that they had unwittingly wandered into a pit of vipers. Dread and anxiety were written plain across all the children's faces – all except Kenneth's – but they all knew that they were trapped now, and that there was nothing they could do to escape. Chuck noticed that Alejandro now had a pistol tucked into his belt. With a sinking feeling in the pit of his belly, he realized that he and his friends were now these men's prisoners.

"Come with me, lil' amigos and amigas," Alejandro said, grinning. "There's a friend of mine you gotta meet. He's gonna be *real* happy to see you, yeah, *real* happy."

"Great!" Kenneth said, seemingly oblivious to the threat and danger. "What's his name?"

"His name … is Pablo."

16

*B*y what seemed like a miracle from the Almighty, Frank had taken out the man with the RPG with the final bullet in his magazine. The danger had by no means passed, though, and the Humvees that were pursuing them showed no sign of slowing down or easing off the chase.

"The turn's coming up!" Diana yelled to Clay. "There, on the right!"

"Get him back in the car or he's gonna get flung out like an empty can of beer when I hit the turn!" Clay yelled back as he started to brake for the sharp right-hand turn onto the dirt track.

Diana didn't have to work too hard to get Frank back in, though. He'd used up all his bullets and there was nothing more he could do at this point. He threw the M-16 back into the Humvee and scrambled back inside the vehicle just as Clay hit a hard right.

He went in fast, almost too fast, and the rear end of

the Humvee skidded across the dirt track, with Clay almost losing control. He managed to pull it in just before the slide worsened into a full-on spin, and then they were off, speeding down the bumpy dirt track through the desert at high speed. They had put some distance between them and their pursuers, but not nearly enough to outstrip them.

"How far till the canyon?" Clay yelled, his hands wrapped around the steering wheel in a white-knuckled grip.

"It'll be coming up in two miles!" Di said.

"How many smoke grenades you got back there?" Clay asked Frank.

"Looks like six or seven," Frank answered. "Enough to do the job."

"You'd better start tossing some now," Clay said, "or it's gonna be obvious that we're setting a trap for the bastards when we get close to the edge of the canyon."

"Good point," Frank said. "I'll drop one or two now so they don't get suspicious, and I'll blast a couple more bursts of AK-47 fire at 'em to distract 'em. Di, reload the rifle, please."

Diana got busy reloading the AK while Frank got two of the smoke grenades ready to toss at their pursuers, who were again starting to gain on them. He pulled the pin on the first grenade and dropped it out of the window. It bounced and tumbled along the dirt road behind them, belching out a billowing tower of smoke as it rolled and jumped. The smoke billowed out fast and thick, and quickly made quite an effective screen, but it only took a few seconds for the first pursuing Humvee to blast through it.

It didn't matter that the smoke was ineffective now, though, for it was only a distraction, a psychological setup that, Frank hoped, would work perfectly and trick their pursuers into literally driving themselves off a cliff.

"The rifle's ready!" Di said, handing Frank the freshly reloaded AK.

Again, Frank knew that the bullets would be mostly ineffective against the bulletproof vehicles, but it was all an act, one that would hopefully result in their enemies' swift demise. He half-leaned out of the window and sprayed a burst of automatic fire at the Humvee behind them, peppering the windscreen and hood with bullets.

In response, a terrorist leaned out of the passenger window and unleashed his own burst of fire on the Humvee. Frank barely managed to get himself back inside the window before bullets hammered the back of the vehicle.

"The canyon is coming up!" Di said to Clay. "You can't see it yet, but trust me, it's there!"

"Toss another grenade," Clay said to Frank.

Frank pulled the pin of another grenade and chucked it out the window. It bounced along the first track, spewing out thick clouds of smoke, and as it did this, he leaned out the window and took aim with his AK, waiting for the enemy vehicle to emerge from the cloud. The moment it did he sprayed it with bullets, and then he ducked back inside the vehicle before they countered with a burst of their own fire.

"You're going to have to start braking soon," Di said to Clay. "When that turn comes up it's gonna be really tight, and we don't want to be the ones flying off the edge of the cliff."

"Got it," Clay said. "Frank, you'd better get ready to drop the rest of those grenades if we want to pull this stunt off. We've got one shot at this, and if we blow it, I don't know what we're gonna do with these assholes on our tail, getting closer and closer…"

"Don't worry, I'm on it," Frank said grimly. "Di, you're gonna need to help me if we want to give them a blast of smoke that's as thick as a sandstorm in the damn Sahara Desert."

"What do I need to do?" she asked.

"Take these," he said, pressing two smoke grenades into Di's hands. "When I say so, pull the pins and drop 'em out the window. If we can drop all four at once, it'll make one hell of a cloud. They won't be able to see two feet in front of 'em … and hopefully that'll be enough to send 'em blasting over the edge of the cliff into the canyon, if we time it just right."

"I think I see the canyon coming up!" Clay yelled from the driver's seat.

"Di, now!" Frank yelled as he pulled the pins of his two grenades and dropped them out of the window. "Drop 'em!"

Diana did this, and four smoke grenades, belching out great, thick plumes of smoke, were bouncing behind the Humvee. Clay, meanwhile, had come off the gas and was holding off hitting the brakes – in case his pursuers saw the brake lights through the smoke and figured that something was up – until the last possible second.

"Hit the brakes, man, we're gonna fly off the cliff if you don't!" Frank yelled as they barreled toward the edge of the cliff.

"Not yet … not yet…" Clay muttered, his focus locked on the road ahead, which bent into a sharp curve to the left, hugging the edge of the canyon.

Finally, at the last possible moment he slammed on the brakes, stomping on the pedal with all his might. The brakes locked up and the Humvee skidded along the dirt track, throwing up clouds of dust and pebbles in its wake. They slid across the stony, sandy path, hurtling toward the edge of the cliff, which was racing toward them at an alarming speed.

"Oh no, oh no, we're not going to make it, we're not going to make it!" Di gasped, watching in helpless horror as they skidded rapidly toward the cliff.

Clay said nothing; he was utterly focused on the task at hand. At the final moment, before it seemed they would fly off the cliff into the canyon in a mere handful of yards, he yanked the steering wheel to the left, whipping the back end of the Humvee around in a vicious skid that flung Frank, Boris, and Diana's bodies into a heap against the right-hand side of the vehicle.

They had stopped a few inches from the edge of the cliff. Yawning before them was a sheer hundred-foot drop, the bottom of which was lined with jagged boulders. Clay waited here, leaving the motor idling, perfectly calm and collected despite coming within inches of death.

"What are you doing?!" Di screamed. Terror was blasting icy jets through her veins. "Don't wait here, go, go! They'll slam right into us and push us over the edge!"

"No, they won't," Clay said calmly. "This is a little insurance policy, to make sure that the assholes *do* go over the edge."

Frank's first instinct was to punch Clay in the back of the head for this seemingly suicidal stupidity, but then he realized that the bounty hunter was right, and instead of snarling with anger, he grinned. "He's right, dammit!" he said to Di.

At that moment the pursuing Humvees came speeding out of the smoke cloud – and found themselves mere yards from plowing at high speed into the parked Humvee. As Clay had predicted, the drivers, upon catching sight of the obstacle ahead, reacted on pure instinct, swerving hard to avoid hitting him – and in the process, they launched themselves over the edge of the cliff into the canyon, all three flying through the air in quick succession.

A few seconds later came the sounds of crunching metal and shattering glass smashing on the jagged rocks below.

"Oh my God," Diana gasped. Her whole body was trembling violently, and she could barely breathe. "I thought I was going to have a heart attack. How did you know they'd do that?"

Clay shrugged. "Instinct and timing," he said. "Think about it; you're driving at high speed through a patch of thick fog on the interstate, and suddenly you emerge from the fog and discover you're inches away from smashing into the back of a broken-down truck. What's your first instinct?"

A smile of understanding spread slowly across Diana's face, and she nodded. "Of course … I'd swerve out of the way. Anyone would, acting purely on instinct."

"That was good thinking, Clay," Frank said. "It was a risk, because if they hadn't swerved, we'd be the ones smashed up like broken eggs on those boulders down there … but it was a good, calculated risk. And it worked, thank God."

"We aren't out of danger yet," Clay said. "When those three Hummers don't return to town, their buddies will know something happened and they'll send more men out to hunt us down. We have to get as far from this place as possible, as quickly as possible."

"How much gas is in the tank?" Frank asked.

"Plenty," Clay said. "Where were you folks planning on heading? Di mentioned you had a homestead in the hills outside town, Frank, but I wouldn't advise going back there, not for a while at least. I don't know who those clowns were or what their objectives were, but I suspect they'll occupy the town until they've looted it completely. After they move on somewhere else, you could probably head back to your homestead."

"I have to head south," Frank answered. "Deep into the desert, close to the Mexican border. My grandkids are down there somewhere, stuck in the desert after that EMP strike with some greenhorn hiking club teacher who doesn't know his ass from his elbow, from what my grandson tells me."

As if to emphasize this point, Boris, who had been quiet up to this point, aside from a yelp of pain when Clay's sharp turn had flung his body against the side of the Humvee, let out an excited bark.

"I see," Clay said slowly, thinking about what Frank had just told him. "You see, I'm headed that way too, probably in the same area you're gonna be looking in. I guess we can stick together for the time being, at least until I've done what I have to do."

"Why are you going down there?" Frank asked. "You got a woman or family down that way?"

A dark look came over Clay's face, and he shook his head. He told Frank the same story he'd told Diana, about how Pablo had murdered his best friend and his friend's wife, and how he'd sworn to avenge their deaths.

Everything Clay had just told Frank about Pablo and his cartel made him even more worried than ever about the safety of his grandchildren. From the sound of it, Pablo was heavily involved in smuggling people as well as narcotics, and this did not bode well for the children stuck in the desert.

"I guess that's it then," Frank said. "We're all going south, and we'd better not waste any more time hanging around here."

They took one last look over the edge of the canyon, with the ferocious sun beating down on the boulders and the crushed, shattered remains of their enemies' vehicles a hundred feet below, and then they sped off into the heart of the desert.

lejandro led the children around the back of a large, boarded-up building, which looked like it had once been a trading store. Chuck was walking along slowly and compliantly, and trying to act as calmly as possibly, but his eyes were darting around everywhere, searching for escape routes. His grandfather had told him to do this if he was ever kidnapped. Melissa was also quietly scanning the terrain for possible escape routes, following Frank's advice.

Unfortunately for the siblings, there were no obvious escape routes, and with the big, tattooed man breathing down their necks with his shotgun at the ready, any attempt to suddenly bolt off would likely end in tragedy. All they could do for now was comply.

"Man, it's one fucking, um, I mean, real crazy hot day today, huh kids?" Alejandro said, lifting up his shirt to fan some of the hot air onto his belly, which did little to cool him. "I bet you can't wait to get those sodas and ice creams, huh?"

Even Kenneth, though, was starting to feel suspicious about this whole thing, and he could no longer muster his former enthusiasm. "Uh, yeah," he mumbled nervously, staring sullenly at the ground as they walked.

As for the others, Joe and Priscilla were both completely silent, and their eyes were full of fear. They knew now that they had been duped, and that there was nothing they could do to escape whatever terrible fate lay in wait for them in the abandoned trading store.

Alejandro took them around the back and then knocked on the door in a peculiar pattern that seemed to be some sort of code. After a while, they heard the door being unlocked from within, and it swung open.

Instead of the boarded-up building being completely dark, as they had expected it would be, it was brightly lit inside, with dozens of gas lamps burning everywhere. A rough-looking Mexican man in his forties was standing inside the door. In his scarred hands was an AK-47. Alejandro spoke to the man in Spanish, and he turned and beamed an evil grin at the children, flashing them a mouthful of rotten and missing teeth.

"Is uh, is that your friend Pablo?" Kenneth asked nervously.

Alejandro chuckled. "No, this ain't Pablo, lil'

ROBERT J WALKER

hombre. We call this guy El Caníbal. Do any of you know what that word means?"

"It means … cannibal," Melissa murmured.

Alejandro chuckled darkly. "Ah, so you know a lil' Spanish, chiquita? Hehehe. Maybe you know what the word means, but I don't think you really want to know *why* we call this man El Caníbal, eh? Hehehe."

"Uh, mister, I uh, I changed my mind," Joe stammered nervously. "I don't want any ice cream or soda, I, uh, I think I'm just gonna go, we've got a long hike ahead of us and, uh—"

"You ain't going *nowhere*," the big man, Carlos, growled. Any pretense of friendliness had vanished from his face, and it was now contorted into a monstrous and terrifying snarl. He pointed his shotgun at Joe. "Get the fuck inside, you fat little shit, before I remove some of those excess pounds with this hot lead!"

The children hurried into the building, whimpering with fear, and when they were all inside, El Caníbal slammed the door shut behind them and locked it. Chuck, as attentive as ever despite how stressful and frightening the situation was, noted that it was a simple deadbolt lock. Although it was a very large and sturdy one, if he could find the right moment to escape this place, at least opening the door wouldn't involve picking any locks, he noted.

The inside of the derelict trading store consisted of a very large room, which had formerly been the store area, with a big room, formerly the stock room at the back, and two smaller rooms which had once been offices. The back door, via which the children entered, led into a small room which had once been a kitchen. Alejandro took them through the kitchen – which was filthy, and stank to high heaven, with piles of opened cans of beans, spam, and other such food rotting in the corners – and into the main area of the store. The children were shocked to see large tables with mountains of what looked like hard drugs on them. The drugs were being packed into plastic bags by more rough-looking men, presided over by a man who looked quite different to the other thugs.

He was dressed in an expensive, spotless suit, despite the sweltering heat, and his black hair was perfectly styled. He didn't look particularly dangerous, rough, or threatening, not like the other men in here did. But the moment his eyes met Chuck's, Chuck knew that this man was far more dangerous than any of the others in here, even the one called El Caníbal. In this man's eyes there was a hardness and a malicious cruelty the likes of which he had never seen in a human being. It was the kind of look he imagined one would see in the eyes of a truly psychotic serial killer.

"Pablo, here's the gringo kids I found in the desert," Alejandro said.

Pablo smiled at the children, but there was no warmth in his grin, only a chilling iciness, devoid of any emotion. He had a rolled-up hundred dollar bill in his right hand, which sparkled when he moved due to the number of jeweled rings on it, and he used this to snort up a line of whatever drugs were on the table. He threw his head back and gasped as the chemicals hit his brain, and he shuddered, almost to the point of convulsing, when the chemicals tore through his system. The children trembled in fear as they watched this; being innocent middle-class kids, none of them had ever seen anyone do drugs like this.

Pablo wiped the excess powder off his nose with the back of his sleeve and then walked over to the children, taking slow, deliberate steps. Now that he was high, his eyes looked even scarier than they had before.

"Well, well, well," he said slowly. "Look at this ... look at this. Five lil' gringos, come wandering into the gingerbread house, like a bunch of lil' Hansels and Gretels, eh?" He paused here to chuckle darkly. He walked around the children in a slow circle, looking each of them up and down. He paid particular attention to Priscilla and Melissa, who felt his predatory eyes roving unabashedly over their bodies.

"What do you wanna do with 'em, boss?" Alejandro asked.

"I like this one," he said, nodding his head in Melissa's direction. "She's a real pretty lil' chiquita, ain't she? Mm, yes ... very pretty. And my amigo Hernan in Tijuana, he likes Asians, and you bet he'll like this lil' Asian," he added, giving Priscilla a good looking over. "We'll take 'em across the border."

"What about the boys?" Alejandro asked.

"Hmm," Pablo said. "Maybe they can be … slaves. Or maybe their blood can feed Tlaloc, when I perform the ceremony with the captured federales." He smiled darkly and stepped in front of Chuck. "Do you know who Tlaloc is, lil' hombre?" he asked.

Chuck's mouth was dry with fear, but he did his best to put on a brave face. He shook his head. "No sir, I don't," he said.

"He's one of the gods of my ancestors," Pablo said. "You heard of the Aztecs? You know my people?"

"They um, they lived in Mexico before the Spanish got there," Chuck said. "That's what we learned in history class, sir."

"Yes, yes, that's right," Pablo said. "But here's something you don't know, boy: I am the last Aztec emperor!" he suddenly bellowed, raising his hands to the sky, his voice booming through the room. "I am the last living descendent of Montezuma! This is my land! I am the ruler … I am the fucking ruler of *everything!* And I will feed Tlaloc the rain god the way my ancestors fed him … with the *blood of my enemies!*" His voice had taken on a maniacal tone, and his eyes looked even crazier than before. He was clearly in the grips of whatever madness the drugs had stirred up in him.

Neither Chuck nor any of the other children had any idea how to respond to this terrifying madness. They were so caught up in the surreal terror of the situation that they simply stood in shocked silence, rooted to the spot. A dark patch of warm wetness spread across the front of Kenneth's pants, while vomit rose up the back of Joe's throat. Priscilla burst into tears, but Melissa simply stared at the ground, hardly able to process what was happening and what this evil man had said about her.

Pablo's left eye was twitching from the drugs, and his movements had become jerky and erratic. He paced back and forth in front of the children, muttering to himself in Spanish. Then he suddenly stopped in front of Chuck and opened his expensive suit coat. Inside he had a gold-plated .45 pistol in a holster which was encrusted with diamonds and other precious stones. The garish firearm was not what he wanted to show the boy, though. Instead, he pulled out another weapon from a pocket inside his jacket.

It was a stone dagger, fashioned from black obsidian, and Pablo held this item mere inches in front of Chuck's eyes. "Look at this, lil' gringo," he said softly, almost whispering. "Do you know what this is?"

Chuck swallowed slowly and shook his head.

"This is what my ancestors' priests used to feed the god Tlaloc. It's a sacrificial dagger, made of obsidian. It's a stone weapon, hombre, but did you know that the edge of this blade is as sharp as a surgical scalpel? My friend stole this from a private collector … it's the real deal; this dagger was used to feed Tlaloc. This beautiful black blade has probably killed thousands, maybe tens of thousands of people…"

"Okay…" was all Chuck could say. His limbs were ice-cold with fear, and he felt as if he could hardly move.

"Do you know how my ancestors used to feed Tlaloc?" Pablo asked, staring directly into Chuck's eyes, his face only inches away from the boy's. Sweat was pouring off his face now.

Chuck shook his head.

"The priest would use this dagger to cut open the victim's chest," Pablo said. "And then they would pull the motherfucker's heart out – still beating – and hold it to the sky. The last thing the victim would see was his own beating heart in the priest's hands…"

Chuck swallowed again. Terror was ripping through his veins, paralyzing him with its intensity.

"That's how I'm gonna feed Tlaloc," Pablo whispered. "Just like my ancestors did in the old days. You see, this whole fucked-up power outage thing that's killed all the cars and TVs and phones and shit … it's a message. It's a message from the old gods of my people! They're saying that it's time for the Aztecs to rule this land again. The blood in my veins, the blood of the emperor Montezuma … it's been waiting five hundred years for this moment. And now, the time has come. Did you hear that, everyone?!" he roared. "The time has come!"

His men cheered, and the children cowered and whimpered.

"Lock these little fucks up," Pablo growled, shoving the obsidian dagger back inside his coat. "We'll deal with them later. We've got plenty of product to finish packing, so get your lazy asses back to work, mother-fuckers!"

The men got back to work sorting and packing drugs, and Alejandro and Carlos grabbed the children and dragged them off to the room in which they would be locked up to await whatever terrible fate was in store for them.

18

"*L*ooks like a storm's brewing up ahead in the distance," Clay remarked as they drove through the desert.

"Yeah," Frank said. "I don't think it'll hit for a few hours, though."

The heat of the morning was ferocious. Before the EMP had hit, weather services had issued warnings stating that the next few days would be the hottest of the year. Everyone in the vehicle could believe that.

"I hope the kids are okay," Diana said worriedly.

"I've taught 'em well," Frank said. "Especially Chuck. He knows how to survive and stay safe in conditions like these."

"Even so, anyone out in the desert without shelter on a day like this is going to be in real danger," Diana said. "I hope they've managed to find somewhere to hide from the sun."

"I think Chuck will have done that," Frank said. "I know the weather's bad, but I'm more worried about danger from people than from the sun and the heat."

"If those kids are anywhere near Pablo," Clay said, "you have good reason to be worried."

"All the more reason to get there faster," Frank muttered. "I think we should cut across the desert instead of sticking to roads. This thing is as capable an off-road vehicle as any other, and I've got a compass to navigate by, and a few US Geological Survey maps in my bag. It'll save us a few hours of driving."

"Are you sure that's wise, Frank?" Diana asked.

"He's right," Clay said, "it will cut a few hours out of our travel time, and this Humvee can handle just about any terrain nature throws our way, except for sheer cliff faces and other extreme things like that. Also, it'd be safer in that we're less likely to encounter terrorists than we would be by sticking to the roads. We've still got plenty of gas in the tank, so there's no danger of getting stranded, not for a few hundred miles anyway."

As if to add his opinion, Boris let out an eager bark. Frank chuckled and ruffled the dog's fur.

"See, even Boris thinks it's a good idea," he said. "I say we do it."

"Agreed," Clay said.

"I'm not so sure," Diana said, "but I guess it's two against one, so that settles it." She shrugged and shook her head.

Boris barked again.

"Three against one," Frank said, giving Diana a

wink. "Before we strike off into the desert, though, I need to feed Boris and give him some water."

"We could use some food and water too," Diana said. "Let's take a quick break to stretch our legs. We've been driving for almost three hours now."

They pulled off the road. There was no shelter or shade, just scrub, cactuses, and towering rocky outcrops dotting the landscape. The bright blue sky above was edged with a rim of ominous black storm clouds on the far horizon.

They got out of the Humvee to stretch their legs and were hit with a wall of fierce heat.

"Man, it's gotta be over 110 degrees out here," Frank muttered.

"Maybe closer to 120," Clay said. "I don't think I've ever felt heat like this, not in all the years I've lived out here."

"I think whatever storm breaks later is going to be a big one," Diana said, shooting a worried glance over at the horizon, where the storm clouds were growing darker and bulkier.

"We'll have to be wary of flash flooding," Frank said. "That's one disadvantage of driving across the desert. We don't want to be caught in a floodplain area at the wrong time. I've seen walls of raging water ten to twelve feet deep come out of nowhere when flash floods break."

"Let's hope we're not caught in the wrong place at the wrong time then," Clay said.

They ate some of the food Diana had packed for

them in her house, and Frank opened a can of dog food for Boris and gave him a bowl of water.

"He's a good-looking mutt," Clay said, smiling as he watched Boris wolf down his food. "Reminds me of a dog I had when I was a kid."

"Boris ain't no mutt," Frank said. "He's a purebred German Shepherd. And you'd better believe he's one of the best-trained dogs you ever laid eyes on."

"It's true," Diana said. "Frank entered him into a couple of sport and agility contests, didn't you Frank?"

"I sure did, and we took first place at two of 'em, and we had couple silvers and bronzes in others. If there's a dog I'd trust with my life, it's this one. He'd fight a damn rabid grizzly bear to protect me! Hell, he was ready to take on a hungry mountain lion last night."

"A mountain lion!" Diana exclaimed. "You didn't tell me anything about a mountain lion!"

Frank chuckled. "With all the crazy stuff that's happened since then, it almost slipped my mind. But yeah, last night me and Boris almost became cat food for a big, mean, hungry mountain lion. One of the biggest I've ever seen. We were lucky to escape without so much as a scratch." Frank went on to describe his encounter with the mountain lion in detail, while the others ate their food and listened with rapt attention.

"You were lucky to get out of that situation," Clay remarked. "If you believe in luck, of course. Me, I'd say it was something else. And not just skill and an ability to think logically and act cool under extreme pressure, which are all qualities you obviously have."

"Frank was a Green Beret for many years, and I wouldn't have expected any less of him," Diana said, staring at Frank with both admiration and affection in her eyes.

Frank chuckled. "Sure, sure. I think it was more luck than anything," he continued, being modest, as he usually was, "but what do you mean you think it was something else?"

Clay smiled. "My ancestors believed that if a man encountered a dangerous wild beast like a bear or a mountain lion, and he came away from the encounter unscathed, like you did, it meant that the spirits had marked him for something special, to do something extraordinary. Maybe that sounds like a bunch of bullcrap to you," he said, shrugging, "but to me, maybe it means that you've been blessed by the spirits."

"I don't think it's nonsense," Diana said. "I think it was God watching over Frank."

"I still think it was luck," Frank said, bending down to pet Boris, who had finished eating and drinking. "And this good boy's sharp senses. If he hadn't alerted me to the mountain lion's presence when he did, I probably wouldn't be standing here today. Anyway, enough about that. I'm being cooked alive in this heat. Let's get back in the car and get moving."

They piled back into the Humvee, and with Frank navigating with his USGS paper maps and a compass, and Clay driving, they took off, heading into the vast, scorching heat of the desert. On the horizon, the bulging storm clouds grew heavier and darker.

19

The room the children were taken to had formerly been a stock room. It was grubby and windowless, with only a small air vent near the ceiling for ventilation. The children were surprised to see that they were not the only prisoners in the room. There were two white men, both in their 30s, who were handcuffed and gagged, sitting on the dusty floor. Both men's faces were heavily bruised and swollen; it looked as if they had been badly beaten up.

"Get in there," Alejandro muttered, pointing inside the room. Any pretense of friendliness was gone from his face and voice, and only a cold hardness remained.

The children obeyed in silence, slinking sullenly into the room.

"Should we tie 'em up?" Carlos asked.

"Nah, they're just dumb kids, they're too shit-scared to try anything. Leave 'em for now," Alejandro said.

"All right," Carlos said.

"There's your soda," Alejandro sneered at the children, pointing at a grubby plastic bottle of water. "And you'll find that your hotel room has an en-suite," he added sarcastically, pointing to a filthy bucket in the corner, which was obviously the toilet. "I hope you enjoy your stay, lil' gringos."

Once all the children were inside, the door slammed shut behind them, and they heard a key turn in the lock. This door, Chuck realized, would be far harder to get through than the one that led outside.

The men stared at the children through their swollen, purple eyes. Chuck recognized the uniforms the men were wearing at once: they were border patrol officers. He hurried over to them, while the other children cowered in the opposite corner of the room, and pulled the gags – which were just dirty rags – out of the men's mouths.

They spit and coughed after the rags came out, but they both mumbled thanks to Chuck.

"The last thing I expected to see was a bunch of American kids," one of the men said. "How'd you end up in this sorry situation?"

Chuck explained to the man about their camping trip, which had been cut short by the EMP. Neither of the men seemed to understand what an EMP was, so he explained it to them.

"Ahh," the first man said. "Well, that explains why our trucks cut out last night, and all our equipment stopped working. That's how Pablo's thugs were able to capture us so easily."

"Who are these people?" Chuck asked. "They're gangsters, right?"

"Some of the worst of the worst, kid," the man said grimly. "This guy, Pablo Cortez, he's the head of one of the most brutal cartels in Mexico. We've been fighting this guy for years. He and his boys have been smuggling drugs and people across the border for the last ten years, and as many of them as we catch, three times as many get away."

"The guy's a psycho," the other man muttered. "A cold-blooded killer. I don't know what he's planning to do with us ... but based on what he's done to other border patrol officers in the past, I—"

"Shut up, Bill," the first man said. "We don't wanna traumatize these kids."

Of course, Pablo had already explained to the children what he was planning to do. Chuck wondered if these officers had heard Pablo talking about making blood sacrifices to an ancient rain god with an obsidian dagger, and his rants about being the last living heir to Montezuma.

"You guys look badly hurt," Melissa said. "Is there anything I can do to help you?"

"You're a sweet kid," the man called Bill said, shaking his head, "but unless you've got a key to these handcuffs and an M-16 rifle to hand me, there ain't much you can do for us."

"Would you like some water, at least?" Melissa asked. She picked up the grimy plastic bottle, which was full of tepid, dirty-looking water.

"I wouldn't drink that," the first man said to her. "It's probably battery acid or something. That's exactly the sort of thing Pablo would pull."

"I don't care," Bill grumbled. "With everything that bastard has already done to us – excuse my French, kids – I couldn't give a damn if it's pure rat poison in that bottle. I'm parched, my tongue feels like a freakin' potato in my mouth, and my throat is so dry the sand in the desert outside would be like wet mud in comparison. So yeah, sweetie, if you don't mind, I'll have a drink of whatever's in the bottle."

Melissa took the cap off the bottle and sniffed the liquid. It had no smell. She was about to pour some of it into the palm of her hand to test it further, but Chuck yanked the bottle out of her hands.

"Are you crazy?!" he snapped. "What if it is battery acid or something?"

"I uh, I know how to test it," Kenneth said nervously. He was sitting cross-legged on the floor with his backpack in his lap, so that he could cover the shame of having peed himself earlier.

Chuck spun around and glared at Kenneth. He wanted to explode with fury and ball his hands into fists and beat Kenneth mercilessly, for it was Kenneth's fault that they were in this mess in the first place. Seeing the other boy looking so scared and pathetic, though, caused the heat of his wrath to diminish, and instead it morphed into a rather different emotion: pity. Kenneth truly was a pathetic little creature, Chuck thought. It wasn't worth wasting precious energy by beating him up. "And how exactly are you going to test this liquid, Kenneth?" he asked coldly.

"I've got a whole bunch of crap from school in my bag," Kenneth said. "I didn't really clean it out properly before we went on this trip. I've got one of those pH testing kits from last week's science class in here. I uh, I figured we could test it with that."

Chuck had to chuckle. For once, Kenneth's laziness and sloppiness had proved useful. "Good idea," he said. "Gimme the kit."

Kenneth dug around in his bag – which was crammed full of trash, crumpled-up test papers, and other garbage from school, and eventually found a small pH testing kit from some experiments they had done in science class the previous week. "Got it," he said, holding it up.

"Well what are you waiting for, bring it over here," Chuck said.

Kenneth bit his lip and shook his head, and his cheeks blushed hotly. If he stood up now, all of the others would see the humiliating wet patch on his pants. Chuck was the only one who had noticed that Kenneth had wet himself, and while part of him wanted to humiliate the boy by forcing him to stand up – as revenge for Kenneth's devious plot to make it look like he'd stolen an oat cake – he realized that his grandfather would never approve of such pettiness.

"All right, I'll come and get it," Chuck said. He walked over to Kenneth and snatched the test kit out of his hand, glaring at him as he did. He may have decided not to humiliate Kenneth, but he certainly hadn't forgiven him for what he'd done just yet.

"Okay, let's see what this stuff really is," Chuck said, and poured a little of the liquid into the bottle cap. He then dipped one of the strips of litmus paper into it, waited a few seconds, and then checked the color on the scale.

"What does it say, kid?" Bill asked, licking his cracked, swollen lips. He was desperate for a drink of water.

"It's got a pH of seven," Chuck said. "So I'm pretty sure it's just water."

"I don't care anymore," Bill said. "Like I said, whether it's rat poison or hydrochloric acid or anything, I gotta drink something, I'm dying of thirst over here."

Chuck took the bottle over to Bill – who couldn't take it himself, owing to the fact that his hands were cuffed behind his back – and raised the bottle to his lips. He tipped a little of the liquid into Bill's mouth, and everyone waited in suspense, half-suspecting that even though it had passed the pH test, it was infused with poison of some sort.

Chuck, however, realized that it was probably safe, although the reasoning behind this understanding was rather grim. If Pablo truly did intend to use them as human sacrifices in some evil ritual, he wouldn't want to poison them now. He would need them to be alive and healthy in order to sacrifice them later. He didn't say any of this out loud, though.

Bill smiled. "It's water, everyone," he announced after gulping a swig down. "Tastes like it's been sitting in that bottle for a few months, but it's water, pure, delicious, safe water!"

"In that case, uh, I'll have some too," the first man said.

"Told ya, Wayne!" Bill said.

The other man – Wayne – was too busy gulping down water to respond.

Just then, thunder rumbled ominously outside. Since there were no windows in the room, there was no way of seeing what the weather was like outside. The rumble was deep and long, though, and it sounded as if a major storm was on the way.

"Hopefully it'll bucket down and wash away some of this damn heat," Bill muttered. "Man, I hope the boys get to us soon. I can't wait to see the look on Pablo's face when our troops come charging in."

"What do you mean?" Chuck asked. "Is someone coming to rescue you?"

"You bet!" Bill said. He glanced at the door, as if he was suspicious that someone might be listening in on their conversation. Then he lowered his voice to a whisper to speak to Chuck. "Our boots," he whispered. "They've got tracking devices in the soles. Brand-new tech, installed just two weeks ago. Pablo's goons tossed our phones and radios into the desert when they captured us, so that our location couldn't be traced, but they don't know about our boots ... US troops are gonna be swooping in on this place soon, real soon," he said. "Just you wait."

"Okay," Chuck said, hoping that Bill didn't see the obvious disappointment on his face. It seemed that Bill didn't quite understand the full scope of what the EMP meant. The tracking chips in their boots would have been fried, as well as whatever computer system had been used to track them. He didn't have the heart to tell Bill this, though, and rob him of what little hope was available to cling to.

"Just you wait, son," Bill whispered. "The full might of the US military machine is about to be unleashed on these scumbags. They'll be arriving soon, I bet. These pricks won't know what hit 'em."

"I um, I hope so," Chuck murmured.

A sudden, violent thunderclap boomed like an exploding bomb through the humid, stifling silence of the room. This one sounded as if it had come from a lot closer. It was so loud that everyone jumped and started from fright.

"I thought Pablo's thugs had just rolled a stick of dynamite under the door!" Wayne exclaimed. "Damn, it's gonna be a monster of a storm when it breaks."

There were a few more thunderclaps, each louder than the one that preceded it, and the last two were so loud they actually rattled the walls. Then the first drops of rain began to fall – big, fat drops that hit the tin roof above them like stones. Soon the rain started to grow in intensity.

Kenneth was about to say something, but before he

could, everyone heard a key turning in the lock. They watched, with dread percolating deep in their stomachs, as the door opened. Alejandro, Carlos, and El Caníbal barged into the room. Pablo, meanwhile, waited in the dark hall behind them. Chuck shuddered when he saw the obsidian dagger in the drug lord's right hand.

"Take that one," Pablo said, pointing at Wayne. "The time is right; Tlaloc is ready to be fed…"

"What the hell is Tlaloc?" Wayne growled as the three goons grabbed him and hauled him up from the floor. "What are you assholes doing?! Get your damn hands off me!"

"Tlaloc is hungry," Pablo muttered, ignoring Wayne's protests. "Bring the victim…"

"Let him go, you sons of bitches!" Bill yelled from the floor, but Carlos lashed out a steel-capped boot, and the vicious kick caught Bill's jaw and whipped his head to the side, stunning him. He slumped over in a daze.

The children watched in horrified silence and shock as the three gangsters dragged Wayne out of the room. They knew what was about to happen to him, but none of them could even begin to wrap their minds around the true horror of it.

The door slammed shut and the key turned in the lock.

Outside, the storm began to rage.

20

"Man, it's a good thing we managed to get this vehicle," Clay said as they drove through the desert. "I can't imagine how tough it'd be to be hiking through the desert on foot on a day like this."

"The sky's getting real black over there," Diana said. "When that storm breaks, it's going to be an intense one. Fiercest storm we've had in these parts for years, by the look of it."

Lightning flashed across the dark clouds in the distance, illuminating their bulbous contours in a brief burst of brilliant violet. A low rumble of thunder rolled across the desert plain, and it was loud enough to get Boris whimpering with fright.

"I've trained him to be okay with gunshots," Frank said, gently petting Boris, "but he still doesn't like thunder."

"Let's hope we avoid the worst of the storm," Clay

said. "I'll sure be grateful for the cooling down it'll bring, but I hope we don't get caught in it."

They drove on. Hours had passed since they had escaped from their pursuers, and they had not seen any signs of any other terrorists, or anyone else at all out here in the middle of the desert. The Humvee's fuel had dipped down to about a quarter tank, but they would still be able to cover plenty of miles.

"How long before we get close to the border?" Diana asked.

"I'd say we could get there before sunset," Clay answered. "If we keep going at this pace and don't stop anywhere."

"What are we going to do when the fuel runs out?" she asked.

"Continue on foot," he said. "We'll be close enough by then, and I'm sure that Frank's grandkids will be easy enough to find when it's dark; they should have enough sense to get a fire going, and we'll able to spot it from miles away."

"So will Pablo and his gangsters," Frank muttered. "And I sure as hell hope they don't see my grandkids' fire before we do."

"Whatever happens, Pablo is going to die," Clay growled, tightening his grip on the steering wheel and clenching his jaw as thoughts of revenge against the man who had murdered his best friend floated around his mind. "Don't you worry about Pablo, Frank. I'm gonna make sure I take care of that bastard. He won't be hurting your grandkids or anyone else, not after I deal with him."

They were driving across a flat section of the desert with a rocky floor. It looked as if this had once been a riverbed, hundreds or perhaps thousands of years ago. Now, however, it was as dry as a bone, scattered with boulders, scrub, and cactuses.

"Looks like the storm is breaking on those hills in the distance," Frank remarked. "Maybe we won't get any of it after all."

The clouds were indeed emptying their issue over the hills in a ferocious deluge. The three of them watched as they drove, but soon turned their attention back to the path they were on, ignoring the raging storm in the distance.

"Frank, check your map," Clay said. "Should I be heading southeast or south-southeast here?"

Frank checked his map. "South-southeast is a more direct route," he said. "It should shave off an hour or so."

"South-southeast it is then," Clay said, and they continued along the ancient riverbed.

They were so focused on getting to their destination that none of them noticed the tiny trickle of brown water that was starting to flow along the ancient riverbed. It was barely perceptible at first; little more than an inch-wide snake of water beginning to worm its way along the riverbed.

Someone in the vehicle knew that something was wrong, though – someone whose senses were far sharper than any human's, and far more attuned to the ebb and flow of natural phenomena. Boris could sense that something bad was on the way, and he sat up straight and started barking.

"What's up, boy?" Frank asked.

Boris continued to bark, and his barks started growing more frantic. Even though he was in a vehicle, separated from the dirt beneath his paws by the seats and the rubber of the tires, he could feel a deep vibration in the earth … the vibration of a massive, raging torrent of tumbling water that was barreling down the ancient riverbed from the hills where the huge storm was gushing out rain.

"Something's wrong," Diana said, looking worried. "He's not barking like that for no reason."

"I know, I know," Frank said. "But what?"

Boris's barking became even more frantic, and he jumped up and started pawing at the doors and windows, trying to get out of the car.

"Stop the car, stop the car," Diana said. "We have to get out. Something is terribly wrong."

"Get out?! Here?!" Clay said. "I don't see anything wrong, and…" he trailed off, for he had just caught sight of something in the rearview mirror – something so terrifying he could hardly believe it was real. "Oh my God," he gasped, his jaw dropping with shock and disbelief. "Oh my God…"

Frank turned around slowly, following the gaze of Clay's eyes in the rearview mirror … and saw, a few hundred yards behind them, a tumbling, raging wall of brown water racing down the ancient riverbed, plowing across the landscape and obliterating everything in its path. "Drive!" he roared. "Stomp on the gas pedal and drive!"

"Oh God!" Diana screamed as she too caught sight of the wall of water racing toward them. "Oh God, Jesus, save us!"

Clay saw that there was higher ground to their left, perhaps a hundred yards away. Getting up onto it was their only chance at surviving the coming flash flood. Clenching his jaw tight with determination, he swung the steering wheel hard and stomped on the gas, desperately praying that he could reach the riverbank before the tumbling wall of water slammed into them and carried them away to a watery grave.

The vehicle surged forward, and they barreled toward the high ground ... but there was no way the Humvee could out-accelerate the wall of raging water. They got to within twenty yards of the bank when it hit them, and the force of it almost rolled the vehicle. By turning with the flow of the water, though, Clay managed to keep the Humvee on its wheels instead of ending up upside down.

The water raged around them, hammering the doors and growing deeper with every terrifying second that passed. The Humvee was dragged along with the flow of the flash flood, and despite all the motor's power, there was no way Clay could fight the immense force of the water. The massive vehicle was about as helpless as a rubber duck in an emptying bathtub, getting sucked toward the drain.

"We have to bail out!" Clay yelled. "There's no other way to survive!"

Frank realized that this was the case. If they stayed in the vehicle, they would all be drowned in it. Of course, trying to swim through the fury of the flood water, even across as short a distance as twenty yards, also meant a high chance of drowning – but at least it was only a chance, compared to a certainty if they stayed in the vehicle.

"Go! Open your windows and swim before it gets any deeper!" Frank yelled.

Everyone opened their windows – at which the top of the tumbling brown waters were now lapping – and scrambled out into the churning water. There was no time to grab anything, not even the most crucial supplies; this was a situation in which even a second's hesitation could mean certain death. The water level was growing deeper by whole inches with every passing second, and the force of the flowing current seemed to double with every moment that passed too.

Frank's first priority was not to save his own life. It was, instead, to save Diana's. And his second priority was, again, not his own life, but Boris's. He and Boris went out the same window, while Diana went out the window on the other side. Clay piled out of the driver's window into the churning water.

Frank had always been a strong swimmer who had always taken naturally to oceans, lakes, and rivers, but as seal-like as he was in the water, he felt as powerless as a piece of driftwood in the flood. He had managed to keep a grip on Boris's collar when the two of them had plunged into the water, but now he could barely keep himself above the surface, let alone get to Diana, who was floundering a few yards away from him.

They were being carried downstream at an incredible rate, and were being dunked and thrashed around like helpless rag-dolls in the furious brown water. Frank was trying to swim with all his might while keeping one hand on Boris's collar, but he was hardly able to stay afloat like this. Boris was paddling as strongly as any dog could, but he too was having great difficulties in keeping his head above the water, even with his master doing his best to hold him up.

Diana screamed and went under, and Frank watched in horror as she stayed under. He realized that he had a terrible choice to make – and he could not hesitate in making it. "Swim to the bank, boy, swim to the bank!" he yelled to Boris, and then released his collar. He prayed that his faithful companion would be able to make it out under his own power. Now, though, he had to focus all of his strength on saving Diana.

He swam through the furious waters, being pummeled and hammered by the awesome force of it, searching desperately for any sign of his lover's presence in the waves and troughs of the tumbling flood. He was hardly able to keep himself afloat, and it took all of his strength to do this, but he knew that he had to do his utmost to save Diana.

Then, suddenly, her head broke through the surface a mere yard away from him. With the irresistible force of the water, though, it may as well have been a mile away. Even so, just the sight of her, and the agonizingly brief eye contact they made in that single second before she went under again was enough to spur a boost of almost superhuman strength into his veins. He surged forward and dived under the water, flailing blindly in the murky, tumbling depths of it, desperately seeking Diana's body.

His breath was running out fast – he had only been able to gulp in a small amount of air before going under – but he wasn't about to give up. He pushed through the water, fighting the immense force of the current, seeking until it felt as if his lungs were about to explode … and then his hand gripped an arm – a familiar arm.

He clamped his fingers around Diana's arm and pulled himself closer to her, and then kicked as hard as he could, pushing himself to the surface. His head broke the water and he sucked in a lungful of air, and then he used all his strength to haul Diana's body up, gripping a handful of her hair and yanking her head up above the surface of the water.

She was limp and unresponsive, and Frank had no idea if she was still alive, but he knew he had to do everything he could to save her. He was only five yards from the bank now … but that five yards felt like having to swim a mile in choppy ocean waters. He roared wordlessly with effort, kicking as hard as he could, getting slowly closer to the bank even as the raging river continued to carry them downstream.

Suddenly, a tremendous impact smashed through Frank's side, knocking the wind out of him. He had hit a log, but this proved to a lifesaver, for the log was jammed against the bank, and it stopped him and Diana from being carried any farther downstream.

Groaning with pain and gasping for breath, Frank levered his body against the log and managed to drag both himself and Diana out of the water. He dragged her limp form up onto higher ground, aware that the raging waters might creep up the bank, and then started administering first aid. In his military training, he'd learned how to handle drowning victims, and he started by getting the water out of Diana's lungs.

He was hoping that she would cough and splutter, but she remained still and limp, and her eyes stayed closed.

"No, dammit," he muttered. "You're not leaving me like this, Diana Smith, not like this!"

He pinched her nose and clamped his mouth over hers, giving her the breath of life. He then pressed his hands over her chest and pumped. She coughed up a lungful of water and her eyes flickered open, and relief rushed through Frank in a tremendous wave.

"You're alive!" he gasped, tears of joy and relief rimming his eyes. "Thank God, you're alive!"

He helped Diana to sit up – she coughed up some more water – and held her hand tightly, immensely grateful that she was alive. She couldn't speak yet, but she squeezed Frank's hand tightly in a gesture of thanks.

"Are you gonna be okay sitting here for a few minutes?" he asked. "I need to try find Boris and Clay."

Diana nodded. She didn't feel great, but she knew she would survive, and she was also worried about Clay and Boris.

"I'll be back soon, sweetcheeks," Frank said. He gave her a kiss and then got up and started jogging along the side of the raging river, searching both the banks and the tumbling brown waters for any sign of Clay or Boris. He found Clay soon enough; he saw him on the opposite bank. Clay had just crawled out of the water and was on all fours, coughing up water from his lungs. He saw Frank on the other side of the river and gave him a weak wave, indicating that he was okay, if a little worse for the wear.

Now Frank had to find Boris. He had a bad, sinking feeling in the pit of his belly about his dog. He knew that he couldn't have held on to Boris, because then Diana would be dead now, but even so he felt a terrible, gnawing sense of guilt. He knew this feeling would not be assuaged until he found his dog and was sure that he was alive and well.

He continued jogging down the river, desperately searching for Boris, but there was no sign of the dog either in the water or on the banks. Frank ran down the side of the river for over a mile, but with each step he took, his hope for finding Boris grew dimmer, and a sense of despair and sadness began to grow within him.

"Boris!" he yelled every few steps. "Boris, where are you?! Come here boy, come here!"

He stopped every hundred yards or so and stuck his fingers in his mouth to give a high-pitched whistle. If Boris was anywhere nearby, he would come running at the sound of the whistle. However, even after Frank had done this whistle over a dozen times, there was no sign of Boris at all.

After some time, Frank had to stop. The sun was out in full force, beating down on him mercilessly, and he had neither food nor water. He gave one last whistle, staring around him at the desolate landscape and the tumbling flood waters, which were finally beginning to die down as the flash flood passed, and then he turned around, crushed by a feeling of defeat, and headed back to where Diana was.

When he got back to her, she was feeling much better and had moved from where she was to a position of shelter from the sun in the shadows behind a large shrub.

"Where's Boris?" she asked. She knew that Clay was safe, for he was now across the river from them, waiting for the waters to die down in intensity so he could cross.

With tears in his eyes, Frank shook his head. He couldn't speak, couldn't say what he knew was true. Boris, one of his best friends in the world, was gone.

Diana didn't need to hear the words; she could see it plainly enough in Frank's eyes. Tears filled her eyes too, and she got up and threw her arms around him, hugging him tightly. "I'm sorry, honey, I'm so sorry," she whispered hoarsely.

Things had taken a turn for the worse, now. Three of them had survived, yes, but all of their equipment and provisions had been swept away. Now, alone and virtually unarmed, they had to take on the vastness of the desert and the dangerous enemies who lay ahead.

21

A bloodcurdling scream echoed through the abandoned store. The children sat huddled together in terrified silence; they knew what had just happened, and although none of them had seen it, they were all able to picture Pablo's evil hands slamming the obsidian dagger into Wayne's chest and ripped out his beating heart.

"What the hell was that?!" Bill yelled. "What are those bastards doing to him?!"

None of the children wanted to tell Bill what had happened, but Chuck knew that the man deserved to know the truth, as ugly as it was. "They've killed him, sir," he said sadly.

"They've ... they've what?! How do you know that?!" Bill demanded.

Chuck explained what Pablo had said to them, about his drug-induced delusions of being the true

Emperor of Mexico, and his desire to sacrifice people to an ancient rain god.

"My God," Bill murmured, his face a mask of horror and disbelief. "I knew that Pablo was crazy, but never realized just how crazy he really was. Wayne, oh my God, what have they done to him?!"

"I'm sorry," Chuck said. "I wish there was something we could do…"

"Do you know how to pick handcuff locks?" Bill asked.

"No…"

"Then there's nothing you can do," Bill muttered darkly. "Nothing but wait for those sick bastards to do the same thing to the rest of us. We're all going to die, we're going to get our hearts cut out by that maniac, and—"

Priscilla burst into tears, and Kenneth started whimpering too, his eyes welling up with tears.

"Shut up, man," Joe muttered. "I don't usually talk to grownups like that, but man, you need to shut up. Look what you've done!" he added, pointing at Priscilla.

"I'm sorry you're feeling like this," Chuck said to Bill, "but we can't give up hope now. We can figure out a way to get out of this situation. There has to be a way, if we all put our heads together."

"You're just a bunch of kids," Bill muttered, scowling. "What the hell do you think you're gonna be able to do against bloodthirsty cartel killers?! We're all dead! Just accept it."

"Just leave him," Melissa whispered to Chuck. "His

ROBERT J WALKER

friend just got killed. He's not going to be any help to us, not for a while. We're all scared, Chuck, and there's not much we can do right now."

Chuck wasn't about to give up so easily, though. There had to be a way to outwit the gangsters. He knew that if his Grandpa Frank had been in his place, he wouldn't have given up without a fight. He sat down in a corner of the room and started to think, determined to come up with a plan for escape.

"They're not going to kill all of us," he murmured to himself, thinking about what Pablo had told them. "They want to keep the girls alive … and that's something I can use to my advantage somehow. I just have to figure out how…"

Then an idea hit him. "Melissa, come here," he whispered. "I'm gonna need your help."

She crawled over to him. "What's up? Do you have a plan?"

"Sort of," he said. "Look … Pablo *likes* you. You know what I mean?"

Melissa cringed, and a look of pure disgust and horror came over her face. "Yeah, I know what you mean, and it's … it's totally gross and disgusting," she muttered.

"He's not going to kill you or hurt you, though, and that's what counts," Chuck said. "I need you to pretend to be sick … real sick."

"Then what?" she asked.

"They'll take you out of this room, I hope," Chuck

176

said. "Then you need to get your hands on a key … or a gun."

"Chuck, are you insane?!" she spluttered. "Just how am I supposed to do something like that? This isn't an action movie or a video game, this is real life! If I even try something like that, they'll kill me! These people are crazy, Chuck, they're truly crazy and evil. They just … they murdered a man! And you expect me to try and get a gun or steal a key off one of them? No Chuck, I … I can't do it, I'm too scared. It's just, it's too crazy to work. We can't pull something like that off."

"It's either that or we sit around waiting for another person to die," Chuck said, "when Pablo wants to feed the stupid rain god again. And I don't feel like sitting around and letting another person die. Not if there's a way to get out of this."

They both sat in glum silence. Melissa knew that there was a valid point in what her brother was saying, but the thought of having to try to deceive and steal from these evil, ruthless men was absolutely terrifying. She had never been a good liar, and to try to lie to men who lied for a living was surely a suicidal idea. These men would surely be able to spot a lie from a mile away, especially from an inexperienced liar like her.

Even so, Chuck was right. There were no other real options here. It was either play sick and try to dupe the gangsters or, like he said, sit around waiting helplessly for the next person to die. Melissa sat and thought about this for a while, as the rain hammered down on the tin roof in a relentless, ear-splitting drumming, before she eventually turned to her brother and tapped on his shoulder.

"Don't bug me now, I'm trying to think," he whispered, clearly annoyed with her.

"I'll do it," Melissa whispered back. "I'll try to trick the gangsters." She could hardly believe she was saying this, and it seemed utterly surreal that she was about to do this, but she knew that this might be their only hope of escaping.

"Are you sure?" Chuck whispered back. His tone had quickly changed from annoyed to cautiously hopeful.

Melissa bit her lower lip and nodded. "I'm sure. Like you said, it might be our only chance."

"You're brave, sis, real brave," he said, with genuine admiration in his voice. "Grandpa would be proud of you. And so would Mom and Dad, if they were still in this world."

"I know," she said, with a sudden knot of sadness tightening in her throat at the mention of their deceased parents.

"Don't tell the others," Chuck said, shooting a wary glance across at the other children. "It's not that I don't trust them, it's the fact that if they don't know you're acting, they'll think your sickness is genuine, which will help when it comes to fooling the gangsters."

"All right," she said. "But what do I do when they take me out of here?"

"They'll probably give you some medicine, or at least clean water or something," Chuck said. He knew that this was going to be risky, but he trusted his sister and had faith in her courage. "Act real sick, but keep your eyes open for an opportunity to get your hands on a key or a weapon. When you've got one of those things, tell 'em you're feeling better and you want to come back here with the rest of us."

Melissa nodded. "Okay. But ... what if Pablo ... *tries something* with me?" she asked.

The thought of this made both of them sick to their stomachs. Chuck didn't want to think too deeply about it, but he knew that it was a pertinent concern. "All right," he said, "if he does that, you need to lead him on. Make it seem like you like him. He's someone who loves power, and wants people to fear him. If you make it seem like you like him *and* you fear him at the same time, he'll be like putty in your hands. I know it sounds gross, and crazy, but you have to act like you like him. And if he does want to try any sick stuff with you, act like you want to ... but only after you feel better. That'll buy you some time, and you'll be able to get back here without having to do anything like that. And then, hopefully, we'll have a key or a weapon, and the chance to escape this horrible place."

She breathed in deeply and held the air in her lungs for a while. "Okay," she whispered. "I'm scared outta my mind, and I wanna puke at the thought of being anywhere near that disgusting, crazy Pablo ... but I also don't wanna die, and I don't want anyone else to die. I'll do this."

"I'm ready whenever you are," Chuck said.

"We'll wait until the rain dies down a little," Melissa said. "They won't hear me coughing and stuff with this noise on the tin roof."

"Okay. I'll be ready to play along as soon as you get started."

Melissa crawled over to Priscilla, who was still weeping, and put her arm around her friend. "Don't worry, it's gonna be okay," she said softly, hugging Priscilla. "I know things seem bad, but … it's gonna be okay."

The rain started to die down, and Melissa knew that now was the time to act. She also knew that she had to convince her friends that she was sick; if only her and Chuck were in on the act, it would be much easier to fool their captors. Only Bill and Wayne had drunk the water from the grimy bottle, so this would make her job of faking illness a little easier. She got up and walked over to Bill, whose head was hanging with despair as he stared blankly at the ground, and picked up the water bottle. "Do you mind if I have some of this, sir?" she asked.

"Knock yourself out," he said sourly. "I'm not gonna need any more water if I'm gonna be dead in a couple hours."

She glugged down a few mouthfuls of water. It was tepid and had a plasticky taste to it, as if it had been sitting in this bottle for months, or even years, but it seemed okay. However, she made a show of twisting her face into an expression of disgust, and coughed a few times, as if it had tasted disgusting. Then she went and sat down, biding her time.

Chuck made eye contact with her, and she gave a subtle, almost imperceptible nod, quietly informing him that their plan was now underway. He gave a subtle nod in response. Melissa figured she should wait a while before beginning to put on the act; if the water had genuinely been bad in some way, it would likely take a while to start affecting her.

Everyone waited in somber silence for a while, listening to the pitter-patter of the rain on the tin roof. The deluge was intense and furious for about twenty minutes, but after that it quickly started to slow down and weaken, and soon only the odd drop struck the roof. Then there was silence. Melissa decided that now was the time to act. She gripped her belly and scrunched up her face into a grimace of pain.

"Uh, Bill?" she asked, loud enough that everyone could hear her. "Do you feel okay after drinking that water?"

"I don't know, I don't know how I feel about anything right now," Bill muttered.

"I … I feel sick," Melissa said. "Really sick. My stomach hurts real bad."

"Oh no sis, you shouldn't have had that water!" Chuck said. "You know how sensitive your stomach is!"

"You look really sick, Mel," Priscilla said, sounding concerned.

"Ooh, it really hurts, it hurts bad," Melissa said,

gripping her belly. "I need some medicine or something…"

"You think these goons give a shit?" Bill muttered. "They're gonna kill us all anyway, why would they care if you're sick?"

"They're not going to kill us," Chuck said. "Not the girls, anyway…"

"How do you know that?" Bill asked.

"That's what Pablo said himself. He's gonna take my sister back to Mexico, and one of his friends is going to take Priscilla."

"Oh my God," Bill murmured, the color draining from his face as the implications of what this meant hit him. "I'm … I'm so sorry, girls, I, I wish there was something I could do to stop this … this disgusting monster. Damn it, son of a bitch! These people are *sick*, they're fucking *sick!*"

Chuck feigned innocence about the gangsters' motives. "If they want to keep her alive, they probably will care if she's sick," he said. "And I'm going to tell them." He got up, walked over to the door, and bashed on it. "Hey! Alejandro! Carlos! Are you guys out there? My sister's real sick! She needs some help!"

There was no reply, so he thumped his fist on the door again and repeated the calls for help. Then, finally, there was a response. Chuck heard a key turning in the lock, so he stepped away from the door. Alejandro opened the door and stepped halfway into the room. He had a pistol in his hand and an angry look on his face. His eyes were red and his pupils large and black; it looked as if he was high.

"What the fuck do you want, you lil' punk?" he growled. "You want me to kick your fuckin' teeth in, is that it?!"

"My sister's real sick," Chuck said, doing his best to stay calm despite his fear. "She needs some medicine or something."

"What's wrong with her?" he grunted, clearly suspicious.

"She drank that dirty water, and now her stomach hurts," Priscilla said. She didn't know that this was all an act, so there was genuine concern for Melissa, both on her face and in her voice.

"She's got a real sensitive stomach," Chuck said. "Please Alejandro, she needs some medicine. When she gets like this, her pain can get unbearable."

Melissa doubled over and whimpered, gasping in mock agony for effect.

Alejandro scowled, but he glanced over his shoulder and called out to someone in Spanish. He and the other gangster had a brief conversation in Spanish, and at the end of it, Alejandro shook his head and muttered a curse under his breath. "Come here, you stupid lil' puta," he growled at Melissa. "We got some shit that might help you."

Priscilla and Chuck helped Melissa – who was pretending she could barely walk – to her feet, and helped her to walk over to the door. When she got there, Alejandro grabbed her wrist and yanked her away from the others, and then shoved her out of the room and into the arms of one of his waiting friends.

"Don't try anything stupid," he snarled at the other kids and Bill, and then he slammed the door shut and locked it.

Chuck sat in the corner in anxious, nerve-racking silence, praying he had done the right thing, and that he had not unwittingly delivered his sister into the hands of the devil himself.

22

"*A*ll right, so what do we have left?" Clay muttered.

He, Frank, and Diana had taken shelter in the shade behind a huge boulder a few hundred yards from the ancient riverbed. The flood waters, ten feet deep and raging madly only half an hour ago, had died down into a harmless trickle only a few inches deep. Within an hour or so, the riverbed would be dry again. There had been no sign of Boris, nor of the Humvee, which had been washed away with almost all their weapons, equipment, and provisions.

"You've got your tomahawk and a knife," Frank said. "I've got my .357, but the only rounds I've got are the ones in the cylinder. And I've got my knife, a multi-tool, and a compass."

"And I've got a bow and three arrows," Diana said glumly. They had found these caught in the branches of a dead tree. Unfortunately, this was the only equipment of theirs they had recovered from the flood. There was no food, no water purifying bottles, no clothing, no guns.

"Looks like we're shit outta luck," Clay muttered, shaking his head.

"We might have lost almost everything, but we've still got *these*," Frank said, thumping his fist against his chest, his jaw tight and his eyes bright with determination, his attitude indefatigable even in circumstances like these. "I don't intend to give up or give in to despair or hopelessness anytime soon. My grandkids need me, and I'll be damned if I'm gonna let the loss of a few possessions ... and a good friend ... stop me from getting to 'em."

Diana smiled, and both pride and affection sparkled in her eyes when she looked at Frank. "That's why I love you, Frank," she said, taking his hand and squeezing it gently. "You never give up."

The stony expression on Clay's face crumbled abruptly into a grin. "You know, I do have one vice," he said. "I like gambling. Especially when the odds are high. We've got everything stacked against us now ... and that's the kind of challenge I live for. My tomahawk against Pablo's guns? Bring it on."

Frank chuckled. "I knew there was something I liked about you, Clay. Aside from trying to kill each other in the first few seconds of meeting each other, I think we're laying the foundations for a pretty solid friendship, huh?"

"We sure are," Clay said. "Come on, we need to get

going. It's hot as hell, but that isn't going to slow Pablo and his thugs down, so we can't let it slow us down. Let's get moving."

"We need to protect ourselves from the sun," Diana said. "We could get sunstroke or some horrific burns. I know you two cowboys want to be heroes and strike out into the desert with your arms and faces exposed like that, but if you want to cripple yourselves for the next few days, that's how you do it."

"You're right," Frank admitted. "Let's cut some branches off these shrubs. They ain't much, but they'll work as makeshift umbrellas to keep the worst of the rays off our skin."

They cut some leafy branches off of the nearby shrubs, which made quite effective umbrellas when held in the right position, and set off into the desert with the sun beating relentlessly down on them. There was nothing around them but sand, scrub, and towering rock formations for miles around, and a vast blue sky which, now that the storm had passed, didn't have a single cloud in it. There was no respite from the vicious heat, and almost no shade, and no water in sight. The trek soon became exhausting, but there was nothing they could do but go on. They could have waited for night, of course, but by then they would have been even more dehydrated, and everyone knew Pablo could well have come across and captured Frank's grandchildren by then.

They didn't talk as they walked, for it felt as if even talking would sap too much precious energy, of which they had little. Then there was the thirst, which was not only ever-present, but which seemed to grow in intensity with every step they took. Even though all three were very fit, there was no getting around the fact that Clay was close to middle-age, and that Diana was well into it, and Frank was getting close to the cusp of his geriatric years. Soon a crushing weariness began to sap everyone's strength.

"There's gotta be something to drink … somewhere…" Frank groaned. He stumbled over a rock and almost fell. He was so thirsty now he was beginning to feel disoriented.

"We have to find … liquid," Diana agreed, her voice croaky with thirst.

"Fishhook barrel cactuses," Clay croaked. "Keep your eyes open for 'em. We can drink a small amount of liquid from inside 'em."

They carried on, keeping their eyes peeled for this type of cactus. Finally, Clay spotted a large fishhook barrel cactus. The three of them stumbled over to it, and Clay used his tomahawk to hack it open. Stored in the gourd-like inside of the cactus was a decent amount of a cloudy liquid.

"Are you sure this is safe to drink?" Diana asked.

Clay nodded. "My people have used these as emergency water for hundreds of years. The key is to only take a little, though. Too much will make you sick, but a little will keep you alive."

Frank nodded. "They taught us about this when we did desert survival courses in my Green Beret days.

Clay's right, we can definitely handle a handful of this stuff."

"And after that?" Diana asked, squinting against the bright rays of sunshine that were beating relentlessly down on her face. "This little bit of liquid isn't going to give us much fuel…"

Frank chuckled humorlessly and smiled darkly. "Then we have to drink our own pee. Let's hope it doesn't come to that."

"I'll die of thirst before I go that far," Diana muttered, scrunching up her face with disgust.

They each took a handful of water from the cactus. It tasted quite bitter, and left a bad aftertaste in their mouth, but the simple act of swallowing a mouthful of cool liquid brought psychological and emotional relief, as well as physiological relief from the ever-present thirst that dogged them.

"That's all we can have," Clay said, wiping his cracked lips with the back of his hand. "We'd better keep going."

"There's some shade up ahead, by that big rocky outcrop there," Diana said, pointing to a towering outcrop a few hundred yards away. At its base was a large pool of shadow. "I think we should go lie down in the shade for a while to recuperate some energy."

Frank was reluctant to stop, but he knew that this made sense. They had been pushing themselves through the intense heat and ferocious sun for hours now, with nothing but a sip of cactus water to go on. "All right," he said, "let's take a rest."

They staggered over to the shade behind the towering rock and collapsed behind it. All three of them were parched and exhausted, and despite having used branches to shade themselves from the sun, they still felt as if they were starting to suffer from sunstroke.

"I'm just gonna … close my eyes for a few minutes," Diana murmured, her voice hoarse, as she lay down in the shade.

"Me too," Clay said.

Frank figured it was safe to sleep without someone keeping watch, as the chance of encountering another human being out here on a day like this was negligible. Even if the level of danger had been higher, he wasn't sure whether he would have had the strength in him to stay awake and keep watch. He lay down and closed his eyes. He would only sleep for a few short minutes, he told himself … just a few minutes.

When he opened his eyes again, the sun was low in the sky and the terrible heat of the day had diminished to a more bearable temperature, although it was still very hot. Frank groaned, his throat as dry as the endless desert that surrounded him, his innards aching and screaming out for just a drop of water. He glanced past Diana, who was still asleep next to him, and saw that Clay was also still asleep.

He felt like drifting back into the comfort of slumber himself, but he knew that they had already wasted too much time. He struggled up onto his hands and knees and then gently shook Diana awake.

"Where … are we?" she murmured as she woke, staring around her in confusion for a few seconds before the memory of everything that had happened came rushing back. "Oh, Frank," she groaned when she remembered it all, "it's late! We've been asleep for hours!"

Clay, who was a light sleeper, woke when he heard their voices. "Dammit," he grunted as he got up and dusted himself off. "We've wasted most of the afternoon, haven't we?"

Frank shrugged. "We can't do anything about that now," he said. "And to be honest, I think we all needed a long rest. We can't help my grandkids if we all keel over from sunstroke and exhaustion. But now that we've had a rest, and with the day getting cooler and the sun weaker, we should be able to make better time. How's everyone feeling after the cactus juice?"

"My stomach hurts a little, and I feel kinda queasy, but it's not bad," Diana said.

"I feel fine," Clay said. "It's not the first time I've had to drink from a fishhook barrel cactus, though."

"Come on, let's go," Frank said. "Since we're all okay after that first drink from the cactus, keep your eyes open for another big fishhook barrel. I could do with a little more liquid in me. I'm sure we all could."

They set off into the desert, where the shadows were growing long and dark, stretched across the barren landscape. There were still no clouds in the sky, which would mean a very cold night. While they had sweated and burned beneath the fierce heat of the

191

extraordinarily hot day, Frank knew that in a few hours they would be shivering from the chill of the desert night when all the heat escaped from the sands into the empty sky above. He pushed these thoughts of future suffering out of his mind, though; it would do him no good to dwell on these things.

They pushed on for an hour, moving at a slow but steady pace despite their thirst, aching bodies, and general state of dehydration, and managed to find another large fishhook barrel cactus. Again, Clay hacked it open with his tomahawk and they each took a handful of the liquid within. As bitter as it tasted, they had to stop themselves from taking more, for the thirst within each of them was reaching unbearable levels.

It was getting close to sunset, and the land was quickly cooling. The sun was hovering low on the horizon, and the sky was fading to a deep blue above. There were no stars out yet, but there were lights sparkling on the horizon – not in the sky, but on land.

"What's that?" Diana asked as they stopped to stare at the handful of gleaming dots in the distance.

"They're not moving, so I doubt they're headlamps," Clay said.

"I think it might be a small town," Frank said. "I wish I hadn't lost my maps…"

"We've been on a steady south-southeast course for a few hours," Clay said. "And the compass has ensured that we've been traveling in a straight line. Do you remember there being any towns in that direction on your maps?"

Frank scratched his chin, which was rough with a dense growth of gray stubble after two days of not shaving. "Come to think of it, there was a town in that direction. Well, more of a little village than a town; just a gas station, a couple stores and houses along a long section of desert highway," he said. "I was planning on skirting around it … but we all know that we can't go much farther without water. Some food would be good too. My stomach is twisted in knots."

"So you think we should head into the town … village, whatever you want to call it?" Clay asked.

"Under any other circumstances, I would avoid it," Frank said, "but right now, with things being the way they are, we *have to* get water from somewhere. I know that these pains in my stomach aren't just from hunger; I can't handle another drink of that cactus water."

"Frank's right," Diana said. "We have to find fresh water and something to eat."

"It'll be dangerous," Clay said. "We don't know if those lights mean that the residents are there, or if the place has been taken over by terrorists. But you're right, I guess. We can't go on much longer without food or water."

"It's a risk we're going to have to take," Frank said grimly. "And at least we're not *completely* lacking in firepower," he added, patting his faithful .357 in its holster on his hip. "I may not have too many rounds left, but by God I swear I'll make each and every one of 'em count if we do run into trouble."

"And I've got my bow and my arrows," Diana added. "They're not much against guns, but they're something."

"They could be more valuable than any of Frank's bullets if we need to take someone down silently," Clay said. "So don't dismiss them as useless just yet."

They continued walking toward the distant settlement, and the sun sank behind the horizon. The land was plunged into silence and darkness, and the only lights to be seen were the thousands of stars above and the handful of lights which grew ever brighter as they grew closer to them. Frank prayed that these lights, like the will-o-the-wisps of legend, were not leading them to their doom…

23

"Come here, little chiquita," the man said, beckoning with a crooked finger to Melissa. He was an older man, in his sixties – the same age as her grandfather – but unlike Frank, he looked older than his years. He was scrawny and weak, and his back and shoulders were hunched over, and his fingers and teeth were yellow from decades of chain-smoking cigarettes. His wrinkly arms were covered in tattoos, but time had faded the images into vague blue blurs.

He and Melissa were sitting in one of the smaller rooms, which Pablo used as a makeshift office. They were sitting opposite each other at a crude wooden table, upon which plastic-wrapped bricks of cocaine, marijuana, and crystal meth were stacked. While Miguel wore a 9mm pistol in a holster on his torso, additional protection was provided by Alejandro, who stood guard in the open doorway.

Pablo had ridden off with a few of his men into the

desert on their dirt bikes, and he had left this old man – Miguel – in charge of the abandoned store in his absence. Miguel, like everyone in Pablo's cartel, was a hardened thug, a former hitman who had killed hundreds of people. Now, too weak and frail to fight and kill anymore, he worked for Pablo doing less risky tasks, like packing drugs and testing their purity. Despite his meager frame and general physical frailty, his past reputation still allowed him to command respect from the younger members of the gang. Furthermore, he was a shrewd thinker, sharp and quick to detect any sorts of lies or betrayals on the part of the gang members. This was the main reason Pablo kept him close.

"My stomach really hurts," Melissa said. It was only a half-lie now, since the stress of having to put on this act in front of these dangerous men, as well as the dread of what Pablo might want to do to her, had genuinely made her feel quite ill. "It's from drinking that dirty water in the bottle, sir."

"It was only you who drank this water, chiquita?" Miguel asked.

She shook her head. "Wayne and Bill drank some too, sir," she said.

"Well, Mr. Wayne is ... not with us anymore," Miguel said with a dark, sudden grin, "but this Mr. Bill, is he sick too?"

"I don't know," Melissa said. "I, um, I have a very sensitive stomach, I get sick real easy. I shouldn't have drank that water, but I was so thirsty…"

Miguel asked Alejandro in Spanish whether he thought the remaining border patrol officer was sick. Alejandro shrugged and said that he didn't think so.

"What do you think this little slut is playing at?" Miguel asked Alejandro in Spanish. "I don't think she's really sick. I'd say she's faking it."

"I don't know, but she's a little girl, what the hell is she going to do? Grab an AK and start blazing away like she's fucking Wonder Woman or some shit? Who cares. Just give her an edible and I'll shove her back in the room. Whether she's sick or faking it, a special cookie will sort her out real fast. You know Pablo doesn't want her getting bruises on her pretty lil' face, so I don't want to have to smack her around or nothin'. It'll be easier if you just play along, pretend to believe her, and give her a cookie."

Miguel listened to this and nodded slowly. What Alejandro was saying did make sense. The girl was virtually powerless to do anything against them, and a marijuana cookie would shut her up without really harming her, whether she was actually sick or just faking it. He turned back to Melissa and flashed an alligator's smile at her.

"All right lil' chiquita," he said. "I'll get you and your friends some clean water. And I'll give you some medicine. Here, have this cookie," he said, reaching under the table, where there was a jar of marijuana-laced cookies.

Melissa swallowed slowly and stared with suspicion in her eyes at the cookie. She was terrified of having to eat it; what if it was poisoned? Miguel, who was extremely perceptive, noticed the doubt and fear in her eyes and smiled.

"What, you think there's rat poison in this or something? Look here." He broke the cookie in half and ate half of it himself, and then opened his mouth to show her that he had swallowed all of it. "See? It's good enough for me, it's good enough for you, girl. Trust me, you'll feel better after you eat it. It's got medicine in it, good medicine. Come on, take it."

He leaned across the table and shoved the broken cookie into Melissa's hands. She didn't want to eat it, but knew that she had to. She nervously put it in her mouth and started chewing.

Miguel smiled. "See? Tastes good, eh? It'll make you feel better in a couple minutes." He then looked up at Alejandro. "Alejandro, there, it's done, take her back to the cell and lock her up," he said in Spanish. "And get the gringos some clean water so they don't have an excuse to try and pull any more shit like this."

"Come with me," Alejandro grunted at Melissa.

Seeing as she understood a little Spanish, she knew that she was going to be taken back to the cell now. She pretended to swallow the cookie and walked over to Alejandro, who made her walk in front of him through the building to the cell. She noticed that he kept the key on a string around his neck; this would make stealing it from him nearly impossible. He shoved her aside, unlocked the door, and then told her to get inside. "I'm gonna go take a dump," he muttered. "I'll bring you fuckers some water when I'm done. Maybe it'll be toilet water, maybe it won't, huh?" he added with an evil smile. "You'll just have to taste it to find out." As soon as she was in the room, he slammed the door shut and locked it.

She spit out the chewed-up cookie – she hadn't swallowed any of it, even though it had actually tasted good – and kicked the chewed-up mess across the floor, and then she hurried over to Chuck.

"Were you able to get a gun or a key?!" he whispered.

Melissa shook her head. She was both disappointed and immensely relieved. She hadn't managed to get hold of a gun or a key, but she had also managed to avoid coming into contact with Pablo. Despite her failure to get a gun or a key, she hadn't come back completely empty-handed. She opened her right hand to reveal what she'd managed to steal from the table: a razor blade, which the gangsters had been using to cut their lines of cocaine and meth. There had been a few razor blades on the table, and Melissa had managed to sneakily take one when Miguel had been focused on Alejandro.

"It's not much, but it's something," Chuck whispered, taking the razor blade from her. "How are you feeling? What happened?"

She told him about Pablo and a bunch of other gangsters having departed, leaving Miguel in charge.

"I thought I heard a bunch of dirt bikes riding away," he said. "That's good news for us; if there aren't too many of these people around, it might make escaping easier."

"All we've got is a razor blade, though," Melissa said. "And I don't think they're going to buy any more 'I'm feeling sick' acts. Alejandro's getting clean water for us, so we definitely can't try to pull that trick again."

"Is he, huh?" Chuck said, and Melissa could see that a plan was forming in her brother's mind.

"Chuck ... what exactly are you going to try to do? If you think you can use that little razor blade to take on Alejandro, who's got a freaking *gun,* and who has probably killed people before, you're crazy."

"I'm going to do what Grandpa Frank would do in this situation," Chuck said calmly, turning the razor blade over in his fingers.

"What exactly do you mean by that?" Melissa asked, sounding worried. "Seriously, Chuck, I know we're in trouble here, but if you try anything stupid, you're going to get killed. These people are dangerous, seriously dangerous, and this isn't a video game or an action movie. If you get shot, you die, and you don't come back. You're gone forever."

"Compared to what they're going to do to us if we don't try to escape, I'd rather get shot," Chuck said. "At least it'll be over with quickly."

Melissa now deeply regretted smuggling the razor blade in here. She should have known that Chuck would try something crazy with it, she thought to herself, shaking her head. "Chuck, look, I don't think —" she began.

"I have to do this, sis," he said. "This is our one and only chance to escape this place. Look at the opportunity we have here – Pablo and most of his goons are out, and there are only a few gangsters left here. We're not going to have a chance like this again. It's a big risk, yeah, I know, but if we don't take it, we're all totally screwed. Have you forgotten that Pablo has already murdered someone?! And that he's not going to stop there, he's totally nuts. And they're all high on drugs too, so they'll do even crazier things. Not to mention the fact that he wants to take you and Priscilla away and do … terrible things to you. We have to do this."

"Chuck, no, please—" Melissa said, with tears of fear and anxiety welling up in her eyes.

Chuck, however, ignored her as he got up and pushed past her. He went straight over to Bill, who was still sitting slumped over in the corner, stewing in dread and hopeless misery.

"Bill," he said, the urgency in his tone causing the man to look up immediately.

"What do you want, kid?" Bill muttered, scowling. "Go bug someone else, and—"

Chuck held the razor blade up in front of Bill's face, and his expression immediately changed. "Holy shit, where'd you get that?!" he gasped.

"It doesn't matter," Chuck said. "We're going to have to use it *right now* if we're going to have any chance of escaping this place. One of the gangsters is coming in here to bring us fresh water, probably in the next few seconds. What should I do?!"

"With a blade that small, you've only got one shot," Bill said. "Damn it, I wish I could use my hands, but you're gonna have to do this. And one of your friends is gonna have to help you. I'll do what I can, but my hands are out of the picture."

"Just tell me what to do and I'll do it."

"You're gonna have to slash him across the side and front of his throat," Bill said. "You've only got one shot, so hit him hard and cut deep. You'll cut more effectively if you slash in an uppercut kinda motion, almost like you were throwing a punch. The instant you attack him, your buddy has to go for his gun. If your cut is deep enough, he'll be dead in maybe twenty or thirty seconds ... but in the first five or ten seconds, he's gonna fight like a crazed animal. If you can prevent him from using the gun in those first few seconds, we'll win. If you can't ... it's not just the gangster who's gonna die in this room."

Chuck understood how high the stakes were, and how dangerous this was going to be. However, he also knew what would happen to them if he didn't do this. "I'll do it," he said. "And I'll get someone to help me."

"I'll be ready, and I'll do what I can," Bill said. "You're a hero, kid, no matter what happens. Remember that..."

Chuck nodded and then hurried over to Joe. Joe was chubby, and not particularly fit, but because of his weight, he was quite strong for his age and could move fast in short bursts. Chuck also knew that he could trust Joe, unlike Kenneth.

"Joe," he said, "I'm about to do something crazy, and I need you to help me..." He explained what he was going to do, but just before Joe could say whether he would either act or refuse to participate, a key turned in the lock and the door started to open.

Chuck's heart began to pound like a thumping jack-hammer in his chest. He knew that it was now or never ... but when – *if* – he made his move, would Joe support him, or would more than one person die in this room in the next few seconds?

24

*I*t was dark by the time Frank, Clay, and Diana got to the outskirts of the small settlement. While they were all exhausted and dehydrated, and feeling down after the loss of Boris and most of their equipment and supplies, the fact that they weren't able to see any evidence of the presence of terrorists or their Humvees anywhere gave them a measure of hope.

The lights they had seen were bonfires burning in one or two backyards, as well as gas lanterns burning inside the small, squat buildings. The power and everything electrical here was dead, as it was everywhere, but it seemed that there hadn't been any violence here.

Even so, they decided to approach the settlement with caution. Just because there was no sign of the blue-uniformed terrorists, this was no guarantee that the place would be safe, or that there weren't other dangerous people around.

"What's the plan?" Clay whispered. He, Frank, and Diana were hiding behind an empty toolshed in the backyard of one of the houses that bordered the desert. They had been observing the house for around fifteen minutes, and while there was a light burning in one of the windows, they hadn't seen any signs of life inside it.

"We need to be very stealthy and stay out of the light," Frank whispered back. "We need to find some food and water, then get the hell out of here. Even if it's only residents in this place, they'll all be on edge after everything that's happened, and you can bet that a bunch of them are sitting in their living rooms with shotguns or rifles in their hands, and nervous fingers on the triggers. We don't want to be mistaken for criminals, not at a time like this. We don't want to be seen at all."

"Where do you think we can find some food and water, Frank?" Diana asked.

"Water should be easy enough. At least one of these houses will have a water storage tank in the backyard. Food ... that'll be harder. I guess we're gonna have to see if we can get into the gas station and grab some snacks or canned food, or whatever they've got in there."

"We'd better get moving," Clay said. "I don't know why, but this place gives me the heebie-jeebies. Something about it just ... I don't know, maybe I'm too hungry and thirsty to be thinking straight, but I don't like this place."

Diana nodded, frowning. "I know what you mean,"

she said. "I feel uneasy about this place too. I can't explain it, but the feeling is definitely there, and I can't shake it."

Frank felt it too; it was a deep sense of unease in his stomach, a sixth sense pealing out a silent but potent warning in his mind. Even though he knew that such instincts should not be ignored, if they didn't at least get water here, they might not live to see another sunset. If they had had even one bottle of water between them he would have chosen to give this little settlement a wide berth, but as it was, they simply had to have water. "Follow me," he said. "And stay low, stick to the shadows."

He gripped his revolver in his right hand, ready to squeeze off a shot in the blink of an eye if necessary, and he crept through the empty yard, avoiding the patch of light coming from the single gas lamp burning in the window. The others followed him, hunched over and creeping behind him with two or three yards between them.

They slipped between the two houses – the other was shrouded entirely in darkness, and no lights burned in its window – and got out to the single road that ran through the settlement. Now that they were able to see the front of the gas station, they noticed a number of old dirt bikes parked up outside it.

"I don't like the look of that," Frank whispered to the others. "I think we're going to have to give the gas station a pass and go without food. We find some water, drink our fill, then get the hell out of here before whoever owns those bikes sees us."

The others all agreed with him; the sight of the dirt bikes unsettled them and hinted at the presence of possible hostiles. Staying under the cover of the densest, darkest shadows, they scanned the strip, which consisted only of a handful of small stores and houses, for any signs of water that they could drink.

In the middle of the buildings was a small convenience store. The entire storefront window had been smashed, and once again silent alarm bells pealed within everyone. Since it was clear that the store had been looted, there was undeniable evidence that nothing was as it seemed and that something was definitely wrong here. Frank didn't need to say this to the others; he turned and looked at them, and even in the dark shadows the look that passed between their eyes said it all.

"We'll leave the store unless we have no other option," Frank whispered. "First we'll search the yards for water storage tanks. Only if we have no other choice will we go look in that store."

The others murmured their agreement with this, and they set off along the strip, dashing between patches of shadow and staying well away from any pools of light coming either from camping lanterns or bonfires that were burning in people's yards.

"Why the hell is nobody around?" Clay whispered, half to himself, as he scanned the settlement for any signs of life. There were all these lights and fires, yet they hadn't seen or heard a single other person in the entire time they had been here.

"I don't like this place, I don't like it at all," Diana whispered.

"We just have to find some water, then we'll get as far from this damn place as possible," Frank said.

They got to the end of the strip and found that the only store that had been looted was the convenience store. The other stores were all locked up, their doors and windows unmolested.

"Clay," Frank whispered, "you go around the back of that row of houses and look for water. Me and Di will check the backyards of these places here. Meet back here in around fifteen minutes, okay?"

Clay gave a curt nod in the darkness and glided silently into the shadows like a ghost. Frank and Diana, meanwhile, headed around to the backyard of the nearest house, a small, squat dwelling that was shrouded in darkness. There was no moon in the clear sky, but the thousands of stars provided a little illumination. Even by starlight, Frank could see that there was no water tank in this yard. He and Diana moved through each yard, and every time their quest to find a source of water was unsuccessful.

Finally, they got to the last yard, which was the one they'd entered when they first came to the settlement. The light still burned in the window of the house, but there was still no sign of life.

"Dammit," Frank muttered. "Nothing this side. We need to backtrack and find out if Clay managed to find anything. If he didn't, we're going to have to go into that damn store."

"Frank! Over there!" Diana whispered, her voice unmistakably urgent.

He spun around, peering through the gloomy emptiness in the direction Diana's finger was pointing. There, in the street, Frank just managed to see three figures slipping swiftly and silently through the shadows … and all three were clearly armed with assault rifles.

"Oh shit," Frank muttered. "It looks like they're going after Clay."

"What do we do?" Diana asked anxiously.

"We can't leave him; we have to help him," Frank whispered. "Get your bow ready; you might need to use it. Quick, this way!"

They hurried along the side of the house, moving quickly but keeping their steps silent, in a maneuver that would flank the three dark figures as they went after Clay. The danger wasn't only from these three men, though; Frank knew that the moment a shot was fired, it could bring any number of enemies out of the woodwork. If Diana could take the men down silently with her bow, they still had a chance of getting out of here without getting into a firefight … but Frank knew the chances of this were slim. He gripped his revolver tight, ready to fire it at a moment's notice.

They got to the front of the house, and from there they had a clear view of the street and the three armed men who were crossing it. In the distance, Frank caught a brief glimpse of Clay's outline, silhouetted against the starry sky as he moved through one of the backyards of the houses. It was now completely obvious that the men knew he was there, and that they were hunting him.

"Di," he whispered without looking over his shoulder at her, keeping his eyes instead on the three men. "You're going to have to use the bow on 'em. How fast can you put those three arrows on target?"

No response came from Diana, however. Instead, there was just an eerie silence.

"Di, hurry!" Frank said. "They'll be out of range soon. If you're not gonna do it, then hand me the bow." He half-turned to face her, but instead of seeing her familiar face just behind him, he saw a viciously-swung baseball bat whipping through the air toward his face. He only just had time to half-gasp with surprise before a bright flash of light and a concussive impact rocketed through his skull. Then everything plunged into blackness.

25

*E*verything felt surreal, like a dream … or a nightmare. Chuck couldn't believe he was about to do what he was about to do, but he knew that he had to do it. If that disgusting monster Pablo carried away his sister and Priscilla, he knew that he would never forgive himself. And this, this terrible moment right here, was his only chance to stop that from happening.

Alejandro flung open the door and walked in, carrying a large plastic bottle of clean water in his left hand and a pistol in his right. He saw Chuck standing up a few feet from him, holding his hands behind his back, but he obviously did not consider the boy a threat, and so he ignored him. He squatted down to put the water on the floor, and that was when Chuck moved.

He lunged forward, slashing the razor blade in a diagonal arc upward, putting all of his strength into the cut. His aim was perfect, and the tremendously sharp sliver of steel slashed through the bottom and side of Alejandro's unprotected throat. Blood sprayed in a grisly spurt out of the man's throat, soaking Kenneth with its warm wetness. Alejandro gasped and staggered back, taken completely by surprise by the attack. He could scarcely believe that Chuck had attacked him and wasn't yet able to process the severity of his injury. Joe had already scrambled to his feet and clamped his hand around Alejandro's right wrist and was desperately trying to yank the pistol out of his hand.

Chuck, driven now by a surge of adrenaline and the urgent desperation of their situation, jumped up onto Alejandro's back and clamped a hand over his mouth, stopping him from screaming. Alejandro was in such shock about what was happening that he was barely able to fight back for the first few seconds, but when his brain finally registered what was happening, he began to struggle like a cornered panther.

Bill jumped up from his position in the corner, and with a roar, he charged and slammed his shoulder into Alejandro's midriff, sending both him and Chuck tumbling to the floor. Blood was spraying everywhere from the gruesome cut, and Alejandro was struggling and kicking viciously and biting Chuck's hand, which was clamped like a snapped-shut beartrap over his mouth.

Kenneth sat rooted to the spot, his eyes almost popping out of their sockets, drenched in warm blood, while Priscilla, next to him and also splashed with blood, sat with her mouth open to scream – but no sound came out; she was simply paralyzed with horror and shock. Melissa too was almost crippled with terror and horror, but a single, urgent thought was bouncing around her head: *shut the door*.

She dashed across the room, yanked the key out of the lock, and then slammed the door shut and locked it from the inside, while a few feet away her brother, Joe, and Bill fought in a vicious, animalistic struggle for their very lives against Alejandro.

Bill kept Alejandro's left arm pinned down with the weight of his body, driving his knee repeatedly into Alejandro's groin and stomach with vicious power, every blow exacting vengeance for his murdered friend. Joe kept all his weight on Alejandro's right arm, hanging on for dear life as the man thrashed around. He had wrested the gun out of the gangster's grasp and kicked it across the room. Chuck, meanwhile, kept both hands clamped down over Alejandro's mouth, and he gritted his jaw and whimpered with pain as the man's teeth sank deeper into the flesh of his hand.

The struggle was as short as it was brutal. Blood was gushing out of Alejandro's throat, and his strength quickly faded away. His violent thrashing subsided, and his flailing kicks became weaker and weaker until they ceased completely. His body became limp, and the pressure of his jaw on Chuck's left hand eased off. Finally, with one last shudder, the life passed from his body and he became limp, and lay deathly still on the dirty concrete floor.

"Oh my God," Melissa gasped, staring in horror at the dead body and the blood-spattered living bodies of Joe, Bill, and Chuck. "Oh my God…"

A low cry finally started to emerge from Priscilla's mouth, morphing into a high-pitched wail of sheer terror. Realizing the danger this scream put them all in, Melissa darted her hand out and clamped it over Priscilla's mouth to stifle her howl.

Kenneth, who was utterly drenched in blood, simply sat there with his eyes as wide as saucers and his mouth hanging open with disbelief and fear. He was far too shocked to say anything or even scream.

All of them were, really; they had just watched a man die in front of them in an immensely gruesome manner. Joe, Chuck, and Bill had been fighting, driven on by pure survival instinct and raging adrenaline, but this was now wearing off.

Bill quickly took charge. "Search his body, he's got the keys to these cuffs on him. Hurry! If any of those other thugs heard that scream they'll be coming this way, and if I don't get my hands free by the time they get here, we'll all be dead!"

Intense pain was throbbing through Chuck's left hand, where Alejandro had bitten it in desperation, and blood was flowing down his wrist and forearm, and he was in shock over what had happened and what he had just done. However, he forced himself to act and push through the haze of horror and shock. He rifled through Alejandro's pockets and soon found a bunch of keys. He pulled them out with trembling fingers and held them in front of Bill's face. "Are th-, these the right k-, keys?" he stuttered.

"The small gold key, that's the one," Bill said. "Quick, unlock the cuffs!"

"Holy shit, I can't believe we just did that," Joe murmured, breathing hard, his eyes wide and white with shock and horror. "We just … we freakin' *killed* that guy. Holy shit, holy freakin' shit…"

"He would have killed all of us," Bill muttered as Chuck fumbled with the keys and handcuffs behind his back. "Don't feel bad about this scumbag dying. I sure as hell don't."

Chuck got the cuffs off, and Bill groaned with relief, shaking the tension out of his aching wrists. He didn't savor this feeling for long, though, for he understood just how urgent their situation was. He scrambled over to the pistol and picked it up. He quickly popped the clip out, nodded with satisfaction when he saw that the magazine was full, and then he slapped it back in and cocked it. "You got the key, right kid?" he asked Melissa.

She nodded, biting her lip and staring at the ground to avoid the grisly sight of the corpse and all the blood.

"Okay, good, that's good, kid," Bill said. "Hand me the key, and we can get the hell out of this place."

At that moment the door handle turned. Everyone fell silent, and a silent shock wave rippled through the room, as if a grenade had just been detonated inside it.

"Hey, Alejandro! What's going on in there? What's taking so long? Why have you locked the door?" a voice from outside yelled in Spanish. "Open up, you stupid asshole!"

"Get back against that wall, kids, and cover your heads and ears," Bill whispered gravely, taking aim at the door with the pistol. "Things are about to get crazy…"

26

rank woke with a raging headache drumming its dull, painful thumps in regular pulses through his skull. His mouth was dry and sticky, and the metallic taste of blood lingered on his tongue. For a few seconds he was overwhelmed with confusion, and he had no idea where he was, nor any recollection of how he had gotten there. His eyes were open, but there was nothing around him but intense blackness. He could hear breathing in the dark near him, though, and this ominous sound got his heart racing with fear.

He could not speak, for he found that a rag had been stuffed in his mouth and had been fixed there with duct tape. He was seated on the ground, his back against a wall, and his hands were tied behind his back.

When the fog of confusion and fear began to clear after a short while, though, his thoughts immediately went to Diana. He tried to call out to her, but all that emerged from his gagged mouth was a muted, incomprehensible mumbling.

He growled with anger and frustration, furious at his own helplessness. He began to remember patches of what had happened. The three men who were stalking Clay ... following them, planning to take them out silently with the bow and arrows ... then a baseball bat whipping toward his face, and a bright flash behind his eyes. Then ... this.

He forced himself to calm down, controlling his breathing and ensuring that his inhalations and exhalations were slow and regular, as he had been trained to do in situations like this. This in turn slowed his racing heart and allowed him to think more clearly and act more rationally.

The first thing he did when his mind was clearer and his body calmer was to listen carefully. Without eyes, his ears and other senses would have to take over and feed him the information he needed to escape this situation.

Judging by the slightly warmer temperature, the smooth surface beneath him, and the lack of wind, he was indoors. He could hear more than one person breathing nearby. In fact, there seemed to be a handful of people, so it wasn't only himself, Diana, and Clay. This gave him hope, at least, for it meant that his lover and his friend were still alive.

As for who had taken them captive, it didn't seem to have been the blue-uniformed terrorists. He hadn't managed to get a very clear look at the men he'd seen stalking Clay, but from what he had seen, they hadn't been wearing uniforms. Who were these people, then? A chill ran down his spine when one specific thought entered his mind: they may well be Pablo's cartel thugs. This, he thought, might be even worse than if they were the terrorists.

He tried to move his arms, but found that his wrists were bound tight. Judging by what he could feel, it seemed that it was wrapped with duct tape. This was good, he thought; if he could find a rough surface to rub the tape against, he could get through it in a few minutes and free himself. He started shifting his body through the darkness, moving slowly and feeling what was behind and to the side of him, keeping his back against the wall.

Before he could get very far, though, he heard the sound of a nearby door opening, and as it did, light from a camping lantern flooded into the room. The bright illumination burned raw pain through his dark-accustomed eyes into his skull, and he winced and shut his eyes, turning his face instinctively away from the pain.

He heard a number of boots and shoes walking into the room, and he slowly began to open his eyes, allowing them to adjust to the light. With his eyes half-open, he saw the blurry sight of five figures standing in the room. An unfamiliar voice began to talk, speaking in English that was tinged with a heavy Mexican accent.

"Okay, listen up, gringos," the voice growled. "This

here is our little town now. It don't belong to you no more. It belongs to our boss, Pablo Cortez … and soon this whole state is going to belong to him! We don't want you around here, and we don't need you around here. But before you *go*, we got a job we need you to do for us."

Frank didn't like the way the man had said "go". It didn't sound as if he intended for them simply to leave the town. There had been something far more sinister in that word than that.

Frank heard a number of muffled mumbles coming in response from the people in the room; it seemed that everyone else was also bound and gagged. His eyes were now adjusted to the light, and when he opened them fully and looked around him, he saw that there were nine other people seated on the floor. Clay and Diana were among them. The rest all looked as if they were the residents of this settlement.

The men were obviously Mexican cartel gangsters. They were dressed in casual clothes, but each was armed with a firearm. The man who was speaking, a short, rough-looking gangster in his thirties, with greasy slicked-back hair and a badly pockmarked face, was armed with a pump-action shotgun.

"Yeah yeah, you stupid assholes," the man grumbled, "I know y'all can't speak right now, but I don't need you idiots to speak anyway … I just need y'all to *listen*. And if you don't … let's see, eeny meeny, miney, moe … o-u-t spells … out." He casually pointed the shotgun at an elderly man who was sitting in one corner of the room, and without warning blasted a hole through his chest.

The shot roared like thunder through the room, leaving everyone's ears ringing with a shrill whine. Everyone started screaming with terror and shock, their cries muffled by the gags in their mouths, while the old man, killed instantly, keeled over limply, blood gushing from the huge wound in his chest. Frank and Clay, however, did not scream. Instead, their eyes hardened with cold fury, and their jaws clenched tight with anger. There was nothing either of them could do at this moment, though.

"As you fuckin' gringos can see, it don't mean *nothin'* to me to kill a man – or a woman," the short man growled. "So you do what I say, or I kill you. It's that simple. Now get up, all of you. Stand up nice and slow. Yeah, that's it, get on your feet, on your damn feet."

Everyone got up slowly, struggling to their feet. The gangsters leveled their firearms at them, the evil smirks on their faces daring anyone to make a move.

"That's good, gringos, that's good," the short man said. "All right, let's move now. Follow me. And don't try nothin' stupid, coz my friends here, they kill just as quickly and easily as I do." He led the way, walking out of the room, while the other gangsters kept their guns aimed at the people as they filed quietly out of the room in a line, following the short man.

He led them out of the building – which turned out to the looted convenience store, in the storeroom of which they had been imprisoned – and out to the desert behind the back of the store. There, he and his men had made a few bonfires to provide a source of illumination. Frank liked the look of things even less when he saw what was lying on the ground: a number of shovels.

"Okay gringos, listen up!" the short man said. His friends formed a spread-out semicircle behind him between the store and the line of captives. "We're gonna free your hands now, so that you can do a lil' work for us. Everyone's gonna take a shovel, see, and start digging one nice big hole right there in the ground. You work nice and hard, and I'll give you a good reward when you're done, understand?" he said with an evil smirk. "It's very simple ... you just dig, and you keep digging until we say stop. Here, I know you'll all be hungry and thirsty, and you'll need some energy to do this job, so we're gonna give you something to eat and drink before you start work."

He nodded to two of his men, who each set their guns down and picked up large plastic bottles of water. They went to each captive in turn, ripping off the duct tape from their mouths, taking the gags out and holding the bottles up to their lips. They allowed each of the captives to drink generously and slake their thirst.

After that, they opened a few cans of beans and did the same thing, putting spoonfuls of beans into the captives' mouths. Frank took his beans from the gangster, eating them while staring meekly at the ground.

222

Simple beans had never tasted so good, and he felt energy returning to his muscles as he chewed and swallowed the food.

His meekness was an act, of course, designed to get the gangsters to let their guard down. He didn't know when he would strike, but he knew he had to – for the task the gangsters were making them do was no innocent one. He was one hundred percent certain of this.

The shovels were there for only one purpose, and he understood this with chilling clarity: they were digging their own graves.

"*A*lejandro, open the fuck up!" the man yelled in Spanish.

The door handle turned again, and Bill knew that he had to act now, while the element of surprise was still on his side. Also, since the man on the other side was turning the door handle, Bill could pinpoint his position.

He fired three shots through the door, shooting in rapid succession. There was a grunt and then a muffled thud as a body fell to the ground.

"Unlock the door and open it, hurry!" Bill yelled as cries and shouts of surprise from the gunshots began to ring out through the building.

Melissa was in a state of shock, but she forced herself to fight through it. She scrambled up, ran over to the door, and unlocked and opened it – and barely managed to stifle a scream when she saw the lifeless body lying in a pool of blood on the other side of it.

Nonetheless, she had the presence of mind to grab the pistol the man had dropped before she ran back into the room.

Just as she turned, though, a shout rang out to her left. "Hey, what the hell are you doing?!" a gangster roared, just down the hallway a few yards away with a shotgun in his hands.

Melissa didn't bother to answer; she simply dived back into the room, unable now to stifle a scream, which rang loud and piercingly clear through the room. Bill heard the shout and realized that danger was near, and he ran to the door. The gangster had seen his dead comrade on the floor and knew that the captives were trying to break out. He had taken up a position of cover behind the corner of the wall, and the moment he saw Bill, he opened fire with his shotgun.

The blast tore a chunk out of the doorframe, with some of the buckshot hitting Bill in his left leg, but he fired back furiously with the pistol. He and the gangster were engaged in a short but vicious gunfight, from which Bill emerged victorious, scoring a headshot with his final burst of fire.

"Let's go!" he yelled to the kids. "Gimme the other gun, we gotta move!"

The children scrambled to their feet – all of them except Kenneth, who was still completely paralyzed with fear. Melissa ran over to Bill, her heart thumping madly in her chest, and she handed him the pistol. He tossed the empty pistol aside and cocked the fresh one and then ran out into the hallway, where he shot a gangster who came running around the corner.

"That was for Wayne, you sick fucks!" he roared, charged with the energy of doing battle.

"Kenneth, get up, we have to go!" Chuck yelled.

Kenneth, who was trembling with fear, his eyes as wide as dinner plates, simply shook his head. Chuck was still angry with Kenneth about everything he had done, but he knew he couldn't abandon him here. He also knew that Kenneth wouldn't be going anywhere of his own accord. He was charged up on adrenaline from his fight with Alejandro and from the gunfight that was happening just outside the room. He knelt down, scooped Kenneth up, and slung him like a bag of potatoes over his shoulder and carried him out of the room.

"Hurry, hurry!" he yelled to the other kids, who were also almost paralyzed with fear. "We have to go, we have to go!"

Out in the hallway, Bill had used up all the ammo in his second pistol, so he tossed it aside and grabbed one of the fallen gangsters' shotguns. A gangster popped out of one of the doorways, but Bill shot him down before he could squeeze off even a single shot.

They were near the back door now, and Bill had a brief but intense exchange of gunfire with one more gangster before he got to the door. This time, though, he was wounded, taking a bullet in his right thigh. He grunted with pain and stumbled, but recovered and blasted the gangster in the chest with the shotgun.

"Outta the door, kids, go, move it!" Bill yelled,

grimacing with pain. The wound in his leg was a bad one, and a wet patch of blood was rapidly darkening the right leg of his pants. Melissa flung the door open, and the warm light of the afternoon sun and the hot, dry air of the desert came blazing in. She rushed out, her eyes wide as saucers, and scanned the desert beyond the ghost town. There was no sign of anyone nearby. "The coast's clear!" she called out to the others.

They all ran out of the building, followed by Bill, who came limping out after them, dripping blood from the right leg of his pants, his face twisted into a grimace of agony. "That bastard got me good," he muttered, gripping his leg. "He really got me good."

"Which way should we go?" Joe asked.

"I don't care, we just have to get out of here," Priscilla murmured, looking as if she had seen a ghost.

"I have to make sure Wayne is really … gone," Bill said. "I'm going back in."

"What if there are more gangsters in there?!" Chuck said, breathing hard from the exertion of carrying Kenneth. "He's dead, Bill, trust me. We all heard it … come on, we have to get away from this place before Pablo and the others come back."

Bill shook his head stubbornly. "I can't do that, kid. I have to make sure. I'll be back in one minute. You kids just wait here."

The other children shouted and screamed, but Bill's ears were deaf to their protests. He turned around and limped back inside the building, determined to find out what had happened to his fellow border patrol officer.

Chuck, realizing that he had to take charge here, dumped Kenneth on the ground and then ran into the building. He picked up a pistol that one of the dead gangsters had dropped, checked that it had ammo in it, and then ran back out to the others. Just as he got out of the building, a barrage of gunfire thundered through it.

"Get behind cover!" Chuck yelled to the others. "There, those old oil drums, get behind them!"

A few dozen yards away was a pile of rusty old oil drums. The kids ran across to them and crouched behind them. Now that Kenneth was outdoors, he seemed to have recovered his senses somewhat, and he scrambled to his feet and got up from the ground. He ran on shaky legs over to the oil drums and skidded onto the ground behind them with the others.

They waited with bated breath, with Chuck peeking out from behind the oil drums and keeping the pistol aimed at the back door, in case it wasn't Bill who emerged from it.

"How many bullets you got in that thing?" Joe whispered.

"Three or four, I didn't count," Chuck whispered back, his eyes locked on the door through the pistol sights.

"I hope it's Bill who comes through the door," Joe murmured. He gripped the edge of the oil drum with trembling fingers.

The door began to open, and everyone sucked in sharp breaths of suspense. Chuck gripped the pistol tight, his heart racing like a throbbing motor in his ribcage.

Out of the door staggered Miguel, holding an AK-47. The moment the children saw him, they realized that Bill had not survived. He had not gone down without a fight, though; Miguel was bleeding profusely from shotgun wounds in his abdomen and his left shoulder. Two thin trickles of blood were running down his chin from his gasping mouth, and his breath was coming in short, shallow gasps.

Chuck whipped his body back behind the cover of the oil drums and pressed his forefinger against his lips, gesturing to the others to remain silent. Miguel hadn't seen them yet, and if they could stay hidden for the next few minutes, he would probably die before he found them.

"Where are you … little bastards?!" Miguel croaked hoarsely in Spanish. "I'll … kill you … I'll kill … all of you … little shits!"

"Shh," Chuck whispered softly to the others as they huddled quietly together behind the oil drums.

"Come out!" Miguel gasped, staggering forward. His strength was failing him, and he could barely stand now, let alone walk. His rage and hatred propelled him on, though. He was determined to get the children before he died. He still couldn't believe that they had managed to pull something like this off. In a way, he was glad he had been shot; if he had survived, he knew he would have been subjected to a much slower and crueler death at the hands of Pablo. The only way he could partially redeem himself now, he knew, was to find and kill those responsible.

"Little … bastards!" he roared. "Where … are you?!" In desperation he started firing his AK wildly, spraying bullets in all directions.

Behind the oil drums, Chuck and the others lay flat against the ground, their blood like ice in their veins, terror ripping through their bodies. A burst of bullets smashed through the oil drums just above their heads, and Priscilla whimpered with fear, only barely managing to suppress a scream.

"Shh, don't say anything, don't move, don't make a sound," Chuck whispered to the others. He was just as scared as they were, but he knew that all they had to do was wait this out, and then they would be safe.

"Damn … you!" Miguel rasped, gasping and panting. His strength was rapidly failing him, but he was determined to find and kill the children before he died. He lurched around like an inebriated drunkard, blood running from his mouth and dripping in fat, dark blobs onto the dirt from the shotgun wounds that had torn holes in his body. With shaky hands, he popped the empty clip out of his AK and shoved in a fresh one.

"Come out … little … rats!" he yelled in Spanish, and again started firing in random directions, spraying bullets everywhere. Once again, a few bullets punched through the oil drums, but they zipped over the heads of the children.

Miguel dropped to his knees; he no longer had the strength to walk, let alone stand. He coughed weakly, and a gush of dark blood poured out of his mouth. "Little … shits…" he croaked, teetering and swaying on his knees.

Then, finally, he flopped forward, smashing face-first into the hot dirt, and breathed his last.

Behind the oil drums, the children heard the dull thud of his body hitting the ground, but nobody wanted to stick their head out to look just yet. They waited in terrified silence, nobody daring to move. Finally, after a few minutes, with no sound in their ears but the vast silence of the desert, Chuck figured it might be safe to peek out. Gripping the pistol tight, he craned his neck and peered around the side of the oil drums.

He saw Miguel lying face-down on the ground, the dirt around him dark and glistening with the wetness of soaked-in blood. Miguel was completely still – deathly still. Even though it seemed plain that Miguel was now dead, Chuck couldn't bring himself to move. What if Miguel was only faking it, a voice in his head asked. What if this was just a trick to get him to show himself?

He drew in a deep breath and held it in his lungs, then exhaled slowly. He did this a few times, breathing in a calm, rhythmic pattern, and counting to four between each one, just like his Grandpa Frank had taught him to in situations of extreme stress. Then he stepped out from behind the oil drums, and, keeping the pistol aimed at Miguel's body, he walked slowly over to it.

The other children watched him with their hearts in their mouths, also unable to believe that Miguel was actually dead. Chuck reached the body and quickly kicked the AK away from Miguel's hands, just in case. Then he stared at the body for a few drawn-out moments. It didn't feel real. None of this felt real. Miguel wasn't breathing, he could see that plainly enough. And, what was more, there was no sign of even the faintest throbbing of a pulse in any of his veins.

"He's dead!" Chuck called out to the others. "You guys can come out, he's dead!"

The others all emerged slowly and warily from behind the oil drums ... but their relief was very short-lived, for a sound soon shattered the silence of the desert: the sound of a large number of dirt bikes racing toward the ghost town.

*F*rank would have preferred to have a gun in his hands, but a shovel was a far more effective weapon than mere fists. He and the other captives outnumbered their captors, but he doubted that he could rely on any of them to fight alongside him, other than Clay and hopefully Diana, of course. He didn't know when he was going to make a move, only that he would, for he knew that he wasn't going to die like this.

"Okay gringos, start digging!" the short man commanded. "Make that hole nice and deep now, you hear? There'll be a good reward for you at the end of it when you're finished digging. Yeah, a *good* reward."

His men chuckled darkly when he said this. Clay and Frank scowled, but said nothing. Diana, meanwhile, had a worried and frightened look on her face, as did the other captives, all of whom were adults, ranging in age from their mid-thirties to their sixties.

They all picked up shovels, and everyone started digging. Frank could feel the gangsters' eyes on him, watching closely for any signs of rebellion. He knew that they would be extra vigilant for the first few minutes, but he was certain that their attention would drift off after a while, when boredom set in and they convinced themselves that the captives would not attempt to fight back.

And that was when Frank would strike. He would wait until they were at their most lax, and then he would hit them. He figured he could take out at least two of them with quick, brutal blows to the head before he got shot down. At this stage he was prepared to die if it meant saving Diana's life; if he didn't fight back he was dead anyway, and he would rather die fighting with a weapon in his hand than on his knees, being executed in cold blood by these criminals.

"I'm gonna hit you bastards," he whispered to himself as he slammed the shovel into the ground and scooped up the dirt. "I'm gonna hit you bastards real hard, when you're least expecting it."

As he dug, he glanced across at Clay. Their eyes met, and they gave each other a subtle nod. Frank felt a little more confident and hopeful after this, for in that brief moment, the look in Clay's eyes had told him that he had a partner who would fight as ferociously as he would when the time came. Clay too was unwilling to die on his knees, and would fight like a man possessed when the moment was right.

It was no small task to dig a hole deep and wide

enough to serve as a mass grave, and while the captives dug for a solid hour, the hole was only half-done by this time. As Frank had predicted, while the gangsters had been watching them with hawk-like intensity for the first fifteen or twenty minutes, their attention had wandered, and now the thugs were drinking liquor, smoking cigarettes, and joking among themselves, only paying cursory attention to the captives.

Frank knew that the time to strike was almost ripe. He paused digging and looked across at Clay, waiting to make eye contact before he made a move. Clay looked up and saw the gaze in Frank's eyes, and understood that it was almost time. He gave Frank a subtle nod, signaling that he would move when Frank needed him to. Frank then looked across at Diana, trying to silently convey the same message to her.

Her eyes met his, and while there was fear and dread splayed across her face, there was also defiance shining in her eyes. She wasn't about to go meekly to her death.

Despite the circumstances, Frank allowed himself a little smile. These gangsters might win, but they would pay a heavy price for their victory. Hell, if things went his way, he and his friends might even stand a chance of defeating them. Either way, at least some of the gangsters would end up dead, and that was an outcome Frank would be satisfied with, regardless of what else happened.

He resumed digging, but his eyes were not on the dirt. Instead, he was searching for an opportunity. The gangster closest to him was a tall man holding an Uzi. He was around six or seven yards away. The guard closest to Clay was a chubby bearded man with a shotgun. His attention was completely distracted; he and another guard were passing a whisky bottle back and forth between them and laughing over jokes. If Clay could attack them in the next few moments, the captives might just stand a chance.

The man with the Uzi was, unlike the other gangsters, watching the captives closely. Frank decided to use this to his advantage. He dug with his shovel and then gasped with surprise, pretending that he discovered something in the soil.

"Oh my, look at *that!*" he gasped, as if he'd found buried treasure. He crouched down, as if he was examining something valuable he had discovered in the dirt.

"What's going on here, old man?" the gangster with the Uzi demanded, walking over to Frank. "What did you find there?"

Clay and Diana were watching this interaction closely, and they were ready to move.

"I can't believe it," Frank murmured, his tone one of awe and wonder. "I never thought I'd find something like this, not in all my years."

"Move, you stupid old gringo, let me see!" the gangster growled, trying to push past Frank.

That was when Frank made his move. He whipped his torso around, swinging the shovel with all the force he could muster. It slashed through the air and clanged with a powerful thump against the gangster's skull, knocking him out and dropping him immediately.

Clay moved like lightning, jumping up and bringing his shovel down on the nearest gangster's skull in an axe-like woodchopping blow. Before the man had even hit the ground, Clay had bounded over to the next man, who had swung around in surprise, but before he could fire a shot, Clay lashed out with his shovel in a vicious horizontal blow, smashing it into the man's jaw. The force of the blow whipped the man's head to the side and spun his body around, sending him tumbling to the ground, unconscious.

Diana was charging across to lend her support to the fight, while the rest of the captives were yelling with surprise and fright at the sudden commotion.

Another guard close to Frank whipped up his pistol to take a shot, but Frank lunged forward with a swift one-handed hack, using the long reach of the shovel to slap the firearm out of the man's hand. The man yelped with pain, for the blow broke a number of bones in his fingers and hand, but with his free hand he drew his Bowie knife and charged Frank. Frank threw the shovel at him and then, when the man flinched and ducked to dodge the flying projectile, he tackled him to the ground, where he started wrestling for control of the knife.

The short man with the shotgun reacted quickly. He dropped his whisky bottle, grabbed his shotgun, and charged over to where Frank and the gangster were wrestling on the ground. Clay and Diana, meanwhile, were fighting the remaining gangster; Clay had kicked the man's pistol out of his hand, but the man had drawn a long machete from a sheath on his hip, and he was now swinging it in wild slashes at both Diana and Clay.

"You're fucking dead, old man!" the short man growled, running around Frank and the gangster as they wrestled furiously in the dirt. The short man was trying to get a clear shot at Frank without hitting his friend, which was proving difficult because of how furiously the two of them were fighting and rolling in the dirt.

Finally, though, the man Frank was fighting pinned him down, and the short man was able to get a clear shot at Frank.

"Say goodbye, you stupid old gringo fuck," the short man growled, aiming the barrel of his shotgun at Frank's face from just a foot or two away.

29

It was a shot he couldn't miss, and it would have taken Frank's head off ... but before he could squeeze the trigger, a snarling shape came hurtling out of the darkness and launched itself like a missile at the short man. Sharp teeth sank into his arm, and the force of the creature smashing into him knocked the gun out of his hand and bowled him over.

The man on top of Frank gasped with surprise and let his guard down for just a second – and this was all Frank needed. In this brief window of opportunity, he managed to whip the knife out of the man's hands and slam it up under his chin, burying it there hilt-deep. With the knife through his skull, the man's eyes rolled back in their sockets and he flopped to the ground, dead.

Frank scrambled to his feet and grabbed the shotgun, which was on the ground nearby. Then he saw a sight that he couldn't believe was real. The short man was on the ground, being attacked by a dog – a dog Frank knew well.

"Boris!" Frank gasped. "That's it boy, sic him, sic him Boris!"

The short man screamed as Boris went for his throat, trying to throw his arms up to shield his face and throat from the German Shepherd's lunging, snapping jaws. Frank was in a state of shock, scarcely able to believe that his friend was alive and well, but he pushed through this and turned his attention to Clay and Diana, who were fending off the machete man's frenzied attacks with their shovels.

"Hey, you!" Frank shouted at the man, positioning himself to take a shot at him that wouldn't hit Frank, Clay, or any of the other captives if he missed.

The man turned around to see who was yelling at him, and as he did, Clay dropped to the ground, for he knew what Frank was about to do. The moment Clay hit the ground, Frank fired. The shot knocked the man off his feet like a heavy punch, and Frank ran over and put one more shot into him to make sure that he was dead.

Now, with the gangsters almost defeated, Frank ran over to Boris and the short man.

"Boris, stop!" he commanded. "Come here boy, come here."

Boris, supremely well-trained, ceased his attack immediately and ran over to Frank, whimpering softly. The gangster lay on the ground, groaning and bleeding from the wounds Boris's sharp fangs had inflicted on him. Frank intended to keep the man alive, at least for long enough to interrogate him.

"Clay, Diana," Frank said, speaking to them but keeping his eyes and his shotgun trained on the man on the ground. "Tie up the bastards who we knocked out, and take any weapons off of 'em. Then we'll ask our cabron here a few questions…"

"Oh my God … I don't know who you are, sir, but you're a hero," one of the captives said. He was a tall, thin man with graying red hair and a bushy, gray-streaked beard. "You saved all our lives. I thought we were done for."

"Don't thank me now, because it's not over just yet and we're not safe by any means," Frank muttered. "Help my friends to tie up the scumbags who are still alive."

The other captives helped Diana to disarm and tie up the unconscious men, while Clay came over to help Frank with the short man. Clay looked at Boris and grinned, shaking his head with disbelief. "Well, well, well, look who it is," he said. "You're harder to drown than a toad, ain't you boy?" he said, ruffling Boris's fur, which was matted and crusty with mud and debris from the flood. "You showed up just at the right time."

"I still can't believe it's him," Frank murmured, his eyes filling with tears. "I really thought he was a goner … I can't believe he survived those waters."

"He's got a good nose, he does," Clay said. "Must have been tracking your scent all the way through the desert. Good thing it didn't rain again and wash your scent away."

"It's a miracle is what it is," Frank said. Then, however, his face hardened and his smile melted into a snarl. "We'll fawn over Boris later, though. Right now, let's take care of this scumbag. I'll keep the shotgun on him, you make sure he hasn't got any hidden weapons on him. Then we'll ask him a couple questions."

"I'm on it," Clay said. He went over to the groaning gangster. "Looks like the tables have turned, you ugly little piece of shit," he muttered, giving the man a boot in his ribs. "Let's see what you've got on you now…" He frisked the man and made sure that there weren't any hidden weapons on him. He found two knives, which he removed, but there weren't any other weapons. "All right Frank, he's clean now."

"Tie him up," Frank said. "I'm not taking any chances."

Clay tied the man up securely, while Diana helped the rest of the captives and made sure they were all okay. She and the bearded man made sure everyone got enough food and water after their ordeal.

"I don't want to know your name, where you're from, or what you were trying to do here," Frank said to the short man. "I'm just going to ask you a few simple questions, and it'd be in your own best interests to answer them honestly. I can spot a lie a mile away, and if you lie to me, I'm *not* going to be happy. And do you know who else gets unhappy when I get unhappy, punk?"

The short man, scowling, looked up at Frank with venom in his dark eyes and shook his head. Frank pointed at Boris, who bared his teeth and growled at the man.

"You want my dog to finish the job he started on you?" Frank asked calmly. "Because if you lie to me, that's exactly what's going to happen to you."

"Okay, okay man, I'll answer your questions," the man said. "Just keep that fucking dog away from me, okay?"

"Tell the truth and he won't bite again, I promise. Now tell me, where is Pablo Cortez?"

"I don't know man. Him and some others, they're out in the desert somewhere on their bikes."

"The desert is a big place. Be more specific," Frank said coldly. "Someone's getting unhappy here…" Boris growled at the man.

"There's an abandoned town, like a ghost town kinda place," the man said, staring with fear in his eyes at Boris, whose fangs were bared and whose hackles were raised. He then went on to explain exactly where the ghost town was. "It's the place we've been using for years to store the merchandise we bring in from Mexico," he added. "Pablo is using it as his base. It's from there that he's been launching his invasion."

"His invasion?"

The man smiled darkly. "We're taking our ancestral land back, motherfucker. And maybe you stopped me, but you can't stop all of us. This thing that's happened, with all the power going out permanently and the cars all dying and shit, it's a sign … a sign from the old gods of my people. We're taking what's ours back from you. And you can't stop us."

Frank chuckled humorlessly and shook his head with disbelief. "You're crazy, aren't you?" he muttered. "I can't say I'm too surprised, though. Crazy times breed madness in people. Now I have just one more question for you, and this is one is important. If you even add a sprinkling of a half-truth to what you tell me, my dog is going to rip your damn throat out and eat your lungs, and I promise you that that is no exaggeration. Do you understand what I'm saying?"

"Sure. Go ahead and ask, old man. I'll answer."

"Did you and Pablo come across a group of American kids in the desert near this ghost town? Answer me truthfully, or my dog is going to be feasting on your flesh in a few seconds."

The man smiled. "We did. And Pablo took 'em captive."

Rage flashed through Frank, igniting a terrible fury within him, like a spark to a patch of gasoline. He got right up in the man's face and grabbed his collar, staring with vengeful anger into the man's eyes.

"If you filthy animals harmed a single hair on those children's heads, there *will* be hell to pay," Frank snarled. "What did you do to them?! Where are they now?!"

"I left just after they brought the kids in," the man stammered, his voice shaky with fear. "I don't know what Pablo was gonna do with them…"

Frank slapped him viciously across the face. "You're lying," he hissed. "I can see it in your eyes. One last chance, you piece of garbage ... tell me what Pablo is planning to do to those children. Next time you lie, it'll be my dog tearing into your face instead of my hand smacking it, I promise you that."

"Okay, okay," the man whimpered, staring with naked terror in his eyes at Boris. "Pablo is gonna take the girls for himself ... he likes young girls ... but the boys ... he's gonna feed 'em to Tlaloc. He's gonna give their blood to the rain god..."

30

*I*t was clear from the sound of their motors that the dirt bikes and their riders would arrive within minutes. Like an attacking swarm of bees, panic and fear stung and slashed at the children, who were already in a state of shock and terror at everything that had happened over the past few minutes.

"Oh no, oh no, what are we gonna do, what are we gonna do?!" Priscilla whimpered, tears filling her eyes.

"They're gonna kill us when they find us," Joe murmured, his dark face growing pale with fear. "When they see what happened here, they're gonna kill us."

"We have to run!" Kenneth screamed. The blood which covered half of his body – Alejandro's blood – combined with the raw fear in his eyes and the animal panic on his face made him look utterly deranged. "Run, run!"

He started to bolt off toward the desert, but Chuck darted out a hand and grabbed his shirt, stopping him in his tracks. Chuck was as fearful and terrified as the rest of them, but he knew that he had to keep a level head here. "Stop," he said coolly. "We can't run; there's nowhere to hide out there in the desert. The first thing they'll do when they see what's happened here is to search the ghost town. But they'll figure that we ran off into the desert, so while they're searching the buildings, they'll send guys out on dirt bikes to search the desert. And I don't know about you, but I know I can't outrun a motorcycle."

"So … what *are* we going to do?" Melissa asked softly. Her lower lip was quivering, and fear filled her eyes. "If we stay here, we're dead, but if we try to run, we're just as dead."

Chuck's mind was spinning at a tremendous speed – almost too fast, in fact. Despite this, however, a cool sense of calm resolution suddenly sliced through the hyperactive panic like the blade of a scalpel. A plan popped into his head, inspired, bizarrely enough, by the drug use he'd seen the gangsters engage in. It was a crazy plan, he knew … but just crazy enough that it might work.

"We need some money," he said.

"Money?!" Kenneth shrieked, looking as if he was about to tear his own hair out. "Have you lost your freakin' mind, Chuck?! What the hell are we going to do with money when there are these crazy, psycho murderers coming to kill us?!"

"Trust me on this," Chuck said, and then he explained his plan to the others.

Around fifteen minutes later, Pablo and his gangsters rolled into the ghost town on their dirt bikes. At first, they had no idea anything was wrong, but the moment they got around the back of the old general store and saw Miguel's body lying face down in the blood-soaked dirt, they whipped their guns out and got into fight mode.

"What the fuck has happened here?!" Pablo growled. A dark fury exploded within him, and the urge to kill someone became almost irresistible. "Get the fuck inside, see if anyone is still alive!" he roared in Spanish to his men.

The gangsters obeyed his command swiftly and charged into the building with their guns at the ready. It didn't take them long to discover what had happened. El Caníbal and Carlos, the big man, came out with looks of both anger and dismay on their ugly faces.

"That American border cop, he got hold of a gun," El Caníbal said to Pablo. "Shot up the place. And Alejandro, he got his throat slit somehow."

"He's dead, though," Carlos added.

"What about the fucking American kids?!" Pablo demanded through clenched teeth. "Where the fuck are they?!"

Both men shrugged and shook their heads.

"They're gone, boss," El Caníbal said. "No sign of the little fuckers."

Pablo looked up at the clear blue sky and roared out an animalistic howl of pure rage, screaming hoarsely until his lungs were completely empty of air. Then he dropped to his knees next to Miguel's body and lifted the dead man's hand, feeling his wrist. "The body is still warm," he growled. "This happened very recently. Those little fucks are around here somewhere. Carlos, get some of the boys on bikes and search the desert in all directions; if they ran, they can't be more than a mile or two away. El Caníbal, you get three men and help me search the town. We're gonna turn every fucking building upside down. They're around here somewhere, I can smell the little motherfuckers. And when I find them, I'm gonna skin the little shits alive…"

"Will do, boss," Carlos said, jogging off to round up some men to form a search party on the motorcycles. El Caníbal, meanwhile, ran off to get a few men to search the buildings of the ghost town.

Pablo stood in the blazing sun in his expensive black suit, seemingly immune to the fierce heat. He squatted down next to Miguel's body, taking note of the many AK-47 shell casings scattered all over the ground nearby. "You were shooting at something, my old friend," he whispered to the corpse. "You were shooting like a fucking madman on crack … but what were you shooting at, eh? If I had my full powers, I could resurrect you from the dead, and you could tell me … but I need more blood, the god Tlaloc needs more blood, to get to that level. Until then, I'm just gonna have to rely on this," he said, slowly tapping the side of his head with his finger.

His eyes roamed across the landscape … and then his gaze fell up the rusty old oil drums nearby. Oil drums that were easily large enough for children to hide inside. He smiled and started to walk slowly over to the drums. "The best place to hide something is in plain sight, isn't it?" he muttered to himself. "I'm sure you little fuckers know that, don't you, eh? Well, let's see how well you can hide, like a couple of little cock-roaches under a kitchen counter. Let's see…"

He got to the first of the oil drums and knocked on it with his fist. "Hello, anyone in?" he asked in English in a mock-friendly voice. "Any little children hiding in here? I know if I was a scared little American child running from Pablo Cortez, I would want to hide … and this looks like a good place to hide, doesn't it?"

He took a step away from the barrels, aimed his pistol at it, and then started firing, roaring with vengeful fury and maniacal glee as he emptied his entire clip through the oil drums, filling them with as many holes as a block of Swiss cheese. "You little fuck-ers," he growled, breathing hard as he reloaded. "You little motherfuckers … let's see if you were able to hide from Pablo's bullets."

He ripped the lid off the first of the oil drums … and found that it was empty. "Fucking puta!" he roared, his face crimson with rage. "Where the fuck are you, you little motherfuckers?!" He tore the lid off the next drum and found that it was empty too. He kicked the third one, and the ease with which it fell over told him that there was nothing inside it. In a blind rage, he kicked the final three drums and found that they were all empty as well.

"No! No! Where are you, you little fucks, where the fuck are you?!" he howled, jumping around with vicious, crazed wrath.

The children were nearby, but they weren't hiding anywhere near the oil drums. And, like Pablo had suspected, they were indeed hiding in plain sight. Plain enough that he hadn't noticed them, although if he took a few steps in the right direction, he certainly would come across them.

Buried shallowly under a pile of sand nearby, the five children waited in hot darkness, terrified of being discovered. They had dug frantically in the fine sand with their hands and had covered themselves with a thin layer of it – just enough to provide concealment. If anyone stepped on the pile, though, their hiding place would rapidly be revealed. If even a strong wind blew, the thin layer of sand covering them could be blown away, exposing them. All they could do was wait and pray, breathing through rolled-up hundred dollar bills in their mouths, which stuck inconspicuously through the layer of sand.

After a while, Pablo spent his wrath. He stormed off, muttering to himself, and went back into the building. The sound of motorcycles racing all over the desert in all directions rang loud and clear in the children's ears, but all they could do was sit tight and wait for the cover of darkness to fall in a few hours and pray that they wouldn't be discovered before then.

"My God," Clay murmured, after having heard what the prisoner had said to Frank. "Pablo has gotten even crazier than he was before."

"All the more reason to find my grandkids before that monster does," Frank said. "We need to leave right now."

"Frank," Diana said, "I know how serious this is, and how urgent it is to find Chuck and Melissa, but I can't walk another step tonight. After all that digging, and after everything else that's happened today, I can't go on, I just can't, not without a rest and some food and water. It'll kill me, and that's no exaggeration."

Frank was also beyond exhausted, and now that the adrenaline of the fight was wearing off, he was feeling it too. The weariness was beyond crushing, and it was beginning to feel as if he barely had the strength to hold on to the gun in his hands, let alone set off on another trek into the depths of the desert.

"She's right," Clay said before Frank could say anything. "I'm finished too, man. I can't go on, not without a rest and a meal. And I'm almost twenty years younger than you. I don't know where you're finding fuel in your body to push on, but I wish I had a reserve of energy like you do. But seriously, Frank, as much as I want to help you, I'm done for the night. I just can't go on."

Frank looked at both of them in the firelight. They were both wan and haggard, and the exhaustion, hunger, and dehydration they were suffering from was written plain across their faces. He was sure that he looked just as finished and beaten up as they did, for he felt it in his bones. "I'm just as tired as you are," he reluctantly admitted. "I guess we need to rest up and head off in a few hours."

"Excuse me," the thin bearded man said to them, "but I couldn't help overhearing your conversation. You three saved our lives, and we owe you a debt we can never fully repay. But we can offer you food and a bed for the night at our place. My wife and I have a small off-the-grid homestead a mile out of town, and we ran a little bed and breakfast there, before the whole world went crazy, anyway, so we have plenty of space. And we're preppers, so we have a ton of food and water stored up in our cellar."

Frank was usually the type of person who reluctant to accept help from anyone, especially strangers, due to his pride and strong spirit of self-reliance. However, under these circumstances, he knew that it would be wise to accept help from these people. "Thank you sir," he said, "we'd be real grateful for that, and we'd really appreciate it."

"I'm Lars, Lars Reese," the bearded man said, shaking Frank's hand and smiling warmly. "And this is my wife Nancy," he said, introducing them to a short, plump woman around Diana's age, with curly brown hair and a pleasant round face.

Lars introduced Frank, Diana, and Clay to the rest of the small settlement's residents, most of whom had lived in this tiny place their whole lives. They hadn't experienced any trouble here until the night of the EMP, for the aftereffects of which most of them had been sorely unprepared.

"What are we gonna do with this scumbag, and his KO'd friends?" Clay muttered, pointing at the prisoners. "Remember, they were about to execute all of us and dump us in a mass grave…"

"I know that," Frank said, "and they deserve death, it's true. But even so, I can't bring myself to execute these men in cold blood."

"There's a cargo train that comes past here every two days," an elderly man said to them. "And it'll be coming past in the morning. The train tracks are three miles west of town. We could dump 'em on the train, and they'd get taken hundreds of miles away and never bother us again. What happens to them when they get to their destination is their problem."

Frank shook his head and explained that because of the EMP, no trains would be coming past here anymore – possibly ever again.

"Let's just tie their hands up and have 'em march off into the desert," Lars suggested.

Again Frank shook his head. "As soon as they get their hands free, they'll come back for revenge, I guarantee it. You can see the hate in their eyes. These aren't the type of men to forgive and forget."

As if to confirm what Frank had just said, the short man glared at them all with murderous wrath in his eyes. "You know the old man is right," he said, jerking in head in Frank's direction. "You're gonna have to kill us … because if you don't, we'll come back and get you motherfuckers. All of you."

"Shut up," Frank snapped at him. Boris let out a snarl and bared his teeth at the man. "Nobody asked you, scumbag." He turned to the rest of the people. "I think we should just tie 'em up and lock 'em up securely for the night. We're all too tired and stressed out to think clearly right now. We'll figure out what to do with them in the morning."

"We can put them in the cage in the gas station!" a middle-aged man said enthusiastically. "They won't be able to escape from that."

"There's a cage in the gas station?" Frank asked quizzically.

"It's an old, rusty cage, but it's a big one," the man said. "My grandpa owned that gas station, it's been in my family since the '40s, and back then they used to have a mountain lion in the cage as a roadside attraction. Of course, the lion died decades ago when I was a little kid, but the cage is still in the storeroom at the back. It's full of boxes of auto parts and oil, but we can move some of those out and put these bastards in it. I've got a good, hefty padlock we can use to make sure they don't go anywhere."

Frank turned and smirked at the short man. "A cage is exactly where animals like you belong," he muttered. "Come on, get up on your feet, let's go."

The people got the other men – who were now groggily coming to, after having been knocked out by the shovels – up onto their feet, and marched them down to the gas station. There, they cleared out a section of the old cage and locked the men in it. After that, Lars and Nancy took Frank, Clay, and Diana out to their homestead in the desert.

After a hot meal – simple canned food, heated up on a gas stove – and plenty of water, everyone staggered off to their beds, where they fell asleep within minutes, dreaming of the nightmarish day they had survived, and tossing and turning as they subconsciously worried about what the next day would bring.

32

*I*t felt like being entombed, being buried alive. This was the recurring thought that ran repeatedly through Chuck's mind as he lay beneath the shallow layer of sand – all that was keeping him and his friends hidden from the murderous gangsters who were searching the desert and the ghost town high and low for them. He lay as still as he could, breathing through the rolled up hundred-dollar bill. As immediate as the danger was, and as important as it was to remain utterly still, every passing moment of being buried like this that he had to endure felt like horrendous torture.

He wondered how the others were holding up, particularly Kenneth, who had seemed as if he was on the verge of losing his mind even before they had had to hastily bury themselves like this. He knew that Melissa had the mental fortitude to hang in and stay calm under difficult circumstances like these, and perhaps Joe too, but he had doubts about Priscilla, and no faith at all in Kenneth's strength of will. And if either of those two cracked, the game would be up for all of them.

Because of the sand covering them, it was difficult to hear clearly what was going on out there. Sounds came through in muffled tones; the distant buzzing and droning of dirt bikes as the gangsters scoured the desert, and the muted, unintelligible yells of Pablo and the men who were searching the ghost town.

All the children could do was wait, in these agonizing conditions, and pray that Pablo and his goons would give up searching for them soon. While the sand served to keep them cool, even being burned to a crisp with a square inch of shade or a drop of water under the fierce sun seemed preferable to this terrible claustrophobic, suffocating darkness.

Chuck was weary and exhausted after everything, and he knew that the others had to be as well. However, as tired as he was, there was no way he could sleep in a situation like this. Not when he had to concentrate on every breath, not when he felt as if he could be suffocated to death at any moment.

Every minute that passed felt like an eternity, and with the slow, tortuous passage of these trickling seconds came a mounting frustration, building up like a head of steam in a pressure cooker. Every passing moment made it increasingly difficult to stay hidden under the sand, and soon Chuck began to have disturbing thoughts; he started to think that he would rather just get it over with and get shot than have to endure this torture for much longer. What was worse, he knew that the others had to be having similar thoughts, and was sure that they would reach their breaking point sooner than he would – which, judging by his increasingly fragile mental and emotional state, would be very soon, he thought grimly.

Just as he thought he couldn't possibly last another second, though, he heard the sound of many dirt bikes congregating in the street on the other side of the building. He listened intently, but could hear little but the muffled sound of voices. However, soon the sound of the bikes was cut off, and all that remained was a few voices. And then, after that, there was silence.

At this point, it felt as if the weight of the entire planet was pushing down on him, even though it was only a thin layer of dirt. Was this what being buried alive felt like? If so, it was something he never wanted to experience, and he could hardly imagine a worse way to die. He knew that he couldn't last much longer like this, but more than this, he knew that the others had to be at their breaking points, especially Kenneth and Priscilla. He realized that he had to take a look and see if the coast was clear before either of those two had a complete freak-out and blew their cover.

He sucked in a deep breath through the rolled-up hundred-dollar bill and then pushed his arms through the layer of sand and brushed it off his face. The first thing he saw was Kenneth's wild-eyed face, sticking out of the sand. A wave of anger and panic smashed into him; how long had Kenneth had his face out like this? Had any of the gangsters seen him?

Before laying into Kenneth, though, Chuck had to make sure they were safe. He scanned his surroundings, focusing particularly on the building, and felt a wave of relief rush through him when he saw that there was nobody around. Now that his head was out of the sand, he could hear a lot more clearly, and he could hear voices inside the building, but there didn't seem to be anyone outside.

There was no telling when someone would step outside the building, though, so if they were going to move, they had to do it fast, and they had to do it now, making use of this brief window of opportunity. "Joe, Mel, Priscilla!" he whispered, loudly enough for them to hear, he hoped, but not loud enough that anyone in the building would hear. "We have to move!"

Their heads immediately burst out of the sand, and the expressions on them were a strange mixture of both relief and agony. Chuck knew that they had to have had just as bad a time as he had under the sand.

The children scrambled out of the sand, their hearts pounding and their blood cold with fear in their veins.

"Where do we go?!" Melissa whispered, her tone urgent.

There was only one place they could go right now, Chuck realized, one place where they weren't likely to be discovered. If they fled into the desert while it was still light, their chances of being recaptured were high; they had to wait until it was dark before they could make a move. And to do this, they had to continue to hide.

"The oil drums!" Chuck whispered. "Everyone move, get inside one and pull the lid on!"

There was no time to argue or debate; everyone felt terribly exposed and vulnerable out here in the open, just a few dozen yards from the back door of the building, out of which Pablo or one of his men could step at any moment. They sprinted across the hot sand and each scrambled into an oil drum. Thankfully, by this time the oil drums were in the shade, so the children wouldn't slowly be roasted alive in them.

Just as the slowest of them – Joe – scrambled into an oil drum, Pablo and some of his men walked out the back door. "Get the fuck on your bikes," Pablo muttered. "Find those American brats. They're around here somewhere, probably hiding like little rodents in the desert. There's still a couple hours of daylight left, so you'd best use your fucking eyes! If those lil' fucks aren't found by nightfall, I swear I'm gonna cut someone's head off! Go, find them!"

The men hurried out front to their bikes, and the children sat in the oil drums in terrified silence, only a few yards from Pablo, who was high again and pacing around and muttering to himself in Spanish.

Chuck watched the gangster through one of the bullet holes in his oil drum. He was both terrified of and fascinated by the man. Chuck still had the pistol on him, and he aimed it at Pablo through the bullet hole. It would be so easy to pull the trigger … but then the other gangsters would hear, and even though Pablo would be dead, it wouldn't matter if that meant that Chuck and the other kids would end up getting shot a few seconds later. No, as tempting as it was to turn the tables and gun the evil Pablo down, Chuck knew that the wisest thing for him to do right now was to simply sit tight.

After some time Pablo went back inside, and aside from the sound of the dirt bike motors in the distance as they prowled the desert, searching high and low for the children, an eerie quiet settled around the ghost town.

"All right," Chuck whispered to himself in the hot darkness of the barrel. "Now we wait … now … we wait."

33

*F*rank usually woke at dawn every day, but because of his extreme exhaustion and dehydration from the previous day, on this day when he awoke, the sun was already high in the sky. "Dammit," he muttered, rolling out of his comfortable bed in the guest room where he and Diana had slept. "We're wasting precious time here."

Diana, awakened by his movement and the sound of his voice, opened her eyes and yawned. "I haven't slept that soundly for a long time," she murmured, blinking against the light, "and after everything that's happened, I feel like I could sleep until nightfall."

"I'm hoping that by the time the sun sets today," Frank said, "Chuck and Melissa will be safe and sound with us. And the only way that that's going to happen is if we get moving right now. Come on Di, I know you're tired, and Lord knows I could use a couple more hours of sleep, but those kids are in danger."

Diana struggled out of bed. Boris, who had been sleeping on the floor next to the bed, stretched and yawned as he too awoke. While Diana got dressed, Frank fed Boris; there had been plenty of dog food in the convenience store, so that, at least, was something that wasn't in short supply. As for water, there was a well on Lars's property. Usually the water was extracted via a mechanical pump, which the EMP had destroyed. However, there was an old hand-cranked pump as a backup, so everyone had plenty of water.

Frank pulled on a shirt and headed outside to find Clay, and to get a look at Lars's homestead and off-grid facilities in daylight. Lars and Nancy were already up, cooking breakfast for their guests on gas stoves.

"Morning Frank!" Lars said cheerfully. "Did you sleep okay?"

"Like the dead," Frank said. "Thank you again for your hospitality."

"Thank *you* for saving our lives," Nancy said. "We thought we were goners for sure last night. We owe you a debt we can never fully repay. You and your friends are welcome to stay here as long as you need to. And your grandkids too, when you find them."

"Thank you, I appreciate that," Frank said. "If everything goes according to plan, we'll be coming back here with them tonight. This is an impressive setup you guys have here, by the way. How much of it survived the EMP? Are those crop tunnels over there? You're growing produce out here in the middle of the desert?"

He, Lars, and Nancy chatted about the homestead

and the challenges of growing crops in the desert while they finished cooking breakfast. A lot of their infrastructure – particularly the solar panels, which had provided all their power – had been destroyed by the EMP, but a lot of their cultivation methods relied on older, non-powered and non-technological techniques, which meant that they would still be able to grow many of their crops. Frank told them about his own homestead in the hills, which was even more ideally suited to post-EMP conditions.

"Looks like you guys will be mostly all right, despite what's happened," Frank remarked, impressed. "You're in a better position than, well, the vast majority of the population of this country. I'd hate to see the sort of chaos that's been going down in cities and other densely populated places. What little we saw of the anarchy with the terrorists in Di's small town was enough to convince me to stay far, far away from anything but the tiniest settlements."

"But even here," Lars said, frowning, "those crazy Mexican thugs came and did what they did. We might not have some rebel army in blue uniforms and Humvees harassing us, but we do have a bunch of drug-crazed cartel maniacs to worry about."

"Hopefully we can help you take care of that problem," Frank said, resting his hand on the grip of his faithful revolver. "That brings me to my next topic of conversation. How much firepower do you have here? We're going to need a lot of it to take these people on. According to what those goons told us last night, there are a lot more of them deep in the desert, and they're heavily armed."

"We've only got a single rifle here," Lars said. "It's pretty ancient and hasn't been fired in years. We uh, we're kinda hippies, peaceniks, you know."

Frank had gotten this vibe from them when they first met, and seeing the surroundings and décor in daylight – lots of tie-dye, Native American art, dream-catchers, flowers and other such items – had confirmed this suspicion of his. He had never liked hippies, and as a military man he had always had a unique dislike and distrust of peaceniks, but despite their vast differences in ideologies, he knew that these were good, honest people. They would be next to useless in a fight, but perhaps, he figured, he could get them to perform a non-combatant role that would nonetheless be useful.

"Don't worry about that," Frank said, smiling. As a younger man, he probably would have mocked and goaded these people, but age had both cooled his fiery temper and pride and brought to him a welcome wisdom and acceptance of people who had a very different outlook on the world to his. "I'll take a look at that rifle; with a good cleaning, it should be good as new. Do you know if anyone else in around here has guns? I know you two don't like violence much, but I'm afraid our cartel buddies don't give a shit about your beliefs. Sorry to be so blunt, but that's how it is."

"We understand that," Lars said. "These are strange times, and people, well, they're not gonna play nice.

Especially not those cartel gangsters. We saw that plainly enough from what happened last night."

"I'm glad you understand that," Frank said.

Clay came strolling over to them, stretching and yawning. "Thank you kindly for your hospitality," he said to Lars and Nancy. "I slept like a baby last night, and I'm feeling fully recharged. Well, almost. Breakfast will get me back up to 100%, I think."

"We've got bacon, eggs, and mushrooms frying in the kitchen," Nancy said with a smile. "Plenty cheese too, and ice cream. I think I'll make some milkshakes with my hand shaker; since the fridge is dead, we have to eat everything perishable today and tomorrow, before it spoils completely. Eat as much as you can handle; it'll just go to waste otherwise. Speaking of food, I'd better go check on it before it burns."

"Thank you kindly, Nancy, we really appreciate that," Clay said to her with a smile. Then, as Nancy hurried off to the kitchen, he turned to Lars. "I thought I saw a bunch of horses in the distance when I got up. Are they wild, or do they belong to someone around here?"

Lars smiled. "No, those are all Peter Ankerson's horses," he said. "He lives on the other side of town – the old guy from last night, with the big bushy mustache. He used to take tourists on horseback tours through the desert."

Clay nodded. "That's good. You think he'd be willing to lend us a couple of his horses? You and Di can ride, right Frank?"

Frank nodded. "She grew up riding horses, and I've spent my fair share of time in the saddle. Some horses would definitely be a useful asset when we head out into the desert – especially horses that are used to desert conditions."

"Oh, those horses are tough, believe me," Lars said. "Peter's been taking them out into the desert for multi-day trips for many years. They're just what you guys need for your mission. And Peter's a generous man; also, considering the fact that you saved his life last night, I'm sure he won't have a problem letting you take some of his finest mounts."

"Great," Frank said. "By the way, can you bring out that old rifle of yours and whatever ammo you've got? I'll clean it up while we eat."

Diana joined them, and they all sat down to a hearty breakfast, which left Frank, Diana, and Clay feeling energized and ready to take on the many challenges the coming day would no doubt bring. After they had finished eating, Lars accompanied them on the long walk to Peter Ankerson's ranch. As Lars had predicted, Peter was only too happy to lend the three of them some of his finest horses. He also gave them two extra horses to carry the children, if they were able to find them.

He kitted them out with tack and saddlebags for supplies, and lent them his hunting rifle and a .45 caliber pistol. One of the settlement's residents lent them a 9mm pistol and some ammo, while another loaned them a shotgun and couple shells. Lars and

Nancy gave them plenty of food and water to carry in the horses' saddlebags. They also gave them sunscreen and hats to protect them from the sun. Also, because of Peter's former business, he had plenty of USGS paper maps of the area for them to use.

Now, each of them at least had a firearm and a handgun, and a relatively decent store of ammunition. By the time they were ready to depart, the sun was high in the sky and it was almost midday. The day was scorching hot and dry, and there wasn't a single cloud in the sky, but it was at least not as hellishly hot as the previous day had been.

"Good luck!" Lars said to them as they prepared to leave. "I hope you find those kids, and that you all get back in one piece!"

"We hope so too," Frank said. "And if we're not back by tomorrow," he said, a grim frown darkening his face, "you'll know that the worst has happened, and that we're not coming back. And if that happens, I suggest that you all leave town before Pablo and his men get here, because what happened last night will be nothing compared to what that psycho will do to you all." Then he whistled to Boris, who came running obediently over to the side of his horse, and the three of them and the extra horses set off into the ominous emptiness of the desert beyond the settlement.

34

---

*C*huck awoke with a start, opening his eyes to find himself in near-complete darkness. This overwhelmed him with a terror that almost caused him to scream and thrash around in an animal-like panic. He quickly remembered where he was, though, and restrained himself from doing any of these things.

He wasn't sure how long he had been sleeping in the oil drum, but it had to have been a few hours, based on how intense the pain and aches in his joints and muscles were, and the fact that it was now dark outside. He felt around the rough, rusty interior of the oil drum, his fingers seeking out the bullet hole so that he could get a glimpse of the outside world.

He found it quickly enough and lined up his eyeball with the hole. He could see the light of gas lamps shining inside the nearby building, and a bonfire was burning outside. Miguel's body was gone, but the dirt was still dark where his blood had soaked into it. As far as Chuck could see, there was nobody outside. This was as good an opportunity as any to make an escape, so he quietly climbed out of the oil drum and, crouching low and staying behind the cover of the drums, he went over to each of them and whispered to the other kids that it was time to go.

They all climbed out of the drums, stealthy and nervous, and whispering complaints about their aches and pains from having been stuck in the cramped space for hours.

"What do we do now?" Melissa asked Chuck.

"We leave, quickly," he said. "I'll navigate by the stars. We walk as fast as we can, and we keep going until we can't walk anymore – and then we walk some more. We want to put as much distance between us and these maniacs as we can before sunrise."

There was no time to argue, and neither was there any point in disagreeing; fleeing as far and fast as possible was the only option available to the children. Even the querulous Kenneth kept his mouth shut. Chuck took a quick look up at the night sky to get his bearings, and then, with one last cautious glance over his shoulder at the derelict building to make sure that nobody was stepping outside, he set off at a jog.

He didn't bother to look behind him to see if the others were following him; he knew that they had no choice but to keep up, and that the fear of what Pablo and his men would do to them if they captured them would propel fresh energy into their tired and aching limbs.

They jogged steadily across the desert under the dim light of the moon, which was not quite full, but bright enough to provide enough illumination that they weren't running in complete blindness. Chuck prayed that they didn't step on any rattlesnakes, or that nobody tripped over anything and sprained an ankle, but right now these were risks that they simply had to take if they were to escape.

After they had jogged for two or three miles, they were all feeling tired and out of breath, but were at least a lot less nervous and fearful of being caught by Pablo and his men. Even so, the fear was still clearly present, and none of them asked to stop or rest. On the horizon, the bonfires burning in Pablo's ghost town were an ominous reminder of how close he and his men still were. The children knew they wouldn't feel safe until they had put a much greater distance between themselves and their former captors.

"Is everyone okay to keep going?" Chuck asked, glancing over his shoulder at the others for the first time since they had set off. He knew the answer to this question before anyone said it out loud, but he wanted to make sure.

"Yeah," everyone panted as they tried to catch their breath.

"Okay, come on, let's keep going then," Chuck said, picking up the pace after quickly checking the night sky to orient himself.

They kept jogging for another half hour, but after that Joe was unable to run any more. Kenneth and

Priscilla were also exhausted, and Chuck and Melissa, as fit as they were, were also struggling. They sat down on the cool ground to rest for a while and catch their breath. Nobody said a word about what they had seen and done; it was all too immediate and upsetting. All they wanted to do was get home, somehow, and forget any of this had ever happened.

Of course, in this strange and scary new world, in which civilization had been dealt a greater and more severe blow than those of even the worst wars of the twentieth century, none of them knew if they would ever be going home again – at least, to the state of being they knew as "home". Everything was so radically different now than it had been just a few days earlier, it was as if they had passed through a portal and entered another dimension.

None of them could vocalize these thoughts, or really wrap their minds around them. Instead, there was just an eerie feeling of disquietude and dread percolating in their guts that, no matter what they did, they could not get rid of. So, at this moment, all each of them could do was sit in worried silence, shivering against the chill of the night desert air beneath the vast, bright starry sky.

Eventually, Chuck heaved himself up to his feet. He was as tired as anyone, but he knew that they had to keep pushing, as grueling and as exhausting as the journey was. The darkness of night was their only shield against Pablo and his men, and they had to get as much use out of it as they could.

"Let's keep going," Chuck said softly.

Everyone groaned as they struggled to their feet, but nobody voiced a single word of complaint. As tired as they all were, they wanted to get as far from the terror of Pablo as possible.

They pushed on through the night, walking on tired and aching legs. After a few hours they were barely walking, simply limping and dragging their feet, staggering and lurching and swaying, barely able to keep their eyes open, whimpering softly and wordlessly against the pain in their feet, ankles, knees, hips, and legs. But still they kept going.

Eventually, after walking for almost the whole night, with the eastern sky starting to grow lighter on the horizon, they came across a large rocky outcrop, from which there jutted out an overhang. Beneath this overhang was a sheltered space in which they would be able to rest and sleep and take refuge from the fierce sun of the dawning day.

Chuck had a plastic cigarette lighter in his pocket, one of the items he'd taken from Miguel's body. He flicked it on and by the light of the tiny flame, he scoped out the hollow beneath the overhang, making sure there were no rattlesnakes or scorpions or any other dangerous creatures hiding there.

When he had ascertained that it was safe, he wearily called the others over. All of them were parched, starving, and utterly exhausted.

"Sleep," was all Chuck could manage to croak from his dry, burning throat and cracked lips.

They all got into the space, lay down in the dirt, and were asleep within seconds.

Chuck wasn't sure what time it was when they were awoken, but the sun was shining brightly outside. It seemed to be early afternoon, or perhaps even late afternoon. He wasn't concerned about the exact time of day, though. Instead, what immediately caught his attention was the fact that he had been woken up by the sound of a dirt bike motor idling nearby.

He groggily rubbed his eyes and tried to get up, trying to remember where he'd put the pistol – but before he could grab it, a harsh voice, colored by a Mexican accent, echoed through the hollow.

"Well, well, well, look what I found ... a couple lil' gringos."

Chuck looked up, his heart racing, and saw one of Pablo's gangsters staring into the hollow, grinning an evil smile. He had an AK-47 in his hands, and it was aimed at Chuck's chest.

"Don't even think of trying anything stupid, you lil' shit," the man growled. "Get your friends up, all of 'em, and get out of there. Hehehe, Pablo is gonna give me one hell of a reward for this! Get up!" he yelled. "Get up now, all of you lil' punks, get your damn asses up!"

Chuck wanted to cry. He and the others had come all this way, had gone through such effort and pain ... only to be caught at the end of it all. He was too exhausted to shed a tear, though. Instead, he simply crawled out of the space, staring glumly at the man's boots, while the other children all came out after him.

"Hehehe, you lil' fuckers thought you could get away, huh? Ooh, Pablo's got some good shit planned for you kids, I promise you that," the gangster said. "First, with the girls, he's gonna—"

Blood sprayed all over Chuck – the gangster's blood, from a wound that had just exploded through his torso. The crack of a rifle echoed across the desert a second later. The gangster dropped his gun and staggered backward, his face a twisted mask of agony and surprise. Then another shot blasted through his torso, and he flopped to the ground, dead.

Chuck and the others stood there in complete shock, rooted to the spot and unable to move. Finally, Chuck turned to look in the direction from which the two rifle shots had come … and the sight he saw filled him with hope and joy.

For there, galloping toward him, was his Grandpa Frank on horseback.

35

*J*t was dark by the time Frank, Diana, Clay, and the children got back to Lars and Nancy's homestead. Large bonfires were burning in the nearby desert to serve as beacons for the group on horseback. Everyone in the settlement was waiting there, and they let out a cheer when they saw Frank and his group enter the firelight on weary horses.

The ride back had taken a long time and had worn the horses out, since some of them had had to carry two children. Also, since neither Kenneth, Joe, nor Priscilla had ever been on a horse before, they had had to move at a slow pace.

The riders were exhausted from both the long ride and the heat of the day they'd ridden though, but thanks to plentiful provisions and frequent water and meal breaks, they were in good health. One of the residents of the settlement had a swimming pool in his backyard, and the children stripped down to their underwear to wash themselves off in the cool water, which in time would become green and murky owing to the fact that the EMP had taken out the pump and filtration system.

When the kids were all cleaned up, they were given fresh clothes; Peter Ankerson had grandchildren of the same age who visited regularly, so there were clothes for both the boys and the girls. The clothes didn't fit too well, but they were something, at least.

Despite eating and drinking regularly during the ride, the children were still famished and dehydrated from their ordeal, and they all wolfed down the many plates of hot food Nancy handed to them, as if they all had bottomless stomachs. She treated them to milk-shakes as well, since the milk had to be used before the desert heat soured it owing to the lack of refrigeration. While Chuck was drinking his milkshake, he reflected on the fact that this might be the last milkshake he would have for quite a while, since there were neither cows here nor on Frank's homestead. He didn't mind this much, for he had never been much of a fan of milk anyway.

There were spare beds at Lars and Nancy's place for Melissa and Chuck, while the other children went to sleep at Peter Ankerson's, for he had bunk beds in one of his rooms, where his grandchildren slept when they visited.

Chuck was exhausted, but he couldn't fall asleep. He lay in his bed – the most comfortable place he and the others had slept in in a long time – tormented by the memories of what he had had to do to escape. Over and over, he kept seeing the spray of blood that had shot out of Alejandro's throat when he had slashed the razor blade across it. He saw the men Bill shot doubling over in agony and dropping to the ground, and kept seeing visions of Miguel's dead body, with the ominous darkness of blood spreading through the dirt beneath it.

He knew that the others would also likely be reliving the trauma they had been through. He wished there was something he could do to help them, but since he could not even get these images out of his own head, he didn't know how he would get them out of their minds. He knew that the killings had been justified; if he had not killed Alejandro, he, Joe, and Kenneth would likely have been murdered by Pablo, and unspeakably disgusting things would have been done to the girls, but even so, it was a difficult mental and emotional burden to have to deal with.

After many hours of tossing and turning in the bed and wrestling with these memories of violence and trauma, Chuck finally drifted off to sleep.

He awoke the next morning not to cheerful chatter outside, but instead to dark murmurings. He got up, cleaned himself up and got dressed, and then went to see his grandpa Frank.

"That's why I said we should have had a man watching the bastards all night," Frank was saying to Lars, Nancy, and two other residents of the settlement, who all looked worried. "I told you people this would happen, I told you last night, but you didn't listen to me. Now look what's happened."

"Uh, what's happened, Grandpa?" Chuck asked, walking up to them.

Frank sighed and shook his head, but the sight of Boris running over to Chuck and jumping excitedly all over him and licking his face while the boy laughed with delight was enough to get him to smile, despite the current circumstances. Once Boris had finished his enthusiastic greeting of Chuck, though, the grim frown returned to Frank's face.

"What's happened, my boy, is that we've gotten ourselves in danger. Those thugs who were locked in the cage in the gas station, Pablo's boys, they escaped last night. I guess one of 'em was handy with a lock-pick, because they picked the lock on the cage. They also chewed through each other's bonds to free up their hands. Must have wrecked their damn teeth, but I guess they were desperate enough to do anything."

"They've run away, though," Lars protested. "They didn't try to hurt anyone or take any of our guns, they just escaped."

"These are evil men, my friend," Frank said grimly. "Evil men with evil hearts. Do you think they're just going to run back to Pablo with their tails between their legs and move on? No. There's no chance of that, not a chance in hell. They're going to tell Pablo exactly where we are, how many of us are here, how many guns we have, and how much food and water is here. And Pablo is going to bring his army of cartel thugs here, armed to the teeth, to take it all away from us. You can bet your ass on that."

Chuck's formerly buoyant mood was rapidly deflated. He had thought that he had escaped Pablo and his thugs forever, but now he knew that it had only been a temporary escape. And what was to come might be worse than what they had escaped from, especially if Pablo brought his entire force out here to the settlement.

Frank saw the glum look on his grandson's face, so he walked over to him and put his arm around Chuck's shoulders and gave him a reassuring squeeze. "I know things sound bad, Chuck," he said, "but not all is lost. You see, I've got a plan…"

"You do, Grandpa Frank?" Chuck asked, looking up at Frank with a hopeful glint gleaming in his eyes.

"I sure do," Frank said, smiling.

"What is it?" Chuck asked.

"Simple," Frank said. "We don't wait around here like sitting ducks. No. If we're to have any hope of defeating Pablo and his goons … we have to *take the fight to them.*"

36

*F*rank had known that the hippies, Lars and Nancy, and some of the older residents of the settlement wouldn't be useful in a gunfight, but he had suspected that they could be put to use in another manner. Now that he had a battle plan laid out in his mind, he realized exactly how useful these people could be. It all came down to timing and signals. Those who were not going to fight could nonetheless take out plenty of Pablo's troops … as long as they did exactly what Frank told them to, when he told them to.

Lars, Nancy, and the other residents, as well as Clay and Diana, listened with rapt attention as Frank laid out the details of his battle plan. They were all sitting and standing in Lars and Nancy's large living room.

"It's like we're about to travel back in time one hundred and fifty years," Peter Ankerson mused. "There hasn't been a battle like this out here since the days of the Indian Wars, when my great-great grandfather was fighting the Indians. Uh, no offence to you, sir," he said, glancing at Clay, his cheeks reddening with sudden embarrassment.

"None taken," Clay said, grinning. "Sure, your ancestors fought mine, but like you said, that was a hundred and fifty years ago; ancient history, friend. We're on the same side now."

"I bet you never thought you'd see your horses used in a cavalry battle, Peter," Lars said. "Hell, none of us could have seen that coming."

"To be fair, honey," Nancy said, "none of us could have seen what would happen with this whole EMP thing. Almost every item of machinery and technology destroyed, the electric grid knocked out of commission, pretty much every car turned into a useless, stationary lump of scrap metal, phone and cell networks ruined and communication with the rest of the world totally shut down ... It's not just this upcoming fight that makes it seem like we're traveling back in time to the 19th century. It's ... well, it's *everything*."

"I want to help fight Pablo," Chuck suddenly said. He and the other children were also at the meeting. "I can shoot well, Grandpa, you know I can."

Frank gave Chuck a sympathetic smile, and pride sparkled with undeniable brightness in his eyes, but he shook his head. "You know I can't allow you to do that, my boy," he said. "It's just too dangerous. I have faith in my battle plan, that much is true, but the truth is we're going to be outnumbered and outgunned, and there's a very real chance that Pablo might win. And you and the other kids need to be ready to flee if that happens. And that means waiting far away from the battlefield, so you can have a real good head start on them."

The plan for the children was for them to wait at Lars and Nancy's place, with horses and supplies ready to go. The battle would take place in the twilight of the day, and if Frank's side won, they would shoot a huge firework rocket into the sky, which would explode in an eruption of bright colors.

If they lost to Pablo, however, the last survivor would fire a red signal flare into the sky, warning the children to flee immediately. Of course, if things went particularly badly for Frank and his people, there wouldn't be a signal flare … and if neither a firework rocket nor a signal flare had been shot into the sky by the time darkness had fallen completely, the children would know that the worst had happened and everyone had been killed by Pablo. At this point they would flee.

Chuck knew that this plan made sense; most of the people who were fighting on Frank's side were either elderly or middle-aged, with the youngest people being in their thirties. Most of them had lived full lives and were ready to die, if necessary. The children, however, had their whole lives ahead of them, and Frank had insisted that none of them risk this potential by being anywhere near the battle, which, even with Frank's expert strategy, could go either way.

Even so, Chuck wanted to take part in the fighting.

He wanted to show his grandfather, who was his hero, just how tough and brave he was. And he wanted to play his part in protecting his sister and his friends. "Come on, Grandpa," he protested, "you need all the fighters you can get your hands on. And I can shoot well! I've already fought those guys once, and I'm ready to do it again."

Frank was firm on this, though. He shook his head. "No, Chuck. We all appreciate your courage, and believe me, I know how good a shot you are with a rifle, but I can't allow it. If anything goes wrong, your sister and your friends will need you around to protect them and guide them. That's where your duty lies, my boy … not with us. With them – with the future of this nation, after the terrible disaster that's befallen us and brought civilization to its knees. Remember that, Chuck: you and your friends are the future. And that future *must be protected* at all costs."

Chuck nodded glumly. As much as the memories of what he had seen and done haunted him, he none-theless wanted to join the fight against Pablo. He realized, though, that what his grandfather was saying made sense. He and his friends had their whole lives ahead of them, even if those lives would play out in a world much more similar to that in which his great-great-grandfather had lived, technology-wise, than the world they had known up to this point. They were the hope for the future of America, and it would be foolish for them to throw their lives away fighting against a maniac like Pablo.

"All right," he said reluctantly. "I'll stay away from the battle."

"You *do* understand why I'm saying this, don't you?" Frank asked.

"Yeah, I do," Chuck said. Then he turned and ambled off, staring at the ground, his hands in his pockets, while the adults continued to discuss and debate over the strategy for the coming battle.

He headed over to the back room of Lars's place, where the other kids were playing cards. If someone were to have briefly glanced at the children, everything would have appeared to be normal with them. As soon as that person took a closer look at their haggard, worry-worn faces, though, they would have seen that the children's state of mind was anything but normal.

"What are they gonna do?" Joe asked, setting down his hand of cards. "Are they gonna let you fight?"

Chuck shook his head. "I gotta stay with you guys," he said.

"Too bad," Kenneth said, putting on a flimsy act of bravery. "I would have kicked those gangsters' asses with a gun in my hands. It'd be just like *Call of Duty* or something like that, except with real bullets. Did you know that the army uses video games to train soldiers? I'm already the best *Call of Duty* player in my neighborhood, and those skills—"

"Shut up, Kenneth," Chuck grumbled. "If you hadn't pulled all the crap that you did since the night of the EMP, we would never have even met those crazy people."

"Guys, don't fight," Priscilla said softly. "We've all been through a lot, and arguing over whose fault this was or whose fault that was isn't going to help anyone right now."

"Exactly," Melissa said. "We've been through some seriously bad stuff, and the worst of it might not be over, and we need to stick together now more than ever."

"But he—" Kenneth whined.

"Sorry, Kenneth," Chuck hastily mumbled, realizing that his sister and Priscilla were right. He decided to be the bigger man and apologize first. "I didn't mean to snap."

"Oh uh … okay," Kenneth said, frowning. All the other kids stared expectantly at him, until he too mumbled a barely audible, reluctant apology to Chuck.

"You wanna join in the game, Chuck?" Joe asked, offering Chuck some cards, eager to have a distraction from the looming threat of the battle. "Man, with all the video games and phones and all that stuff broken for, like, forever, I guess this is what games are gonna be like from now on! Just cards and stuff."

"Sure, I'll play," Chuck said. He sat down and took the cards from Joe, but his mind wasn't on the game. The only thing he could think about was the battle … and whether his grandfather and the others would survive it, or whether they would all be killed, leaving Chuck and the other kids all alone to fend for themselves in this strange and terrifying new world.

37

"This is gonna be fun," El Caníbal said with a dark chuckle as he slapped a fresh clip into his AK-47. He was with Pablo and the entire contingent of the cartel, who had gathered on the main strip of the ghost town on their motorcycles. They had gathered all of their weapons and ammunition together, and were preparing to set off into the desert in the sweltering afternoon heat.

"Those old gringos are gonna pay for killing some of our boys," said the short man, who was the leader of the group who had previously attacked the small settlement in the desert. "They're gonna fucking pay. And even with that old army motherfucker helping them, they don't stand a chance in hell. I'm gonna make that son of a bitch pay personally … mark my fucking words, he's gonna pay for humiliating me."

"Don't kill them all," Pablo growled, fingering his gleaming gold-plated pistol, his fingers trembling from the amphetamine high he was riding. "We need to take as many alive as we can. Tlaloc is hungry ... he's been speaking to me in my dreams. He needs blood ... if I'm gonna be the Emperor of Mexico, I have to feed Tlaloc the blood of a beating human heart. So if you mother-fuckers don't get at least one living captive, I'll start cutting *your* fucking hearts out to feed to the rain god."

"Don't worry, boss, we'll take some of 'em alive," Carlos said, grinning evilly. He was wielding a machine gun, with the ammo belt draped over his powerful shoulder. "I might cut 'em in half with this machine gun, but they'll still live for a little while without legs ... long enough that you can cut their beating hearts out, anyway."

"Get on the damn bikes," Pablo muttered. "We've wasted enough time talking already. Those old gringos are probably running into the desert as we speak. We don't want 'em to get too far away, because I don't feel like riding this fucking bike all afternoon to find them. And those damn kids ... I want them alive. Do you all fucking hear me?! I want the fucking kids alive! And those little shits can move quickly. The more time we waste here, the better chance those little assholes have of escaping. Start your engines!"

Despite their unruly, rebellious individual personal-ities and bad attitudes, the cartel gangsters were surprisingly well-disciplined. As soon as Pablo gave the order, they stopped their chattering, slung their weapons over their shoulders, and kickstarted their bikes. In a few seconds, the great silence of the desert was shattered by the ominous sound of dozens of revving motorcycle engines.

Pablo squinted his eyes against the brightness of the sun and stared at the distant horizon. There, barely visible but growing thicker and more prominent with every passing minute, dark storm clouds were massing on the horizon.

"Tlaloc," Pablo murmured, his jaw hanging slack with awe, his drug-high eyes bulging from their sockets. "The rain god is with us! We will honor his power with the blood of our enemies!"

The gangsters all raised their firearms, fired a couple of shots into the air, and cheered savagely.

"Ride!" Pablo roared. "In the name of Tlaloc and me, the last living Emperor of Mexico, ride!"

The gangsters whooped and yelled and tore off into the desert, the thick plumes of dust thrown up by their wheels a reddish-brown echo of the masses of dark clouds growing on the horizon. A storm was coming … a storm of gunfire and blood.

Back in the settlement, Frank and the others were preparing to fight. Frank, Clay, Peter, and three men in their forties were on horseback. All of them were armed with rifles as their primary weapons, pistols or revolvers as sidearms, as well as carrying melee weapons; machetes, clubs, and axes.

Diana was dressed in desert camouflage gear, which one of the men, who hunted in the desert, had lent her. She was carrying her bow, which she would be using in an unconventional manner. She also had a pistol on her, but her main goal for the first phase of the battle was stealth. She looked like a child dressed in an adult's clothes, dressed in the light brown and tan desert camouflage fatigues, but as baggy as it was, it would provide the necessary cover to keep her hidden until she could unleash her arrows.

Lars, Nancy, and a few other residents who were either too old, too inexperienced, or too unathletic to fight were on horseback too, but they weren't armed; the fighters had taken all the available firearms. Lars, Nancy, and the others who wouldn't be involved in the gunfight, though, had a vital role to play in the battle – one which, if it worked out exactly as Frank imagined it would, could cut the attacking force in half in one mighty blow. Those who wouldn't be fighting would not be mounted on their horses when the battle started, but the horses would be used to set up the trap Frank had planned for Pablo and his men.

And for this trap, a couple of Peter's strongest draft horses were pulling two cars along the road behind the group. They were the smallest and lightest cars in the settlement, two little econoboxes, and the group had stripped them of their seats, fluids, and everything extraneous to make them lighter for the horses to pull. Even so, they were heavy burdens for the animals to drag through the fierce heat of the afternoon, even though they were traveling on the smooth surface of the road.

As for the rest of Peter's horses, they had been left behind at Lars's place, saddled up and ready to go, where the children would wait for the signals to tell them the result of the battle. If Frank and his force lost, the children would just have to hop onto the horses and take off, thereby getting a good head start on Pablo's forces. Everyone hoped that it wouldn't come to this, but they knew they had to be prepared for such an outcome.

After a few hours of riding, the group came to the place where Frank had planned to set up his ambush. It was a bridge over a shallow but broad canyon, where an old dried-up riverbed cut across the landscape.

"You're sure they'll come this way?" Lars asked, reining in his horse next to Frank's. Lars had a worried expression on his face and was looking doubtful. "They've got a whole desert, tens of thousands of square miles of mostly flat terrain to ride across ... and you're sure they'll come on the road, here?"

Frank smiled confidently. "I spent a few hours studying those geological maps. You're right that they could cut across the desert in any number of places, but right here, this section, they're going to use the road, I'm sure of it. Their bikes would have a tough time getting up and down the sides of the canyon. They could veer off a few dozen miles north or south of here, where the canyon flattens out and the sides get less steep, but then they would add two or three hours to what's already a long ride in this intense heat. Also, these punks aren't expecting to meet us this far away from town. They'll probably expect us to either be fleeing in the opposite direction, or, if they think we've got the balls to fight them, they'll expect us to be in town, fortifying buildings which we would use as defensive positions. Us coming all the way out here to meet them in the desert, midway between our place and their base, is something that I really don't think will cross their minds."

"If I were them," Clay added, "going up against a bunch of old and middle-aged folk who weren't experienced fighters, I sure as hell wouldn't expect anything like this. And given how overconfident they're likely to be, all hopped up on meth and coke, which those degenerates consume by the pound, they're going to be expecting us to be running scared, not coming out toward them to meet them on open ground. No, Frank's right; they won't expect this at all, and they're going to use this bridge instead of adding a couple hours to their journey. If I were them, that's what I'd do."

"Okay," Lars said, still looking doubtful.

They crossed the bridge, and then Peter dismounted and, with the help of two of the other men, began maneuvering the draft horses and the cars they were pulling into place, while the others got the equipment needed to set the traps ready.

While Frank supervised the setting up of the ambush, Clay rode out ahead on his own to do some scouting. The group needed to be informed of Pablo's approach well ahead of time in order for everything to go smoothly.

Clay rode up the road for around two miles, until

he was out of sight of the group, and alone in the vast, hot emptiness of the desert. Even though the landscape seemed devoid of life, he remained vigilant, with his senses on full alert. He noticed that a storm was brewing on the western horizon, and this worried him; if it broke before or during the battle, it would put one of their major traps out of commission and put them at a severe disadvantage.

Still, regardless of whether the storm came or not, there was no way to escape or postpone this fight – a fact that was made even more stark when Clay noticed a brown cloud of dust billowing on the distant eastern horizon, growing steadily larger and denser with every passing moment. There was only one thing that could be generating such a massive cloud: dozens of motor-cycles racing across the desert.

Soon enough they would reach the road, and when they did, they would get to the bridge in mere minutes.

With the first stirrings of adrenaline kicking in, Clay turned his horse around and spurred the beast into a gallop, racing toward the bridge.

"Pablo's coming!" he yelled as he got within sight of his comrades. "Pablo and his men are coming!"

"Ambush positions!" Frank yelled, running to mount his horse. "Everyone, get into ambush positions!"

The battle was about to begin.

38

*P*ablo was riding out in front of the pack of motorcyclists, leading them as, in his eyes, a true ruler should: from the front. However, just as they reached the road that would take them over the canyon via a long bridge in a few miles, his motor started to sputter and struggle, and then, just as the bike rolled onto the blacktop, it died completely.

The pack of bikers pulled up behind their leader as he dismounted. His face was crimson with fury. He tried the kickstarter a few times, but even his most fierce and frenzied kicks brought nothing but an impotent and weak coughing from the motor.

"Fucking puta!" he roared, kicking the dead motorcycle off its kickstand. It toppled over and hit the blacktop with a crunching thud. He cursed and swore some more, kicking the broken-down bike until it felt as if he might sprain his ankle or start breaking some of the bones in his foot.

"You can ride with me, boss," Carlos said. His motorcycle had a dual seat, with space for a passenger on the back.

"An emperor isn't supposed to ride with his fucking soldiers!" Pablo snarled. However, he was too hot and annoyed to work out an alternative solution, so, grumbling and cursing, he climbed up onto the passenger seat of Carlos's bike. "Get moving, you motherfuckers know where we're going!" he yelled once he was ready to go.

When the gang set off, Pablo was now at the back; Carlos's bike was one of the slowest and oldest of the bunch. The fact that he was at the rear of the pack filled Pablo with rage, but being in this position would end up saving his life in the opening stage of the battle.

The storm clouds had moved faster than anyone could have imagined, since a strong, hot wind had started to blow, and in a few short minutes the sky had turned from clear and blue to dark, crowded with black-tinged gray clouds heavily pregnant with rain. By the time the bikers got to within a mile of the bridge, the first few drops of rain were falling, thunder was rumbling across the desert, streaks of lightning were flashing and flickering and lighting up the clouds in hues of bright violet, and the heavens were ready to burst.

As the gang approached the bridge, they had no logical reason to be extra vigilant; the elderly residents of the settlement would have been crazy or even suicidal to attack them out in the open like this since they were so heavily outgunned and outnumbered. This, combined with the darkness that had fallen across the landscape with the crowding of the sky with storm clouds, meant that none of the bikers noticed that there were unusual shapes dotting the desert on either side of the road. Shapes that, upon an initial glance, looked like boulders ... but if one were to look more closely, one would see that these "boulders" were actually riders on horseback, draped with gray and brown sheets, hiding behind shrubs and large cactuses for camouflage.

Nor did they see, because of the angle of their approach, that there were two cars, one on either side of the bridge, parked on the steep slopes of the sides of the canyons, held there by blocks in front of their wheels. And running between the two cars, across the road, was a thin but strong steel cable, looped over the handrails of the bridge.

For the trap to be most effective, it had to be sprung with perfect timing ... and Frank, behind the cover of a large boulder, was planning on doing exactly this as he watched the approaching bikers closely through his binoculars. One hand was holding the binoculars, the other his trusty revolver, with his finger on the trigger. The instant he squeezed the trigger and the shot rang out across the desert, Lars, Nancy, and the other two non-fighters would pull the blocks out from under the cars' wheels, sending them toppling down into the canyon ... and thereby stringing the thin steel cable taut and firm across the entire bridge, at neck height.

Frank's heart was racing as he watched the bikers speeding down what they thought was a safe, empty road. With one move he could take out at least half of them … if everything went according to plan, and if his timing was perfect. He had made a few rough calculations and placed some small rocks as markers on the side of the road. When the first of the bikers passed the first marker, he would fire his revolver.

The first motorcycle sped past the marker, and Frank did not hesitate. He squeezed the trigger, and the boom of his .357 revolver echoed like a clap of thunder across the desert. Hidden behind shrubs on the side of the bridge, Lars, Nancy, and the other two people heard the shot and yanked out the blocks from under the cars' wheels. The two vehicles immediately lurched forward and plunged down the side of the canyon, yanking the coil of steel cable up from the road and pulling it taut.

The first few motorcyclists of the pack were cruising between 50 and 60 miles an hour … and when this cable strung across the bridge abruptly appeared at neck height in front of them, as if by magic, they had no time to react, no time to hit the brakes or duck. They hit the cable at speed, and it had the gruesome effect Frank had envisaged … for it sliced their heads right off their bodies. A dozen motorcyclists were decapitated by the cable in a matter of seconds, while others, farther behind their comrades, slammed on their brakes as they saw the horrific sight of the mass decapitations. Some of them kept their bikes upright, but others hit the brakes too hard, too fast, and went down, tumbling and ragdolling across the road.

The battle had begun, but the gangsters didn't even realize it yet. The moment the first bikers went down, Frank fired his revolver again. This second shot was the signal to attack. The riders on horseback threw off the sheets and blankets they had been using for camouflage and charged out, like cavalry soldiers of old, firing their rifles from horseback at the floundering motorcyclists.

Pablo saw the riders charging out from the desert, cutting his men down like sitting ducks as they tried to grab their own weapons to fire back, and he howled with rage. "It's the gringos!" he roared. "Kill the motherfuckers, kill them all!"

He jumped off the back of Carlos's bike, whipped out his pistol, and started shooting.

Carlos, meanwhile, let out a wordless shout of fury and grabbed his AK-47, and dropped down onto one knee, lining up Frank in the sights of his rifle. "So, you think you're some sort of olden day cowboy on your horse, old man?" he growled. "Well you can suck on th—"

He could not finish his sentence for, out of nowhere, it seemed, an arrow had suddenly skewered his throat. He dropped his rifle and fell to the ground, clutching futilely at the arrow that had impaled his throat as he drowned on his own blood.

At this point, the heavens opened and torrential rain began to fall, cutting the formerly excellent visibility down to a mere few dozen yards. The bucketing rain essentially put the second part of Frank's plan out of commission; he had prepared Molotov cocktails for the non-fighters to throw, but now they couldn't see their targets, and the bucketing rain would probably douse the fires before they could be lethal anyway.

Despite the fact that it had prevented the use of Molotov cocktails, Frank, Clay, and the others were able to use the rain to their advantage, galloping in with their horses, taking a few accurate shots at the floundering gangsters, and then charging off into the rain and essentially becoming invisible in the downpour.

Although the initial attack had hit his men hard, Pablo and his men soon recovered from the shock of it and started fighting back with fury. Pablo, using Carlos's bike for cover, had taken note of his enemies' tactics, and when a man on horseback came charging in from the curtain of rain, he was ready for him. He pumped three rapid shots through the man's chest and laughed maniacally as the rider fell dead from his horse.

And even though Pablo had lost a lot of men, he took the storm to be a sign from his rain god. "Tlaloc is with us!" he screamed as thunder boomed and gunshots crashed all around him. "Tlaloc will give us victory!"

He darted out from behind the bike, taking cover behind another fallen motorcycle, and waited for the horsemen to charge in again. He wanted to kill the old man, the one who was clearly their leader. But he didn't want to simply shoot him down … he wanted the old warrior's heart. He intended to cut it out of the man's chest while he still drew breath. It would be a perfect sacrifice to Tlaloc.

Two riders came charging out of the driving rain, but the old man was not one of them. Pablo pumped a volley of bullets into one of the horses, causing it to crash to the ground and throw its rider – Clay.

Clay hit the ground hard, and the impact drove the wind out of his lungs and left him stunned. His rifle went flying and his sidearm tumbled out of its holster from the violent impact of his fall, leaving him unarmed.

Pablo squeezed off two shots at the other rider, who galloped away, bleeding from a leg wound from one of the bullets, and then ran over to where Clay was lying on the ground. The stunned man was a perfect victim to sacrifice to Tlaloc, and Pablo whipped out his obsidian dagger and dropped to his knees next to Clay, who was groaning and gasping on the ground, with one arm broken and his shoulder dislocated, unable to defend himself.

Pablo tore Clay's shirt open and prepared to plunge the dagger into his victim's chest so that he could rip out his beating heart … but as he raised the dagger high above his head to strike, an arrow zipped through the air and impaled his arm. The shock of it caused Pablo to gasp and drop his dagger, and he jumped to his feet, drew his pistol with his left hand, and took aim at

Diana, who was standing a few yards behind him. She had saved Clay's life with her last arrow, but the bow was still in her hands and she had no time to draw her pistol.

"You fucking puta," Pablo growled, his jaw clenched from the pain in his arm where the arrow had impaled it. "I'm gonna blow a hole through your fucking skull, then I'm gonna eat your fucking heart!"

As he was about to squeeze the trigger, though, a horse came galloping through the rain. Frank was out of ammo, but he didn't care. He charged at Pablo and then dived off his horse, smashing into the cartel leader and bowling him over. The two of them started to wrestle on the ground, both trying to grab the fallen pistol.

Then, just as Frank, who had finally pinned Pablo down, was about to grab the firearm, El Caníbal raced through the rain on his motorcycle, driving straight into Frank and smashing him off Pablo. The impact sent Frank flying and broke his right arm and a number of ribs, and knocked him senseless.

El Caníbal hit the rear brake, locking the rear tire and sliding the bike around in a 180 degree turn, and then he jumped off the bike and let it drop to the ground, still running. He drew his favorite weapon – a 22-inch machete – from its sheath, and walked slowly over to Frank, who was lying helpless on the ground, badly wounded.

"Now, old gringo," El Caníbal growled as he raised the machete, "you die ... you fucking *die*."

Many miles away, Chuck and the other children watched as the storm raged on the distant horizon. It wasn't raining in the settlement, and half the sky was clear and deep blue in the twilight. They knew that it wasn't only a storm that was raging though – a battle was on the go, and they were waiting desperately for the signal that would tell them that their side was victorious.

It did not come, though. Chuck kept checking his wind-up mechanical watch. An hour passed, and complete darkness fell. Another hour passed, and there was no signal. A feeling of both terrible fear and crushing sadness came over Chuck. Too much time had passed, and there had been no signal. This could only mean one thing.

"They're all dead, guys," he said dejectedly to the other children. "They're all dead. We have to ride, now, before the gangsters get here. Getting a good head start on them is the only way we're going to survive."

With tears in their eyes and a debilitating sadness in their hearts, the children mounted their horses and rode off into the lonely night.

EPILOGUE

*C*huck was sitting in the upper branches of his favorite tree, reading a book in the warm fall sunshine of the early afternoon, when a cry of alarm echoed across the hills. "Riders! There are riders coming!" Melissa yelled from another tree a few dozen yards away.

Chuck tossed his book away and grabbed his rifle, and he shimmied out along the branch to get a good look at who was coming. With his heart pounding, he peered through the rifle scope at the road and got a good view of the approaching riders. As soon as he saw who it was, though, a feeling of relief washed over him. "All clear!" he yelled. "We're safe!"

Then, grinning, he slung his rifle over his back and clambered down out of the tree and ran down to the road, where the riders would make their approach. Melissa joined him, laughing and smiling. She too had a rifle slung over her shoulder, but like Chuck, she knew that she wouldn't have to use it right now.

Boris had heard the riders coming, and his senses informed him that they were no enemies; quite the opposite, in fact. Barking with excited joy, he raced down the road to meet them.

Frank, Clay, and Diana came riding up the road a few minutes later on horseback. Each of them had saddlebags on their horses – saddlebags which were bulging with fresh fruit.

"Grandpa!" Chuck yelled, running down the road to meet him.

"I hope you were up in the tree watching the road like I asked you to," Frank said as Chuck reached him. He tried to sound stern, but he couldn't keep a look of joy from his face. They had only been gone for two days to harvest fruit from abandoned farms and deserted orchards, but to the children it had felt like much longer.

Boris ran in excited circles around the horses, annoying them, and Frank laughed with joy. His arm and ribs still ached from the battle months ago, even though the bones had healed. He and Clay had stayed at Lars's place to heal, and had only returned to his homestead here in the forested hills a month prior. Diana, however, had come here with the children two months ago, and had gotten everything ready for Frank's return.

The other children had been reunited with their parents. Frank had invited them to stay on his homestead, even though it would have put a tremendous strain on his resources, but they had declined and chosen to trek to the west coast, where rumors had it there was government help for people. Frank believed they were wrong, but he hadn't been able to stop them.

Clay, however, had taken up Frank's invitation and was in the process of building himself a log cabin on the edge of Frank's land, where he would have some space for himself.

Boris couldn't wait to see his master and was trying to jump up to see Frank, startling the horse the old man was on. "Boris, calm down!" Frank yelled, firmly but not unkindly. "Quit being such an idiot!"

"Hey now Frank, is that any way to talk to the dog who saved all our lives?!" Diana said, admonishing Frank with a smile.

"He took that ugly bastard with the machete down just in the nick of time," Frank said, dismounting and hugging Boris. "I was about to have my head taken off by that son of a bitch. And Boris charging out of nowhere and pulling that big bastard down really changed the tide of the battle."

"I wish you could have told us you guys won us before we rode all night and almost got lost in the desert, Grandpa," Melissa said.

"Come on kids, you know what happened. Lars got so scared during the battle that he dropped the damn signal flares into the canyon! How were we supposed to send you a signal without signal flares?" Frank asked.

"I dunno, I just wish you could have told us somehow," Melissa said.

"It doesn't matter now," Diana said. "We're all here, we're all safe, and we're going to be safe for many years to come. And that, everyone, is all that really matters."

They all sat down and enjoyed the fruit, basking in the warm radiance of the golden fall sun.

THE END